A MURDER IN PARIS

MATTHEW BLAKE is the author of the international bestseller *Anna O*, which is published in 41 territories and being developed for the screen by Warner Bros/Netflix. The book hit bestseller lists across the world and was called 'the most talked about thriller of 2024' by NBC's *Today* show. In addition to his writing, Matthew worked for ten years in Westminster as a political advisor and media strategist. As a screenwriter, he currently has multiple feature film and TV projects in development with production companies on both sides of the Atlantic. He lives in London.

matthew-blake.com
@matthewblakewriter
@Matthew__Blake

Also by Matthew Blake

Anna O

A MURDER IN PARIS

MATTHEW BLAKE

HarperCollins*Publishers*

HarperCollins*Publishers* Ltd
1 London Bridge Street,
London SE1 9GF

www.harpercollins.co.uk

HarperCollins*Publishers*
Macken House, 39/40 Mayor Street Upper
Dublin 1, D01 C9W8, Ireland

First published by HarperCollins*Publishers* Ltd 2025

1

Copyright © MJB Media Ltd 2025

Matthew Blake asserts the moral right to
be identified as the author of this work.

A catalogue record for this book is available from the British Library.

ISBN: 978-0-00-860784-5 (HB)
ISBN: 978-0-00-860785-2 (TPB)

This novel is entirely a work of fiction. The names, characters and incidents portrayed in it are the work of the author's imagination. Any resemblance to actual persons, living or dead, events or localities is entirely coincidental.

Set in Sabon LT Std by HarperCollins*Publishers* India

Printed and bound in the UK using 100% Renewable
Electricity at CPI Group (UK) Ltd

All rights reserved. No part of this publication may be reproduced, stored in a retrieval system, or transmitted, in any form or by any means, electronic, mechanical, photocopying, recording or otherwise, without the prior written permission of the publishers.

Without limiting the author's and publisher's exclusive rights, any unauthorised use of this publication to train generative artificial intelligence (AI) technologies is expressly prohibited. HarperCollins also exercise their rights under Article 4(3) of the Digital Single Market Directive 2019/790 and expressly reserve this publication from the text and data mining exception.

This book contains FSC™ certified paper and other controlled
sources to ensure responsible forest management.

For more information visit: www.harpercollins.co.uk/green

PROLOGUE

THE LUTETIA, PARIS

1945

'There's another body,' says one of the porters. 'Upstairs, Room 11.'

He sighs. 'Murder or natural causes?'

'That's your business, not mine. I told them you'd take a look.'

He is tired of murder and bodies. The war is over, but death goes on. He gets up and leaves the office and enters the lobby. The Hôtel Lutetia, the jewel on Paris's Left Bank, is full of people. There are crowds by the entrance, people mingling in the grand dining hall, standing all the way up the vast staircase and along the corridors. The Occupation is just a memory now, or a nightmare.

Today Paris is full of American GIs, British liaison officers and French resistance fighters.

But no one notices them. They only see the survivors. Each survivor from the camps arrives at Gare d'Orsay with their striped rags, shaved heads, bone-thin and some barely breathing. This grand hotel is their new temporary home. They are like ghosts returning to the land of the living.

He reaches the first floor and finds Room 11. Other residents stand in the corridor hoping for more information. The victim is young. She should have her whole life ahead of her. It is tragic, really, but so are most things in this city after the war. He bends down and puts his fingers towards the neck, feeling for a pulse.

She is dead, right enough. He checks the name on the records.

The Red Cross don't want bodies registered here at the hotel, so he will say she died in transit, one of the many who never made it back to Paris.

He leaves Room 11 and walks down the grand staircase of this magnificent old hotel, past the latest group of survivors heading to their rooms. In the old days, this hotel was one of the most famous in the world. Guests crowded into the bar, dined loudly in the restaurant, conducted passionate affairs in the suites and bickered over cigars in the lounge. He remembers the magic of the place before the fighting started. Paris was always the city of lights. The last five years have changed everything. For too long, it has been a city of darkness.

He returns to his office, writes up the form and stamps it. At lunchtime, he takes a walk along the Left Bank to clear his head. He feels his hand shake as he puffs on a cigarette, the prick of tears in his eyes as he smokes, his whole body wracked with urgent feelings he can't explain.

He wasn't always like this. And, just like the Lutetia itself, the glories of the past seem dead now. They are all survivors here, in one way or another.

Paris will never quite be the same again.

And nor will he.

DAY ONE

PRESENT DAY

1

OLIVIA

The call comes at the worst possible time.

I'm getting TJ ready for school. As always, he's refusing to put his socks on because they're itchy, then also refusing to put his shoes on, and the less said about making sure his geography homework is in his rucksack the better. It's only me and him and he has enough strength as a six-year-old to make the morning routine more like a WWE wrestling match. I sometimes wish I had The Rock as my live-in partner. I'm sure he could ace the no-shoes dilemma in thirty seconds flat. But, alas, it's just me. It always feels like I'm doing a two-person job on my own.

Eventually I corner TJ on the stairs and manage to wedge the shoes on, Velcroing them up tightly before he has a chance to protest, and I find the dog-eared homework perilously close to the marmalade jar on the kitchen table. He's incorrectly identified Asia as Africa and put North America across the shape of Europe. It's too late now. Only the top corner is sticky, so I wipe it clean with my fingers and then put it in his rucksack and end up, as usual, carrying the damn thing myself.

'Right, go, go, go, go.'

TJ is now singing to himself. It's a mangled version of Dua Lipa and Taylor Swift which he must have picked up from the radio in the car on the way to school. I don't remember my mum doing any of this. She was still in a dressing gown at this point in the morning smoking one of her sixty a day. She thought traditional parenting was so passé, an old-fashioned notion that liberated souls like her rejected, and I always had to get myself ready for school. Now I'm standing in my very proper semi-detached house in a grey, bang average London suburb – Redbridge, if you're interested, neither glamorous like Islington or fashionable like Camden; no one has ever used the words 'Redbridge' and 'scene' in the same sentence – holding the door open as my six-year-old sings. I am mum, doorwoman, chauffeur and, last but not least, psychotherapist and memory expert.

The front door is locked. TJ skips to the car. The radio comes on as I force our rickety old Ford Mondeo into life and check the time. We currently have six minutes for a ten-minute journey. I've planned our morning routines like a military exercise, so why does time always go missing on a school day? I am up way before seven, squeezing in ten minutes of stretches and exercise and a smidgen of me time. But getting to the school gates by eight-thirty is like running the hundred metres in under ten seconds. It will always be beyond me, as fiendish as algebra or the perfectly cooked risotto.

'Muuuuuuuuum . . .'

That is another thing TJ's started doing to get my attention. He knows it annoys me which is why he keeps doing it. He learned it from Kyle, his dad and my ex, the master of saying someone's name with serious attitude.

I'm about to tell TJ off when the call rings through the car speaker. The number isn't in my contacts. I'm not expecting anyone to ring. But it could be a patient or someone from the hospital. I answer it and shush TJ. I turn down Sabrina Carpenter belting out 'Please Please Please' on the radio.

'Hello?' I say. 'Dr Finn speaking.'

This is usually the only thing that keeps TJ quiet. He has always been mystified by this other person called 'Dr Finn'. Dr Finn looks and sounds like Mum but has a work voice which is very much its own thing and isn't constantly telling him not to touch sticky surfaces or to wash his hands. In TJ's head, I am the Pepper Potts to Dr Finn's Iron Man, a helpful personal assistant who passes on messages and makes things run on time.

'Is this Dr Olivia Finn of the Memory Unit at Charing Cross Hospital?'

'Yes. Who is this?'

'I am calling from the Hôtel Lutetia in Paris.'

That explains the accent and the odd number. I think it must be a joke at first, despite the tone of voice. One of my guilty pleasures is entering competitions for mini-breaks in the Cotswolds or a five-night cruise round the Med. But I can't remember anything mentioning Paris and the Hôtel Lutetia. I'm half-French by birth, but I've never stayed at the Lutetia. A broom cupboard of a room on the fifth floor is about six figures a night and it's way beyond my budget. I do have one connection to the Lutetia, but that is something else entirely. And it's not my connection, or not really, but my family's.

My thoughts turn to work now. Could it be one of my old patients, perhaps, who still carries my card with them? Or a colleague? But being a psychotherapist isn't like being a software engineer in Silicon Valley and no one I work with has enough spare change to stay in the Left Bank's most famous five-star hotel.

I check the car clock. Paris is an hour ahead of London. If I was a Parisian mother, then my son would definitely be late for school. Then again, I would be Parisian so have a waist like a celery stick and a charmingly carefree attitude to school drop-off times. I'd probably be two espressos in by now and off to meet my sizzling younger lover with a name like Gabriel or Jean-Luc. Instead, I have a nine-thirty with a patient called Alan to discuss distressing memories of school swimming lessons. Glamour is my middle name.

'I'm sorry,' I say, 'but I'm in London on the school run with my son at the moment. It might be better if I call you back.'

The caller pauses. 'Do you know a woman called Sophie Leclerc?'

I've met a lot of people in my life. I remember patient names as long as I'm treating them. Then they become old files. I once read that the human brain can only cope with a hundred and fifty close relationships. Beyond that, we're useless. Some days I feel like even fifty relationships is more than enough for me.

'No,' I say. 'Not that I can remember. Look, I'll give you a ring—'

'Madame Leclerc is waiting in the lobby of the Lutetia here in Paris. She is deeply distressed and insists that only you can help her.'

'I'm sorry, but you must have the wrong number. I'm in London, not Paris. And I've never met a Sophie Leclerc.'

I glance at TJ. He has lost all interest in the caller and Dr Finn and is instead playing with the Chelsea keyring on his rucksack, jamming part of his thumb towards the sharp bit. I am waiting for the cut, the blood, the tears. This morning is proving to be a bit of a nightmare. And it's about to get even worse.

'I'm not sure how to tell you this,' says the caller. 'But the woman sitting in the lobby, well, she . . .'

I am about to end the call and focus on getting my son to school.

Then he says it.

'. . . she claims that she's your grandmother.'

2

OLIVIA

Gran? That explains the Paris connection, at least. I sound completely British but have two passports. Gran on my mum's side is as French as they come, one of those Parisian women I mentioned with the impossible waistline and relaxed attitude to timekeeping. As a teenager growing up in London I used to look out of the window at the rain and think about the Parisian version of me walking along the Left Bank. The French Olivia would be sipping café au lait and talking about existentialism while falling in love and painting devastating watercolours in the evenings. My idealised French men seemed more debonair than the pimpled, brace-wearing Kevs and Mikes and Andys at Oaks Park High School. The fantasy beat biology lessons and compulsory choir practice hands down.

'Can you describe the woman?' I ask.

'Slender, medium height, grey hair in a ponytail, a Japanese-style coat of some sort. I could be mistaken on that last point.'

I sigh. So here we go. It's finally happened. This is the call that every relative fears the most. Gran hasn't been well for a long time, but I've been in denial about how much she is deteriorating. Raising a six-year-old with shoe avoidance syndrome is hard enough. Juggling that with a ninety-six-year-old who can't remember anything is a quick route to a sudden heart attack. I wish that I had someone else around to help. But Kyle has his New Girlfriend, and Mum died when I was a teenager. It's all down to me.

'That sounds like Gran,' I say. 'But her name is not Sophie Leclerc.'

'I'm sorry?'

'My grandmother is not called Sophie Leclerc. She is called Josephine. Josephine Benoit.'

I don't usually say it like that. It's my only claim to fame. And, secretly, I love it. It didn't exactly make much difference at school given Gran was a painter not a centre-forward at Man United or a semi-finalist on *X Factor*. But being the granddaughter of one of the world's best portrait painters has its uses. I hear another pause on the end of the line, as if the caller is looking at the confused old lady again in a new light.

'Like the painter?' he says. 'The person who painted the portrait in the lobby of the Lutetia? The portrait she is sitting under?'

Here we go. Gran's most famous portrait has been the centrepiece of the Lutetia entrance since the 1960s. She's painted other portraits, all of them set in wartime, but this is the one that went big. Guests walk through the revolving doors and then get to see one of the most well-known Parisian portraits since the war. It is on the left before reaching the reception and tourists pose for photos by it. Most probably don't know who painted it, or what it's about. But it has become a thing.

Recently it's had a new burst of life on TikTok. I once tried to explain to Gran what it means to go 'viral'.

'Yes. Well, strictly, not like the painter. She is the painter. And she is most definitely called Josephine and not Sophie.'

'My apologies. She told me she was called Sophie. She said I must ring this number and speak to Dr Olivia Finn.'

'I understand.'

I really do understand. Even people who know nothing about art know one thing about Gran: she is a recluse. She is famous for not wanting to be famous. Gran's shyness ended up being her biggest selling point. Only me and Mum knew the real Gran. The rest of the world just had to guess.

'Can you come and collect your grandmother?'

'As I said, I'm in London at the moment,' I say. 'I'm taking my son to school.'

'She cannot stay sitting here in the lobby, even if she is sitting underneath her own painting.'

I am in full-on Dr Finn mode now. One advantage of my job as a psychotherapist is paying close attention to what other people say. I think back to his exact words earlier.

I am calling from the Hôtel Lutetia in Paris.

He didn't say he worked at the hotel or was calling from reception. I just assumed.

'Do you work at the Hôtel Lutetia?'

'No,' says the caller. 'My name is Captain Vidal. I work for the Paris division of the DNPJ, the Direction National de la Police Judiciaire.'

This doesn't sound good, and I slowly realise how serious this could be. Gran has clearly got confused between her art and her life. It's like a child on their first sleepover trying to find their way home. 'Why would the police be involved?'

'We'll get to that.'

'Gran has an apartment about ten minutes away from the Lutetia. Her carer comes in at seven a.m. every morning to look after her.'

'Surely she has some friends here in Paris who could come and pick her up?'

No, I want to say. Recluses don't have friends. They only have relatives, and I am the last one left. I've sometimes even thought about moving to Paris but Gran likes her independence. She hates people fussing. Any suggestion of round-the-clock care draws a fierce stare.

'All her friends are either old or dead.'

'That just leaves you.'

I know, deep down, that I will end up going to Paris today to sort this mess out. That is what always happens with daughters or granddaughters and elderly relatives, isn't it? I thought my late thirties would be all about baking birthday cakes and opening expensive bottles of wine while staring across my gorgeously designed patio garden. I'd look out at the unstained decking and gather round the patio fire pit and enjoy all those alfresco meals with old friends and charming new neighbours.

'Let me figure something out. Will the hotel be able to look after her until I arrive?'

'I'll ask them.'

'Thank you.' I look at the time and know that TJ is already late for school. Morning assembly starts soon and one of the teachers with a clipboard will be standing at the gates. Never mind scaring TJ, those teachers scare the bejesus out of me. I could tell them that my bohemian grandmother has dementia and that is the real reason I'm late. But I'm not sure they'd believe me.

'What was Gran doing at the hotel?' I ask. 'Why was she even there?'

'That's where things get even trickier, I'm afraid,' he says. 'It turns out that she wants to confess to a crime.'

3

OLIVIA

I'm still stunned by his last sentence, but Captain Vidal doesn't give me a chance to ask a follow-up. I don't like this one bit. It feels like the past is about to be opened up.

'How old is your grandmother?' he asks.

I want to say a woman's age is sacred. But I don't feel like joking now. Gran is part of that wartime generation that still fiddled their ages, sometimes taking off years, sometimes adding them on. She answers to ninety-six.

'She's in her nineties,' I say diplomatically.

'She would have been an adult during the end of the Second World War?'

I don't need to do the maths. Captain Vidal clearly knows Gran's name but hasn't got a clue about her art. Gran is famous for her portraits of Occupied Paris and the hell that France went through during the war. I don't know if she ever tried to paint other subjects, but she didn't succeed.

'More or less.'

'According to the hotel manager, your grandmother claimed to be called Sophie Leclerc and said she must have access to Room 11.'

'Gran has been having memory issues for a while. She's clearly got herself confused. Very confused by the sounds of things. She's mixing up painting and real life.'

'Is that a formal diagnosis?'

This is where it gets trickier. 'She hates doctors and being tested. She always said she doesn't want to know what's wrong with her. But she's been unwell for years.'

Neither of us dare say the D-word itself. It's cursed, like the C-word. It's always easier to say 'senior moments' or 'memory lapses'. I talk about memory conditions for a living and even I have hang-ups.

'You still haven't told me what's happened.'

Captain Vidal coughs. 'About an hour ago, your grandmother entered the lobby of the Hôtel Lutetia. She said her name was Sophie Leclerc. She also made a confession.'

I finally pull up outside the school. It is right next to Oaks Park High School, the same one I went to. TJ has his rucksack on his knee and I lean across and give him a clumsy hug and whisper at him to run to assembly. I have a wave of guilt at not getting him here on time and wonder if I'm more like my mum than I realise. She once said always being late was her way of protesting against late capitalism and the military-industrial complex. She also said that about making me take out the bins.

I turn back to the call. Gran confessed to a crime? She is many things, but definitely not a criminal. She's always quite sensible, despite being an artist. But senior detectives in the French police don't call for minor shoplifting offences or because elderly people have popped in for a comfort break. This feels more dangerous.

'What crime did she confess to?' I ask.

The voice is calm, but ominous. It frightens me.

'Murder,' he says, at last.

4

MYLES

He hears the phone ringing in his sleep. Myles hopes it's a dream. He reaches for it, swipes across. Please, not today.

'Myles Forsyth.'

No, definitely not a dream. It's his boss sounding like he's already on his second espresso having done a punishing workout while also learning rudimentary Japanese.

'Myles, I've got a juicy little nugget for you. Apologies for interrupting breakfast but I know you're going to want to hear this.'

Myles looks at the time. He is not even meant to be on shift today. It is unscheduled, unplanned, spontaneous – all words that Myles hates. But it's part of the job now he is in charge of the joint UK–France investigation into the death of Ingrid Fox. At least he's not still doing his other extra-curricular work too, unlike last year. One job is more than enough to fill his time these days.

'Morning, boss, I'm all ears.'

Today is a personal day. The itinerary has been double-checked. Myles just about resisted printing and laminating it.

But Myles loves order. The world loves chaos. Why can't other people be as organised as he is?

'Captain Vidal from the DNPJ just contacted me,' says his boss. 'He thinks they might have a development on the Fox case. He said it was just a heads-up, but he's sent you an email with the details in case you want to follow up given you're leading the case. It's about lots of the same people connected with the trial, including Olivia Finn. I'm just passing the message on.'

Those two magic words pull him back: Olivia Finn. They also strike fear into him too. If it ever gets out what he did, then Myles will lose everything. He only took on the lead detective role officially after Ingrid's death. She died in her home, bleeding out after appearing to commit suicide. Post-mortem analysis later suggested there might have been third-party involvement and the suicide could have been staged. Myles has plenty of other cases to juggle, but this is one that has stayed with him, and not strictly for professional reasons. He wants to close the file and find the answer. But he can't think too much about that, just like he can't think too much about the events of last year and how far his quest for justice pushed him to break the rules.

He got away with it then. He can't crack now.

He's meant to be playing the fun uncle today and joining his sister, Laura, and her two kids for a catch-up. Technically, she's not his biological sister, but that's the term they used for it in the care system and they've stayed close ever since. He's now an honorary uncle.

Perhaps he can skip the playpark and the film and still make it back for pizza and ice cream. Though, technically, the ice cream isn't for him. He made a kneejerk New Year promise to go sugar-free and has regretted it ever since.

'Okay, thanks for the update. I'll get on it.'

The call ends. Myles checks his emails and sees an update from Captain Vidal. While Myles is the overall lead on the case, Vidal is the point man on the French side. Myles reads about Josephine Benoit, Dr Finn, the Lutetia, Room 11 and a murder confession. He imagines the look on Laura's face if he ducks out of the fun today for work. He hates letting her and the kids down more than anything. Yes, he might get the big stuff right – always on time with birthday and Christmas presents, good for an impromptu game of table tennis or Monopoly – but it's the little things kids remember. He goes back over what Vidal mentioned in his email.

Olivia Finn. Paris. Recovered memories.

Silently hovering in the background, of course, is Louis de Villefort, Olivia's mentor. Which links them all back with Ingrid Fox. No, he has to follow this up. It might be nothing, but he can't take that chance. This is his first big case.

Myles hesitates. He needs a juice or a protein shake. He came in late last night, ignored the leftover salad in the fridge and picked instead at a disappointing chicken and bacon pasta bake. His stomach still feels congealed. The weigh-in today will be a bloodbath. He'll be like one of those ballet dancers dreaming of half an apple or one spoonful of cottage cheese.

Myles tries to think of anything that will make what he's about to say better. But he has nothing. He dials Laura's number and imagines the familiar look on her face. You've let me down, you've let the girls down, you've let yourself down.

'An early-morning call,' she says. 'I take it this isn't good news?'

And so he tells her and makes all the usual excuses.

'I'll try and make it back for ice cream.'

'Ice cream?'

'I'll try and make it back to watch you and the girls eat ice cream. While I reflect on the benefits of my healthier life choices.'

'That sounds more like it.'

He smiles and ends the call, then heads to the shower and, as he starts soaping up, his mind turns to the case again and what happened after the trial.

Ingrid Fox made some shocking allegations about her time as a patient in the therapy room of Louis de Villefort at Quai Voltaire in Paris. Not long after the trial, she was found dead in her home.

Was Ingrid murdered or did she take her own life?

Perhaps today he will finally discover the answer.

5

OLIVIA

Sometimes I find it hard to believe how much has changed in such a short time. Not long ago I was with TJ sipping hot chocolate at Fisherman's Cottage. I hadn't met Tom, the trial hadn't happened, Gran was in Paris and wasn't forgetting things like she is now. There were still problems, but they were pebble-in-your-shoe problems. Then it all went wrong.

The trial changed everything.

I phone the Memory Unit and cancel my appointments for the day and then get home and start packing. I can't believe that Gran has been connected with a murder. I message Kyle and tell him what's happened and then search the quickest route to Paris and book a ticket for the earliest Eurostar from St Pancras. While packing, I look across at the bookshelves in my bedroom and see all the different editions of *Memory Wars*. I wrote the book when Tom and I dated. He would sit with his messy hair, glasses perched on his nose, always a cup of English Breakfast tea to hand and vaping like a teenager, and put squiggles in the margins. He munched on chocolate digestives but always picked up the crumbs. He was a bundle of contradictions like that.

Some days everything begins and ends with Tom.

I finish packing and book an Uber then leave the house while dialling the number for Louis. We used to speak every week or so in the lead-up to the trial. Now it is once a month. The phone almost rings out before his trusty personal assistant, Charlotte Fouquet, answers. She keeps everything running at Quai Voltaire where Louis has his psychotherapy clinic. Her voice has a gorgeous singsong quality to it.

'Olivia?'

'Charlotte, hi, sorry to ring you out of the blue like this but something's come up with Gran. I wanted you and Louis to be the first to know. Apparently, there's been an incident this morning at the Lutetia hotel.'

Charlotte sounds more alert now. The mention of her boss always has that effect. Louis's CV is like something from a Hollywood film. He was a hero in the French Resistance and then became a pioneering psychotherapist after the war. He trained at the Sorbonne and his first patients were the survivors from the concentration camps who were based at the Lutetia after returning to Paris, the sort of unconventional start that happened after wartime. Later, he established a clinic that's become famous around the world in his heyday before age caught up with him and he retreated from the limelight.

He is handsome too, and back in the day looked like a cross between George Clooney and the last Tsar of Russia. He is in his nineties now, but he still has his clothes laid out every night, likes the finest tailoring and, on his rare appearances, looks every bit the gentleman. I've known him ever since I was small and he was the reason I followed in his footsteps and studied psychology. Gran would take us for tea at his luxury apartment on Quai Voltaire which also serves as his clinic. His son Edward – who he had later in life, becoming a dad well into middle age – and I used to play together while Louis and Gran talked.

It seems like a different world from a semi-detached in Redbridge and, in many ways, it was. Later, when Mum died and my life was going off the rails, Louis took me under his wing and helped me find meaning again. I fled London, studied as a student at the Sorbonne, and went to daily sessions in his consulting room, as he slowly put my mind back together. He helped me recover memories of Mum's death, and deal with the trauma rather than repressing it, and to this day I still owe him everything.

'What sort of incident?' asks Charlotte.

The Uber arrives. I check the numberplate against the app, decide the driver isn't an immediate threat to life and limb and then get in the backseat.

'She's having some kind of meltdown. Her memory loss is clearly getting even worse. I'm heading over on the Eurostar to sort it all out.'

I don't mention the confession and the idea of Gran killing someone. The thought is absurd and I don't want to embarrass Gran further. She might be sitting under her own portrait and confusing painting with her own life, but she remains a proud French woman from a generation where no one admitted weakness.

'I had this smug bastard of a detective giving me the third degree like she was a criminal,' I say. 'I should have gone to see her more. I guess I didn't want to acknowledge the fact that this could happen. But all the signs have been there. She needed a proper test. I should never have let it get this far.'

Charlotte, if nothing else, has a voice built for phonelines.

'Don't be silly,' she says. 'Your grandmother is so lucky to have you. We all try to avoid seeing memory loss in others in case we one day see it in ourselves.'

She's right, of course. I spend my life treating patients with memory conditions. But I can't bring all that pain home with me each day and still get up the next morning. No one can.

'I wanted you to be the first to know,' I say. 'TJ's dad is on pick-up duties so I might be able to stay a few nights just to get Gran settled back into her apartment and then look at other options for her to get proper care.'

'And she chose the Lutetia of all places,' says Charlotte. 'And that painting. How ironic.'

I read somewhere that even the greatest stars are one-hit wonders. Gran is the same, I suppose. She has her one portrait that people might have heard of. It is set at the Lutetia when it housed thousands of survivors from the Holocaust immediately after the war. It was the moment when Louis first made his name as a medical student treating them. Despite Gran forgetting what she did yesterday or how to put the kettle on, she remembers the painting that made her career, even if she seems to have confused the woman in the painting with her own life.

If Louis inspired me to train as a psychotherapist, Gran's most famous painting hanging in the lobby of the Hôtel Lutetia helped me choose what to focus on. As Charlotte says, its name seems ironic now.

The painting is called *Memory*.

6

OLIVIA

The first thing to know about Gran is that she is a painter who doesn't paint much.

Her first portrait, *Memory* (1964), is her most famous work. I can still remember seeing it for the first time. I was nine and on holiday with Gran in Paris. Mum often took me to see Gran. She was artsy herself and studied at Central Saint Martins which is where she had a fling with a fellow student. My dad was never involved in my life and died when I was young. Mum stayed on permanently in England because she found she was freer here and not seen as just the daughter of the great portrait painter. For as long as I can remember, though, it has always been me, Mum and Gran, and those frequent trips across the Channel.

On that first occasion, Gran took me to the lobby of the Lutetia hotel to see the original painting. As we stood looking at it, Gran placed her hands on my shoulders and asked: 'What do you see, my darling?' That's what I loved about Gran. She didn't believe that there was a right answer when it came to art.

What did I see, Gran? I saw a young woman sitting in

Room 11 at the Lutetia. The woman is a teenager or early twenties. I remember asking Gran why the woman was dressed in stripy pyjamas, and Gran telling me it was because she had just come from a bad place called a camp. I still thought camps involved tents and sleeping bags, but apparently this was a different sort of camp. I also didn't understand why the woman in the portrait had her head shaved. Was that fashionable at the time?

The room in the painting has been turned into a mess. The drawers are pulled out, chairs overturned and the curtains torn. Paintings on the walls have been smashed. There is a torn swastika symbol glimpsed through the right-hand window and debris left behind by the Nazis. But the mystery woman sits there, defiant.

She has lost everything but her memories. The world might be destroyed, the painting seems to say, but our memories live on inside us. That's when I first realised how important memory could be. My work as a psychotherapist came later, but it started in the lobby of the Lutetia with Gran. That moment turned me into a memory expert.

The portrait was first shown in the 1960s. The Lutetia hotel bought it for their art collection and displayed it for everyone to see in the lobby, as a reminder of the hotel's history.

It was a stroke of genius. Rather than being hidden away in a stuffy museum, the painting was in a public space for everyone to enjoy. Since then, seeing the painting at the Lutetia has been a pilgrimage for art lovers and tourists, the equivalent of taking afternoon tea at the Ritz.

It's why I had a reproduction of the portrait on my bedroom wall and still have it in my consulting room at the hospital. I've looked at it every single day since I was nine. I used to think that the woman in the portrait might be me, somehow, or part of me calling from the past. It's why I still do journalling and monthly therapy sessions and have spent my life helping patients deal with trauma by understanding their own past.

The painting speaks to all of us. It deals with one of life's most important questions.

Without memories, who are we?

7

OLIVIA

I'm not one of life's born commuters. St Pancras looks like the inside of a spaceship but the queue for security could be something from Noah's Ark. It's hard to think that Gran once went to foreign countries without all this. I'm dreading what lies on the other side.

I endure the journey. I'm in Standard rather than Standard Premier or the heights of Business Premier, so there's no Michelin-starred three courses. I make a dash to the Eurostar Café and emerge with a questionable 'light bite' – in this case a chocolate brownie that is already grey at the edges. I have one bite which isn't particularly light and give up.

There are lots of sleepy faces around me this morning. Whenever I use the Eurostar, I gradually switch from being English to French. It's ridiculous, really. I like to imagine I could pass for a French woman, but I couldn't. Gran has that elegance and style, which Mum did too. It's something about being young in Paris. Growing up with Mum in Redbridge wasn't the same. Parisians have the Louvre and high fashion. Redbridge has Redbridge football club and a half-decent Burger King.

As we emerge from the Channel Tunnel, it doesn't feel like being in a foreign country but a home I distantly remember. I've made this journey so many times. I can hear French women next to me bickering about one of their husbands, while two of the Eurostar staff are talking about last night's football game. There are no updates on Gran's situation. Everything sounds worse over the phone and I'm desperate to see her for myself.

We reach Gare du Nord and I walk out of the station doors into the heat of Paris. I haven't checked the temperature but it is several degrees warmer than London. I'm overdressed and wish I had more time to prepare. No matter how many times I vow to stick to one layer, I never learn. I'm stuck in three layers and already regretting it.

I find a taxi at the station and get a chatty driver who insists on giving me his life story. It feels like a long time since I last visited Paris and I've half-forgotten how different it is to London. Everything seems smaller, more ordered, the dusty buildings with their balconies and narrow streets honking with traffic.

I remember that weekend in Paris with Tom just before everything went wrong. I'd just got an advance for *Memory Wars* and splashed the lot on a spectacular room at Le Grand right next to the Palais Garnier. I showed him all my favourite places. We ate creamy foods and drank endless wine and forgot real life existed. Gran wasn't feeling well, and I didn't introduce them, which was for the best ultimately. Did I know then, I wonder? During that honeymoon phase, did I realise how much this man would change my life? I like to think my spidey sense knew. But maybe Tom really did fool me completely. He was good like that.

Eventually, we stop outside the Lutetia. I've left rain and

British gloom behind. Everything now seems sunny. This is what I miss about Paris. It feels like the lights are always on here. It's not quite the fantasy, but it's close. This is the city of love, after all.

I have never stayed at the Lutetia but I know the basic history of the place. It's still the only palace hotel on the Left Bank. It opened in 1910 and then closed in 2014 for a gigantic restoration project. The old Lutetia was slightly scruffy and full of memories. According to the new hotel website, the inside is now more like Harrods.

I spot a police car parked outside. One of the hotel porters offers to help with my bag. I am about to explain that I'm a visitor not a guest and demand to see Gran. But it's too late. The bag disappears into the reception area before I can get the words out and I trail through the revolving wooden doors and into the stone-floored lobby.

There is a young police officer standing by the front desk.

'Dr Finn?' he says.

I reply in French. 'Yes. I'm looking for Captain Vidal?'

The officer nods. 'This way please, madame.'

The police always make me nervous, even as an adult. Some people say I became an expert in recovered memories because of the trauma in my own life. I suppose they're right. Every single day I still think about coming home from school and finding Mum in the kitchen with the empty bottle of pills. And, of course, the secret that I've kept ever since, the thing that no one apart from Louis knows about me, buried at the back of my brain.

The officer leads me down the main hotel corridor. We stop at one of the corporate meeting rooms and the officer knocks. There are footsteps inside. The door opens and a large bull of a man emerges. He is big and hairy and looks like a wrestler about to enter the ring. His voice matches the rest of him.

'Dr Finn?' he says. 'Welcome to Paris. I am Captain Vidal of the DNPJ.'

8

OLIVIA

Captain Vidal is dressed in a crumpled suit with an open-necked shirt and a chin full of stubble.

His voice is gruff. His hair is swept back, but slightly beyond regulation length. He is older than I imagined, late fifties, and smells of cheap cigarettes. There is something old-school, and faintly stylish about him despite the careless clothing. You don't get fag-wielding, glass-in-hand, no-nonsense Parisian cops like this in London any more. This guy could stop a fight, throw in some punches, get a confession and call it just a morning's work.

'Is my grandmother in there?'

'Yes,' says Vidal. 'Before we go in, though, I should fill you in on the background.'

I desperately want to get in that room and give Gran a hug. Selfishly, I think of myself fifty years from now. I wonder if TJ's child will be picking me up after some embarrassing incident where I claim to be someone else. I hate that this is happening to Gran. Dementia is such a horrible disease. She doesn't deserve this. No one does.

'Your grandmother's confession is surprisingly detailed,'

says Vidal matter-of-factly. 'She claims she once killed another woman just after the liberation of the concentration camps in the summer of 1945. And that she was in the concentration camps herself.'

There is a moment of silence as I take this in. I tried to prepare myself, but being told this by a police officer is shocking.

'She even says her victim was called Josephine Benoit and that she killed her to steal her identity and begin a new life after the war.'

'She must be confusing what she painted with her own life,' I say. 'Her *Memory* portrait depicts a camp survivor in a room at this hotel. But Gran spent the war in Paris, or at least that's what she's always implied. She's simply got the two things muddled up.'

Vidal doesn't sound sympathetic. 'She also demanded to be let into Room 11 of the hotel and said that is where the murder occurred.'

'The painting is set in Room 11.'

Despite the bits I do know, I have to admit that there is a lot of Gran's early life that I don't know. Like most of her generation, she never opened up about what happened during the war. I used to tell her to write things down before she forgot the past completely. But she didn't want to talk about it, so I stopped asking questions.

Vidal, though, is persistent. 'Records suggest a woman called Josephine Benoit and a woman called Sophie Leclerc were both here at the Lutetia during the same three days in June 1945. Josephine survived but what happened to Sophie is unclear.'

So that is why he called. This all suddenly feels a lot more serious. What if Gran's senior moment wasn't just the dementia talking? What if it's far, far worse?

Does Gran have a terrible secret from the war? Could it be a repressed memory that has finally spilled out now she has dementia? I've seen it happen with other families, but always hoped it would never happen to me.

Sophie Leclerc and Josephine Benoit both arrive at the Hôtel Lutetia in June 1945.

Three days later, only one of them leaves.

Could Gran have recovered a genuine memory from her own past?

'If she is Sophie Leclerc,' says Vidal, 'what happened to the real Josephine Benoit?'

9

OLIVIA

We enter the meeting room and that's when I finally see Gran.

Pure instinct takes over and I wrap her in a hug. I am so used to seeing her as the adult in the room that it always takes me a moment to realise that I'm the responsible one now. I'm the person everyone looks to. When I was younger, I wanted that. Now I find it exhausting. TJ needs me, Gran is dependent on me, Kyle still acts like a grumpy teenager half the time. I know that I need to be strong for Gran. But sometimes I wish there was someone strong for me as well. Tom was the closest I ever came to that.

'I'm here, Gran. It's Liv. We're going to get this sorted, okay. You've had quite a morning of it.'

Gran has always been spindly, but now her clothes really hang off her. I wonder how long it's been since she had a proper cuddle. I kiss her forehead and rub some warmth into her and realise how much I've missed her. Since my divorce went through, I've wanted to curl up in my pyjamas by Gran's bed and tell her all about what went wrong and hear her withering put-downs about Kyle. No one could cut a disappointing boyfriend down to size like Gran.

'You should have called me, Gran,' I say. 'I would have been here in a heartbeat.'

I keep my arm round her as we sit down. Vidal sits opposite. I keep rubbing her warm again like I used to on all those holidays and weekends where Gran and I would sit at the kitchen table with a glass of wine and put the world to rights.

'I'm not sure how this happened,' I say to Vidal. 'I check in on Zoom most days just to see that she's okay. I've tried to arrange round-the-clock care, or move her to a place with supervision, but Gran always says no.'

'And did you Zoom yesterday?'

'No, she was feeling too tired. But the day before she seemed okay. If there were any obvious signs I would have come over. Gran is a recluse though. I always nicknamed her the hedgehog when I was a kid because she loves to hibernate. Trying to get her out of the house is like trying to get my six-year-old son to stop watching YouTube.'

Vidal nods. 'I like that famous painting of hers. The one in the lobby here.'

'*Memory*,' I say. 'Yes, everyone likes that one.'

I look at Gran and wonder if she is taking in any of this. What must it be like to paint something as a young woman and still be asked about it in your nineties?

'That painting is worth a great deal of money, yes?' says Vidal.

'The Lutetia bought it back in the 1960s for a steal. Experts say it could go for seven figures now. If Gran had held on to it, she could have made a fortune.'

'And has she ever spoken to you about her past?' he asks.

'Do you know about your grandmother's childhood or what happened to her during the war?'

'No, or not as much as I'd like,' I say, feeling ashamed all over again. 'I used to ask her but she never wanted to go there. None of her generation ever really do.'

He is about to ask me a follow-up question when Gran's voice erupts beside me. She is shouting, screaming almost. It is another shock in a day of them. I've seen her disorientated, but never as bad as this. It scares me.

'Who are you?' she says, gripping my hand tightly. 'Who *are* you?'

But she isn't shouting at Captain Vidal.

She is looking directly at me.

10

OLIVIA

I am desperate for a coffee. I like my routine. I always have the same Starbucks Nitro Latte after the school drop-off and occasionally a cheeky almond biscotti cookie before seeing my first patient of the day. Instead, I start messaging TJ, telling him I've been called away and won't be home tonight.

I need the distraction after Gran's outburst. She calms down quickly, but it still shocks me. She has never not recognised me before. It's so heartbreaking, all of this. I hope Kyle remembers it's drama rehearsal tonight for the school's 'bold retelling' of *Cinderella*. TJ's playing Third Footman, complete with tights and an elaborate lacy ruff. Either the drama teacher has never met a six-year-old boy or she is pursuing some kind of elaborate revenge against my son. I favour the second theory.

The uniformed officer who showed me in earlier is sent to find two mugs of black coffee from the hotel kitchens. He looks like a gym bunny with his biceps and washboard stomach and he clearly doesn't like playing waiter. I'm almost tempted to ask for two sugars and a plate of shortbread to go with it, but I resist being vengeful and just smile politely. I don't want to offend the biscuit police or, indeed, the real police.

I stay with Gran, instead. I keep repeating my name and who I am and there is no more shouting. She is confused. She probably hasn't eaten anything for ages. I always worry about Gran's eating habits. She exists on coffee and grapefruit. She was raised in an age where carbs were a mortal sin and fasting was good for the soul. No matter how many protein bars I smuggle across the Channel, she will never change. She could be on death row and her last meal would still be salad with a glass of mineral water.

Once I'm sure Gran is more settled, and there'll be no repeat of the shouting episode, I leave the room and join Captain Vidal outside. The uniformed officer returns with two coffees. He hands one to Vidal, then reluctantly gives the second one to me.

Still processing what's just happened, I gratefully sip the coffee which is stronger than my usual Starbucks. I sometimes see myself packing a bag and moving here with TJ. He could become bilingual and I could finally move on from Tom by meeting some dashing French man with a real flair for grand romantic gestures and a wardrobe to die for. TJ's current French teacher still hasn't got beyond describing what's in their pencil case. I'd be one of those mums who starts dressing their kid like a Ralph Lauren model. My mum always refused to pay more than ten pounds for a haircut, often just scissoring away herself at the kitchen table. I might have been related to the great Josephine Benoit, but I had a pudding bowl fringe all the way into early adolescence.

'I'm sorry about that,' I say. 'I've never seen Gran this confused before. I knew it was coming, but I hoped we might have a bit longer before things got really bad.'

'We know how to stop people dying,' says Vidal. 'But we

don't know how to keep them fully alive. It's sad to see. My father was the same. He was a police officer who worked here at the Lutetia just after the war. He had so many memories. By the end, he didn't even remember my name.'

Tom once made me promise that I would smother him with a pillow if he no longer had his mind. Perhaps it's a male thing. Or just a Tom thing. There he is again. Every day there is a moment when Tom is still beside me, stealing my heart then breaking it in the cruellest way imaginable. I really thought he might be the one. Then he just upped sticks and ghosted me.

'What happens now?' I say.

Vidal shrugs. 'Your grandmother says she killed someone and stole their identity. The murder might be hard to prove, but the identity fraud should be easier. If it's true, then she's been living a lie for decades.'

'She's not in her right mind.'

'According to you, yes.'

'You saw it with your own eyes.'

'Perhaps. Or perhaps I saw what you wanted me to see. Perhaps you are covering for your grandmother because you know she has finally confessed the truth.'

'That's absurd.'

'I'm an investigator,' he says. 'My job is to follow the evidence. How well do we ever really know our grandparents? You only know what she has told you. Perhaps she has secrets you could never dream of?' Vidal finishes his mug of coffee. 'I must ask you to remain in Paris until my inquiries are concluded. I may need to speak to you again.'

I wonder how much he knows about the work I do as a psychotherapist. In London, I would make a scene. But there is something about being in France that puts me on the back foot. In England I work at a hospital seeing patients. In France I'm the granddaughter of one of Paris's greatest living artists. I don't want to embarrass her or the family name. I'm the only person left to protect it.

'How long will your inquiries take?'

'As long as they need to.' Vidal starts to walk away. 'Take care of your grandmother, Dr Finn. Don't let her confess to any other crimes while I'm gone.'

I watch Vidal leave with his sidekick and think about what he just said. How well do any of us know our parents or grandparents?

'Gran' isn't a person but a category. I don't know the girl who discovered her talent for drawing, the teenager growing up in wartime Paris, the young woman who blazed a trail in the male-dominated art scene. I only know the elderly woman who scolded me silently for eating a croissant in a vulgar way or sighed every time I added milk to my tea.

What if Gran is hiding a big secret? What if she is recovering memories buried deep in her own past?

What if everything I know about her is a lie?

11

OLIVIA

I take a moment and walk along the corridor in the Lutetia and try and get my thoughts together. The reception area of this hotel is so shiny, like the set of a 1920s movie. I think of Gran arriving here all those years ago, and the memory of that seems to still haunt the place, despite the refurb and the tourists.

I think about Louis too and wonder if Charlotte has passed on my message yet. Perhaps I should ring him myself. He is not only my mentor but also Gran's oldest friend. When I was growing up without a dad, he was my model for what men were like. In hindsight that was hopelessly misleading. All the accountants and solicitors and insurance brokers I meet on Hinge can't measure up to those old black-and-white photos of Louis de Villefort in his velvet smoking jacket.

When I was a child, meeting Louis for the first time was an experience with his velvet loafers, his signature cologne, even the extravagant rumours of dating film stars or bathing twice a day in goat's milk. That's why he was always Paris's go-to therapist. To be granted an audience at Quai Voltaire with the master therapist himself was an honour. Many famous faces once settled back on the lush velvety couch in Louis's consulting rooms and spilled their biggest secrets. In his prime, from the end of the war to the turn of the millennium, he was said to know more about romantic goings-on at the Élysée Palace or in the bedrooms of Tinseltown than any gossip columnist or divorce lawyer ever did.

With the police gone, I try Charlotte Fouquet again, but no luck. She's probably stuck in a meeting. Instead, I try Louis's private number for the main apartment which sits above his consulting room. The phone is answered by a housekeeper who says Louis is busy.

'Tell him it's Olivia calling,' I say. 'And that it's about Josephine Benoit.'

The housekeeper goes to check. I wait nervously. I think of back-up plans. Gran is still in the meeting room. I need to get her to her apartment and then figure out a plan from there. I hoped the police would move on once I arrived. But Captain Vidal seems determined to take Gran's confession seriously. I need some help before this all spirals horribly out of control. While I might have a French passport, I'm not an operator in this city. Louis de Villefort most certainly is.

'Bonjour.' The change is immediate. Louis always used to sound like he's in charge. But, since the very public defamation trial last year and the subsequent death of Ingrid Fox, one of his former patients, he sounds older. It is a sad end for the Resistance hero and therapy pioneer. 'Olivia?'

'Louis, thank goodness. I need your help. Or, to be more exact, Gran needs your help.'

'Has something happened, my dear?'

'Yes. I'm in Paris. There's been an incident at the Hôtel Lutetia involving Gran and the police. I didn't know who else to call.'

Louis sucks in air. 'Of course of course. Now, the Lutetia, you say?'

'Yes.'

'You are sure of that?'

'Yes. I'm at the hotel with Gran now. She's not in a good way.'

'Has the painting been stolen?'

Louis, as he always says himself, is a psychotherapist by trade but an art collector by divine calling. His consulting room with its view over the Seine is full of contemporary art from his own personal collection.

'No, no, the portrait is fine. It's Gran herself. She's very confused. Her memory problems have been bad for a long time, but now they've got even worse. She came to the hotel, sat underneath her own painting and began making all sorts of confused claims.'

'I see, I see. How distressing for you both. What type of claims has she been making?'

I almost feel embarrassed repeating them. But I have no choice.

'She says she once murdered someone . . .'

12

OLIVIA

When I finish, there is a long silence on the other end of the line. Louis still uses landlines and, as far as I know, has never owned a mobile phone.

As the silence goes on, and I wait for him to reply, I wonder if Louis ever gets tired of his younger self just like Gran does with hers. It's like singers from the 1960s reminiscing about Woodstock or meeting Elvis. No one mentions them doing the weekly grocery shopping or taking the grandkids to Disneyland. They grow old but are always frozen in time.

Eventually, unable to bear the silence any longer, I fill it myself. 'The detective at the scene had some crazy notion that Gran's claims need to be investigated. I kept telling him it was dementia. But Gran has no formal diagnosis from a doctor. So . . . you see . . .'

'Yes, yes. I see the dilemma,' says Louis, at last, sounding very thoughtful indeed. 'What an extraordinary turn of events. And, excuse my manners, how is the delightful TJ? Did you have to leave London in a hurry?'

This is more like it. Louis was always very well-mannered. He is the one person I could say anything to. Gran is family, which sometimes makes things harder, but Louis knows all my failings and my darkest secret. After so many hours of therapy back when he still had his clinic at Quai Voltaire, he knows me better than I know myself.

'TJ's staying with Kyle tonight, and for the rest of the week while I'm away.'

'A small child and a very elderly grandmother. Goodness, I don't know how you juggle it all.'

'Sometimes neither do I.'

'Your grandmother is lucky to have you. I try to still be a good friend, but I'm hardly a spring chicken myself. It's one museum piece helping another, I'm afraid.'

'I know,' I say, treading carefully now. No psychotherapist will ever reveal what they discuss with a patient. It is the oath we take. Though he doesn't do in-person therapy sessions any more, Louis still talks by phone with some of his most treasured patients. Gran is top of that list. I can't help prying just a little bit. 'Have you noticed, well . . . any changes in your conversations with her recently?'

Louis sounds hesitant. 'Nothing to be alarmed at, my dear, no.'

'Has she been more forgetful recently?'

'She has good days and bad days, certainly. I put it down to old age. The Lutetia, of course, is where I started treating my first patients as a wet-behind-the-ears medical student. It was my first taste of what psychotherapy was all about. Perhaps your grandmother got confused because of that. Are you taking her home?'

'Yes. I'm going to get her back in the flat now.'

'Good, good. She probably left without keys. I think I'm right in saying that she keeps a spare set just under the flowerpot outside her apartment door. She started doing that after getting locked out sometimes. Another sign, I suppose, that she wasn't managing. I should have been more attentive. But sometimes it's hard to know where being her therapist ends and being her friend begins. We had our phone calls, but that was all. I should have done more.'

I feel sorry for Louis now. I always hoped old age was a time when everyone became fearless. Bring on the pottery classes and afternoon naps in front of old *Friends* episodes. If only that were true.

'You're the last living link to Gran's past,' I say. 'You were there at the Lutetia after the war. Did you meet Gran there? Is there something she has kept secret about that time for all these years? Whatever it is, however bad, I want to know.'

'I really do love your grandmother, you know, my dear. Not romantic love but real love all the same. I hate to think of her suffering like this. But I'm of little help, I'm afraid.'

That isn't a full denial. It makes me wonder if, even now, Louis is trying to protect Gran as his great friend. Could there really be a secret he knows about her and is determined never gets out? Will he guard it to protect Gran even from me? Will I never get an answer?

It's what cuts me up whenever I think about Tom. It's the idea of him just vanishing and never knowing what happened. They call it ghosting for a reason.

I feel Tom standing by me again now. This is just the sort of situation he would like. He would try and cheer me up with one of his bad impressions. His favourite TV show was *Columbo* and he'd cock an eyebrow at me like an old-school private eye.

Time to buckle up, buttercup.

Then I think of the way he just vanished one day, my calls unanswered, the texts unread, his phone going out of service. It was so unlike him. He always prided himself on having no unread emails in his inbox, or unread texts. He was Mr Efficiency.

'We both love her,' I say, imagining a world without Gran. 'That's what makes this so hard. Life would be so much easier without love.'

Louis pauses and says tenderly, 'Yes. But take this from an old man, my dear. Without love, it would be no life at all.'

13

OLIVIA

It's funny how dealing with Gran is a lot like dealing with TJ. There are moments of overwhelming, starstruck love beyond anything I could imagine. There are also moments of hair-pulling, scream-the-world-down frustration when I want to escape to a beach in Ibiza and wait to be arrested for abuse of the elderly or child neglect. Often those two feelings happen within seconds of each other. That's what no one tells you about being grown up. Happiness and sadness are two sides of the same coin.

This isn't how I'll remember this moment, of course. I will edit out the lack of sleep, Photoshop the stress part, and put a filter on the frustration, until I have the perfect Insta snapshot of TJ as a golden-haired little rascal and Gran as a stately, serene, wise old bird and say these days were the best of my life.

It will be lies. These are days, just like any other days, with ups and downs and everything in between. Nostalgia is the most powerful memory trick. Things really weren't better in the past. We've just forgotten the bad bits.

I try and get my travel bag from the concierge. He apparently needs three trips to the storage cupboard behind the front desk and lots of questions about whether Carl Friedrik is a hotel guest or a brand name. Finally, I'm reunited with my suitcase.

I help Gran into the lobby and down the stairs at the front entrance, convinced that one wrong step and she will fall and break something. I renew my vow to feed her more protein intravenously while she's sleeping. She has become like a bag of bones. We get down the stairs and I hold on to her and realise she hasn't got her usual perfume on. She always wears Chanel No. 5. Ever since I was little, that scent has been linked to Gran. Without it, this feels like the end of an era.

The Lutetia porter hails a taxi. I tell the driver to take us to Gran's apartment in Montparnasse. I feel a sharp stab of sadness as I see the confused look on her face. Does she know where she is? Does she have any idea of what's happened in the last few hours and why she showed up in the lobby of the Lutetia hotel?

I bend down and put her seatbelt on for her and lightly touch her shoulder and smile. She smiles back. I know that, in the blink of an eye, I too will be old one day. Kindness is the main thing I'd want. It's not easy, but I have to keep trying. Touching her shoulder, looking her in the eye, treating Gran as a person and not a task to be completed – the small acts of love.

I squish into the back with Gran and hold her hand during the drive. The traffic is heavy and it's ten minutes later when we stop outside her apartment. Gran has always been slap bang in the middle of the city. She is a lifelong renter, not a buyer. This is her patch, her manor. Josephine Benoit outside the Left Bank would be like seeing Big Ben outside of London. The first sign of the apocalypse.

I pay the taxi driver and help Gran out of the car. It's made more difficult by all the people around us. I like to think I have an optimistic take on human nature, but Gran is nearly knocked over twice by pedestrians with earphones in who are doom-scrolling on their phones. She clings to my hand even tighter and I feel the fear running through her. It almost breaks me. We shuffle away from the busy street and Gran sees the flat and the surroundings and some of the old colour comes back to her cheeks. She is home again.

Gran's apartment is on the third floor of a large shambling building. It hasn't seen a lick of paint for a few decades and I doubt Gran's rent has changed much in that time either. When we finally reach her apartment, I find the spare set of keys under the flowerpot, just as Louis said.

I open the door and see the apartment is in decent shape. At least the daytime carer is doing her job. She certainly costs enough. I help Gran into the hallway and take her coat. There is another smell I remember from childhood. It feels comforting and safe. It was always the old-people smell to me, even though Gran back then wasn't really that old.

As I take her coat and pop it on the coatstand, it's so hard to remember Gran as she used to be. Her devilish smile, her quick wit, her fierce love. Even from the start, Gran was never a conventional beauty. Journalists often talk about her eyes. They see more deeply than I can. Her eyes should be insured, like Taylor Swift's legs or Harry Styles's hair. As a painter, Gran always worried more about her eyesight going than her memory.

I lead Gran into the kitchen and put the kettle on. I make a pot of Earl Grey tea and remember not to add milk for her while adding a teensy drop for me. Black tea is too strong.

That's a British childhood for you. I doubt Gran will notice today.

With my job I've seen so many patients with every type of memory problem. But this is different. Gran is my own flesh-and-blood. Standing in her apartment, surrounded by all my childhood memories, it feels like there's a big black hole in the middle of things. I remember being tall enough to reach this cupboard or trying one of Gran's cigarettes from the side table in her bedroom and Mum catching me. Now Mum is long gone, Gran is almost gone, and I'm still tall enough to reach this cupboard. Sometimes I wish I wasn't.

I finish brewing the Earl Grey and bring the teapot to the table. I rest the mugs on coasters.

Gran looks up at me, and I see the same look of panic in her eyes that I saw at the hotel. I brace myself for another meltdown, and pray that I'm strong enough to get through it.

'What's happening?' she says. 'Where am I?'

14

OLIVIA

'It's me, Gran. Liv. You had a funny turn this morning and the police called me. I got an early train from London to pick you up. They found you at the Lutetia hotel sitting underneath your own painting.'

Gran looks more confused than ever. Then, just like that, her expression changes. She looks at me, finally recognising.

'Olivia.'

'We had a Zoom the other day, Gran. TJ and I check in and see how you're doing. You know TJ. Your great-grandson. He's at school today doing double games and rehearsals for his school play. He's wearing those tights and frills which you know he hates. He's a lot like you, Gran. Six years old and stubborn as hell. He's staying at his dad's this week while I'm here.'

Gran's strength is returning. She picks up the mug of tea. She always likes her drinks hot. 'Why are you here, darling? Why aren't you back in London with your boy? It seems like I haven't seen you both in ages. What day is it?'

I can't avoid it any longer and try not to get frustrated. 'You had an episode, Gran. Last night. A bad episode.'

'No, no. I was here last night, darling.' She looks confused. 'Wasn't I? I got an early night, I was tired, I remember that, an early night and . . .'

'You left this apartment, Gran, and went to the Hôtel Lutetia. You were found in the lobby of the hotel this morning and said you needed to get to Room 11.'

I wonder whether to tell her everything, or just an edited version.

'You told the manager on duty that your real name was Sophie Leclerc.'

That's when her eyes come fully back to life.

15

RENÉ

René listens carefully.

'You're sure?' he says. 'There's no possible confusion?'

'No.'

'Tell me again what happened. From the start, leave nothing out.'

The client goes through the events of a few hours ago.

The old woman arrived at the Hôtel Lutetia. She spoke to the reception desk and claimed she was responsible for a murder on the hotel premises just after the war. When asked to give a name, she said she was Sophie Leclerc and that she killed someone in Room 11 of the hotel.

The woman appeared confused. She was taken to a private room while the manager called the police. Following an initial interview, the police contacted the old woman's granddaughter, Dr Olivia Finn, in London. Dr Finn, a memory specialist, arrived in Paris a few hours later. She talked to the police and then left with her grandmother and went back to an apartment on the Left Bank.

René listens carefully. He doesn't interrupt.

When the client finishes, he says, 'Olivia Finn arrived alone? You're certain of that?'

'Yes.'

'And the old woman definitely said the murder happened in the Lutetia?'

'Yes.'

They talk for a few more minutes, going over the instructions, then René ends the call. He wants to clear his head with a strong drink. But he must stay sober now. There can be no mistakes. Not on something this big.

He sits down behind the magnificent oak desk at the centre of his library. He looks round the semi-circular room. There is a doorway that leads to René's private quarters and a signal jammer for external devices and noise-proof insulation so everything stays private. He can hardly believe he lives here sometimes.

He was the poor boy from the suburbs who made something of himself. He didn't see beyond the outskirts of Paris for the first eighteen years of his life. Then he ended up in every continent, first with the Foreign Legion, then in private security, one of those bulky men with earpieces and tight-fitting suits surrounding whichever A-lister could afford him.

He misses that life of private jets and beautiful people. Since setting up on his own, the money is better but the jobs are lonelier. There is a phone call, a job to do, a body to hide, then it all starts again.

Like today.

René unlocks the drawer at the bottom of the desk and unwraps a new burner phone. The number is answered on the third ring.

'Speak.'

A Murder in Paris

That is always how it starts.

'I need some equipment within the hour,' René says. 'The usual address.'

René says what he needs. Then the call ends. It is not a call he likes making. But he has no other choice. The woman, the hotel, that name. The Murder in Room 11. The secret has been hidden for eighty years. Now an elderly woman enters a Paris hotel at dawn and confesses to a murder and threatens to expose everything.

The client can't let that happen.

And René will ensure it doesn't.

It's like that job last year which still troubles him sometimes – the staging of the murder and the note. René gets up and prepares for the job tonight. He thinks of all those other ex-soldiers he met over the years. Many of them hoped to catch the eye of their big clients and become celebrities themselves, the new Bear Grylls, presenting survival documentaries, running corporate training camps and making overpaid tech executives cry like little boys. He could have a range of keto supplements by now and, of course, a series of children's books about how the class nerd turns into an all-action hero.

As he waits for the next call, René dreams about the path not taken. He imagines himself hosting a TV show about survival or taking the latest non-binary movie star on a trek across the Himalayas to eat liver, sleep under the stars and ignore the fifty-strong film crew following them. He would have to get his chest hair lasered, though, and probably start wearing make-up for the camera. There would be hair stylists, salt depletion diets, endless hours of body sculpting and interviews about his mental health struggles and body-image anxieties.

They say men think about the Roman Empire at least once

a day. René isn't a natural in front of the camera, but he would have been a damn good gladiator. He once thought about a career as a stunt double, but killing in real life doesn't require expensive medical insurance and offers better work-life balance.

So here we are.

It is five minutes later when René receives a second call and gets confirmation of the job and the price.

He stops thinking about the Roman Empire and focuses on the task at hand. He longs for that drink again, but it will still be here when it's over.

The mission is on.

Someone needs to die tonight.

16

OLIVIA

The change is sudden but unmistakable. It's like when I banned TJ from having supermarket breakfast cereals and slowly saw the morning sugar monster turn back into my nice, cheeky son.

She looks at me. 'I told that poor boy behind the desk that I wanted to get to Room 11,' she says. 'That's where it happened, you see, all those years ago. I needed to get inside the room and see if she was still there. Josephine, I mean. She was the one who died in Room 11. I went to sleep and woke up and her body was just . . . there.'

Gran sounds so confused. Parts of her confession sound plausible, but other bits are more like nonsense. Is she really remembering something from the past, or is it all just explained by her memory condition?

'Where what happened, Gran?'

'The past, darling. All the things that happened to me long before you were born. I haven't always been your grandmother, you know. I wasn't always a mother either. It might come as a terrible shock to you, and I'm sorry for that, but I lived a full life. I saw things you couldn't even begin to imagine. I wasn't always a delightful old woman who couldn't remember where she left her keys.'

'You're not remembering things, Gran. You've got yourself confused.'

She looks even fiercer now. I feel like I'm a child again and I've lied about eating a second cookie. 'I'm not confused at all. And there's no need to be impertinent, darling. I might be old but I'm not completely useless. At least not yet. I think I can recognise a memory from my own life when it comes back to me.'

I've become so used to treating Gran like an ill person that I've forgotten how strict she used to be. People think a bohemian artist for a grandmother means no rules and endless ice creams rather than doing schoolwork. But Gran was one of those practice-makes-perfect people.

'I don't think you're useless.'

'But you do think I'm making it up?'

'I just don't understand, that's all. It feels like you're taking things from your painting and turning them into memories of your own. Your name is Josephine not Sophie. You haven't killed anyone. Why would you go round telling strangers that you have? Unless, of course . . .'

'I'm confused.' Gran sighs. 'I know my mind isn't what it was. I know I'm forgetful. But I still have more good days than bad. Who knows how many days I have left to live. I was overcome with a certainty that I would die soon and I just knew I had to reach that painting and I had to see that room again and find out what happened to Sophie and Josephine. They were both there, you see, roommates after the war. We were friends, such good friends.'

'Oh Gran,' I say, as I watch her tearing up and full of

emotion. I must at least pretend to take this seriously. I've known patients with memory loss who become convinced of things in the past that turn out to be things they watched on TV.

I feel guilty too. I encourage my patients to recover memories, so why not Gran? Why is it one rule for them and another for her?

'Did these memories come to you out of the blue? Have you always had them? You've never mentioned anything about this to me before. You always said the portrait wasn't from your own life.'

Gran reaches out for my hand and holds it. 'Paris was a very different place during the war,' she says. 'We reinvented ourselves, wiped away the past, told our children and grandchildren a different story about what happened back then and told ourselves a different story too. I'd forced it down . . . but . . . I see their faces. Sophie and Josephine. I see us both.'

I take a tissue out of my pocket and help dab Gran's eyes. I hate seeing her like this. But she seems so convinced. I can't tell if she still thinks she was once called Sophie, or if Josephine is dead, or what she imagines happened in Room 11. Gran is right though. I've known her for a third of her life at most.

'Gran—'

'Olivia, my darling, I realise this won't be easy for you. You and your boy are the two most precious people in the world to me. You'll have to be gentle, forgiving even. I know my memory isn't good, and that I confuse things, but this memory . . . no, this feels real, darling. I need to get back to that room. You must find out what happened.'

'To who, Gran?'

'Sophie, Josephine . . . me.'

I squeeze her hand tighter. 'Feeling real and being real isn't always the same thing. Did you ever speak to Mum about any of this?'

Gran shakes her head. 'No, no, your mother would never have understood.'

I take a deep breath. 'Just to be clear, Gran,' I say. 'I want to understand what you're trying to tell me.'

Her hand is on top of mine. I remember how I used to sleep in the spare room and wake up with a bad dream. Gran would always soothe me with a glass of milk and a story about my great-grandmother, her mum, growing up on a farm in rural France and her pet piglet called Mignolet. I heard the story so many times, but it never grew old. Sometimes I would pretend to have a nightmare just so I could hear it again.

'You're telling me that before Mum was born, and long before I was born, you think your name wasn't Josephine Benoit but Sophie Leclerc? That is what you're now remembering?'

'Yes.'

'The police captain said you mentioned being in the concentration camps during the Second World War?'

'Yes, yes . . . that is correct.'

My voice breaks. 'You've never said anything about this before.'

'I didn't remember before. My mind had repressed it. Or at least I think that's what must have happened. There was too much . . . trauma.' Gran doesn't blink. 'But this lucid spell could pass, dear. Let's move on to your next question and deal with recriminations later. What else do you want to ask me?'

'Why were you trying to get to Room 11 at the Lutetia hotel?'

'Because that's where I stayed after the camps were liberated, where we both stayed, friends reunited. All of us survivors were taken by train back to Paris and put in the Lutetia hotel for three days to be questioned and psychologically assessed. After that, if we passed the police interview, we got on with the rest of our lives.'

I think of Gran eighty years ago wearing the striped clothes of a camp survivor stepping off the train and looking up at the Paris sky. I imagine Louis, too, as a teenage medical student treating the survivors. It's like the whole story of our family past is being rewritten. As a therapist I deal with recovered memories. But I almost want to push this one back down, repress it all over again.

'And is that where . . . ?'

Gran nods. 'I caused the death of another human being? Yes. I can see how horrified you are. I would be, too. But I only committed murder in order to survive. You would have done the same. Those were the choices we faced back then.'

'So if you're Sophie Leclerc, what happened to . . . the real Josephine Benoit?'

There is silence. I hear a church bell chime outside.

'Josephine,' Gran says '. . . yes, I think Josephine was the woman I killed.'

17

OLIVIA

Just at that moment the apartment buzzer starts ringing.
I look at Gran and see the semi-lucid moment is about to pass, just as she predicted. She closes her eyes then opens them and is lost to me again. The on–off switch has been pressed and her brain has gone into full sleep mode.

'One moment, Gran, I just need to quickly answer the door.' I get up, placing a hand on her shoulder to reassure her. 'I'll be right back, okay.'

Her reaction is immediate. She swats it away, then looks angrily at me.

'Gran, it's me. Liv. Your granddaughter. I'm here to look after you and everything is going to be okay.'

'What's going on? What's happening?'

I hate this so much. I have Gran back and then I lose her every time. She is scared, acting out like TJ does when he's frightened. The buzzer goes a second time. I leave the kitchen and find the apartment intercom by the door. I pick up the receiver.

'Hello?'

'Hello,' says the voice. I recognise it vaguely from the phone call earlier, though it sounds different on this line. 'It's de Villefort.'

Louis said he was sending someone round. But I didn't expect him to check on Gran in person. I wasn't even sure he could manage it. Now in his nineties, and following the very public trial, Louis doesn't go out much. He has a chauffeur, sure, but he's important enough that anyone wanting to see him goes to his deluxe apartment at Quai Voltaire.

'Please come on up.'

I check myself in the mirror. I want to seem presentable after the intense conversation with Gran. The apartment is still a bit dusty and a can of air-freshener might come in handy too. I slide off the chain and open the door and expect to see the figure from the call, the old showman with his Brat Pack tailoring and silver-fox looks.

Instead, the man standing in the hallway is my age. It's not Louis, but his son. He has the casual look I associate with wealthy Europeans, all folded cuffs and immaculate loafers. His hair is wavy and dark, hand-styled into a parting, and his smile is an orthodontist's dream. He is slim and gym-sculpted, muscles dimpling an expensive Armani shirt. Edward de Villefort is totally different from the teenage son I knew twenty years ago but also, somehow, just as I remember him. I should have guessed from the voice.

'Hello stranger,' he says. He has a ridiculously handsome smile which, despite myself, I've never quite forgotten.

Everyone likes a bad boy, and back in the day Edward was the baddest of the lot. He was rich, handsome and . . . French. I thought he'd be divorced and wrinkled and have a major beer belly by now. He'd be one of those boring ex-playboys with his model trainset in the garage, swapping parties for Pilates. But his skin is moisturised, his stomach flat. He doesn't look like he's been battling bed times or doing the school run. Edward was the Teflon charmer who studied psychology at NYU then set up a clinic in Manhattan, trading off his father's reputation while living the good life with rich widows on the Upper East Side. I had no idea he was back in Paris.

'If you're a journalist,' I say, 'then you've got the wrong apartment.'

He keeps smiling at me. As well as getting older, he seems to have got hotter, which is surely not possible.

'Liv Finn,' he says, kissing me on both cheeks. 'Or is it Dr Finn now? Dame Olivia? Baroness?'

'I wish.'

'I've missed you,' he says. 'It's been too long.'

My teenage self would be in heaven right now. But that plane flew from Paris to New York twenty years ago and took my heart with it.

'It's good to see you too, Edward,' I manage. 'Please, come on in.'

18

OLIVIA

I close the door and check whether I have anything stuck in my teeth. Why didn't I spend more time getting ready this morning? Edward was meant to be old news. No, ancient news, stuck in the 2000s folder with iPod Shuffles and 'Mr Brightside'. I've always wondered whether I would run into him again in Paris. But it never happened. I wrote it off as a teenage crush and moved on with my life. But that first, feverish attraction never really leaves you, and he's always been there, the person I compare all the others to.

We stand in the hallway, neither of us sure what to do, both knowing we should make awkward catch-up conversation. There is so much history between us, but we haven't met for so long. It's like running into your school crush while queuing at the doctor's. Do you hide the urine sample or make a joke of it? Welcome to the dilemmas of early middle-age.

'It must be, what, 2005 since we last met,' says Edward. 'Jennifer Lopez and Ben Affleck had already broken up for the first time and you had a third piercing in your ear.'

I smile. 'Well, JLo and Affleck have split for a second time and the third piercing is long gone.'

'I'm sorry to hear that.'

'You might be the only one. Are you still in New York?'

He nods. 'I have my clinic in Manhattan. I don't come back to Europe much these days.'

'So that's why I never bumped into you again.'

'Paris is the city of my father. I needed to find my own place in the world. I'm only back for a brief visit. I'll be heading to New York again soon.'

That was the other thing I fell for as a teenager. Yes, Edward was a bad boy, but he was also stuck with his father's legacy. He could never live up to what Louis did. Edward didn't have a Second World War. He wasn't part of the Resistance. He didn't treat Holocaust survivors after the war or pioneer new treatments in psychotherapy.

When I knew him, Edward took drink and drugs and put as much distance between himself and his dad as possible. He was typecast as the disappointing son and he more than lived up to that. Rumour was that he fled Paris because he was about to be busted on drug charges and Louis had to clean up the mess he left behind. Edward might have a consulting room in Manhattan with his name above the door, but he's never come close to matching his father's achievements. He is the ultimate nepo baby. If you can't beat it, own it.

'You look different,' I say. I'm an only child and Edward was the one person who came close to being like a big brother figure, even though I did fancy the pants off him. I could tease him. He could tease me back. It was banter before banter was a thing. But that was a long time ago. I can't afford to let old feelings lull me into a false sense of trust. 'Back then . . .'

'I drank two bottles a day and snorted anything I could find,' says Edward. 'Yes, yes, I know. I spent most of my twenties doing the same thing. Then my doctor told me I was killing myself and I turned things round. I gave up the booze and the drugs, started working out, eating healthily, hopefully living longer. No one wants a therapist who can't get their own life together.'

'Don't tell me a woman changed you?'

I expect him to laugh, tell me about his long-term partner, say they now live a perfect domestic life with two beautiful Siamese cats and a shared passion for antiquing. But he just looks sad instead. I've hit on something without realising. I'm now desperate to find out what that thing is. I'm sorry, but not sorry. Is he divorced? Does he have a kid? What has happened in the decades since I last set eyes on him?

'Something like that,' he says. 'These days I run marathons and drink kale. I'm a walking cliché. But at least I'm still walking. Some of the people I knew never made it this far. The party scene in New York isn't exactly good for your body, or your soul.'

'Well, I'm very glad you're still here.'

'Thank you,' he says. 'How about you?'

'I have a son now,' I say. 'He's six. He's cheeky but great. I also used to have a husband who was cheeky but not so great so now he's my ex-husband. We share joint custody of TJ.'

'I see.'

'I thought getting divorced would be the toughest thing I had to cope with. Then Gran started losing her memory and, well, other stuff got in the way. So, as it turns out, the divorce was just the appetiser. Life still had a main course and dessert of misery to come. Who knows what it will bring with the teas and coffees.'

'I know my father was very grateful for all your help with

the trial last year,' says Edward. 'Without your support, I think the whole thing might have given him a heart attack. It was a dark time for us all.'

Life is a funny thing. Is this where I thought we'd end up? When I was the self-conscious teenager with braces and Edward was the butter-wouldn't-melt heartthrob who was the result of a very late relationship on Louis's part which made Edward only a couple of years older than me? When I was getting into psychology just so I could listen to him tell me about his plans to study it at NYU and become a therapist, did I guess we'd end up talking about cancel culture and kale?

I did not.

'Dad rang me when he received your call,' says Edward. 'He told me about what happened at the hotel. I'm not sure how much help I'll be. Your grandmother was always very independent.'

'You're a face from the past,' I say. 'She remembers you. She needs all the familiar faces she can find right now. It was kind of you to drop by. Tea?'

'Your sort of tea or proper tea?' he says.

Edward used to tease me about that all those years ago. He was the sophisticated French guy who could name twenty types of tea, while I was the English woman who liked a builder's brew with lashings of semi-skimmed.

'I thought New York might have changed you.'

'It has. I exist on coffee now. But black tea is my last link to home. It reminds me that I'm still French.'

'Welcome home,' I say. 'One black tea coming right up.'

19

OLIVIA

We reach the end of the hallway. I hear Gran in the kitchen. It sounds like she's talking to herself. I wonder whether she will be confused or lucid again. I didn't expect Edward to arrive. But I hope it's a good thing and that it won't upset her more.

'Gran. We have a special guest. You remember Edward, Louis's son?'

I am about to jog her memory, remind her of going to Quai Voltaire when I was little, but she recognises his face straight away. She always did like a man with an easy smile. Those older memories, then, are still there. She can still remember Edward and me playing rock paper scissors in the garden while she and Louis talked about her life and state of mind. It's the newer memories – what she did yesterday, where she is now – that come and go.

I finish making another pot of tea. I make sure Gran and Edward are not given milk. Edward sits down at the kitchen table and I join him.

'Gran,' I say. 'Why don't you tell Edward what happened this morning?'

I blow on my tea. I look at Gran and see she is already having another more lucid episode. She glances at Edward and I nod, telling her she can trust him.

'I remember you as a boy running round your father's apartment,' says Gran now.

Edward smiles. 'It's been a long time since we saw each other. I've been in New York for the last twenty years. How are you? Liv tells me you've had a busy morning.'

'I have dementia, darling boy. My memory problems mean I can't remember what I want to remember but I also can't forget the things I'm supposed to forget. All sorts of things have come loose again.'

'Gran thinks she remembers something from her early life,' I say. 'I suppose nowadays we'd call it a recovered memory.'

Edward looks at me. 'You're the expert on those, aren't you? I even read that book you wrote.'

So, yes, he really is keeping up with my career progress. I can see Edward in his consulting room between appointments googling my name and seeing the reviews for *Memory Wars* on Amazon. Perhaps, deep down, he still thinks about those days, the what-might-have-been if he hadn't flown to New York and stayed with me in Paris instead.

'It's why I painted the portrait,' says Gran. 'Or at least I think it is. The girl in that portrait is me before I became someone else. I was innocent then. I hadn't taken another life. I was Sophie, not Josephine.'

I want to ask so many more questions. Lots of people have debated who the girl in the portrait is. But the mystery has been part of the appeal. The woman is everybody, a symbol for what so many millions of people went through during the Second World War.

Gran looks confused again now. The connection with the past is breaking, slowly then quickly, blinking out like a light. The memories go blank and I know I should let her rest. This isn't family history any more. This is one woman's battle with a terrible illness. I want to bring her comfort and make everything all right.

But I can't, and nor can she. And the reality of that is awful.

The latest episode is already over.

Gran, my wonderful Gran, simply can't remember.

20

OLIVIA

Edward offers to settle Gran down for a nap. She seems to like his company so I leave them to it. He can sit with her for a bit and make sure she's all right.

It is getting dark outside. There is the drum of rain on the window panes. But the Left Bank outside is full of light and noise, and it makes me want to be young again. It seems like only yesterday that I was here, returning from a session with Louis at Quai Voltaire, taking out my course reading and sitting next to Gran and sharing treats from her secret stash of chocolates hidden for dark nights and special occasions.

I start tidying up. As the light fades, the apartment feels creepier now. The place is old and messy. It's small, like a lot of Paris apartments, with the kitchen behind me, the hallway where I'm standing, and then a master bedroom directly ahead and a spare room on the right which Gran uses as a studio and which I used to sleep in when staying over. Gran is from that wartime generation which doesn't like spending money. Waste not, want not.

The spare room is a lot messier than the rest of the flat. It's full of odds and ends. There is an ironing board, several broken lamps, piles of paperbacks and then an oak desk jammed in beneath the main window. There is a typewriter on the desk and what looks like a Moleskine pocket diary. Gran hasn't painted for a long time now and I wonder if she will ever pick up a paintbrush again and whether it might be good for her if she did.

I walk over to the desk and run my hand along the spine of the diary. Gran always used to buy a pocket diary like this at the start of each year. She would jot down appointments, ideas for inspiration and look at it each morning to see who would visit. It's how people lived before iPhones and digital calendars. I flick through the pages and see it is empty. There will be no more diaries to fill, now. It all relies on memory.

I remember as a student wanting to copy Gran, thinking it was the stylish Parisian thing to do. I bought a diary from a small shop near the Paris opera house and filled it in with my teenage thoughts. I was in freefall after Mum died and burdened by the terrible secret I was hiding. I enrolled at the Sorbonne to be closer to Gran, go into therapy with Louis and find myself. The notebook was part of that.

I was already fascinated by Gran's *Memory* painting. I spent most mornings with Gran listening to the radio and talking about my course and spent the afternoons in the consulting room at Quai Voltaire with Louis undergoing daily therapy sessions. That summer was when I decided to become a psychotherapist. Louis showed me how transformative therapy could be in rebuilding broken people.

The apartment hasn't changed much since then. Louis was always telling Gran to move somewhere fancier. But Gran likes the simplicity of this place. She has everything she needs. She isn't interested in celebrities or dinner parties with other artists on the Left Bank. She has a roof over her head, cafés nearby, the excitement of Paris.

I start flicking through the diary. I'm still hoping to find an innocent explanation for all this. Could Gran really have such a major secret in her past? Could she be Sophie Leclerc before the war and Josephine Benoit afterwards? Why did she go to the Lutetia this morning and confess like that?

Gran seems to have taken random facts and turned them into a memory from a past life. Unless the secret is so big, and so damaging, that Louis would try and protect me from it, swearing a vow of silence all those decades ago and refusing to break it even now?

I hear footsteps outside. I put the diary back and return to the kitchen.

Edward is stacking the dishwasher. The old Edward would never have done that. He didn't learn how to use an iron until he was eighteen. He once thought washing machines worked without any washing powder, the stains cleaning themselves. He slots another mug into the back of the dishwasher and looks up as I enter.

'She's sleeping,' he says. 'I hope peacefully. Though it's difficult to tell.'

I try to sound normal. 'You're so good with her. I really appreciate it. If New Yorkers ever tire of therapy, you should try social work. You've clearly got a gift.'

Edward smiles. 'That would be the final transformation.'

'What do you think then?' I say. 'Could she really have recovered a memory from her past? Could Gran actually be a murderer called Sophie Leclerc? Or is this her dementia talking?'

I know that Gran isn't the only one with secrets in her past. We all repress things we don't want to remember. After all, my entire life has been defined by what I once did, that terrible secret buried in my own memory.

'Sometimes good people do bad things,' says Edward, drying his hands on a tea towel. 'Wars are like that. If the only way you could survive was taking another life, would you do it?'

I think about TJ and how far I'd go to protect him. My life has been easy compared to Gran's. I've lived through a financial crisis, a recession and a pandemic. But I haven't yet lived through a world war.

Would I take someone's life if it was the only way to save my family and survive? Would I reinvent myself if I was too traumatised to keep on living? Would I cross a moral line to help the people I loved?

'Yes,' I say, at last, thinking about being in Gran's shoes. 'Wouldn't you?'

21

RENÉ

He waits until evening. Once it turns eight-thirty, he starts to move. He doesn't like to eat too heavily on a working day, and spends the hours before the job chewing macadamia nuts and meditating, while monitoring his pulse and heart rate through his Fitbit. He plays 'Waterloo' by ABBA as a lucky charm. It was played as a joke before his first mission with the Foreign Legion, and he can't break the habit. If he listens to that song, he gets the job done and stays alive. He is superstitious like that.

René goes over the key facts again. The apartment in Montparnasse is a rented property. The monthly rent, René knows, is left in an envelope every month in cash. Josephine Benoit is secretive. She has no internet and doesn't do email. She's probably never surfed the internet and still thinks digital things aren't real. The woman has lived in the same apartment since the end of the war.

She plays up to her hermit status. She looks like a charming old grandmother. René pictures her at the nearest bank branch collecting wads of euros that keep her going for weeks on end. Tracking a recluse is what he does. And they don't come more reclusive than the most camera-shy painter in Paris. She makes Banksy look like the Kardashians.

It's dark outside now, which helps, and René is used to operating with just natural light. Night time is essential for this sort of work. The best is total natural darkness, like those evenings on a mission in a far-flung corner of the world with only the moon and birdsong to guide him. But this will do.

He is up the stairs now. It's a bit derelict, to be honest, and not where you expect a major artist to live. That's what makes her special though. She doesn't have a lavish studio in a fancier part of the city to entertain important sitters for hours. That's not Josephine Benoit's thing at all.

He's got his instructions from the client. The rest is taken care of. There are no security cameras nearby. The other apartments are rented out in the summer and mostly empty. He reaches inside his pockets now and puts on the gloves. There must be no trace: fingerprints, hair fibres, blood spots. He will leave nothing for the police to find later.

He reaches the front door and tries the handle. Then he takes a small device out of his pocket, checks either side and works the lock. There is a click as the lock gives way. A door this old will whine, so he muffles the sound and tickles it open millimetres at a time. He slips through the gap and into the hallway filled with shoes and umbrellas.

It's best not to think too much. He learned that long ago. It seems like yesterday that he applied to join the Foreign Legion. He completed the medical, signed the five-year service contract and left his past behind. He chose a new surname and vowed to become a ruthless, efficient, model killer. He hasn't looked back since.

This, by comparison, is child's play. And yet sometimes he

also aches to go back. He liked having comrades. They were all exiles from the normal world. They didn't have kids, pension plans, a car in the drive and weekly cooking rotas.

Does he ever regret choosing this life? No, he does not.

René stays still and listens. According to the floor plan, it's a small apartment. There is the sound of a radio playing in the kitchen.

He is expecting two targets. The third, he knows, has left the building.

The instructions tonight are simple.

He rehearses the plan again. The primary target will be easy. But the secondary target is different. That's why René charges the big bucks. Those ex-military types on TV might look the part, but they've lost their edge through meetings, mani-pedis and listening to their stylist telling them which shade of tangerine will make their eyes pop. The only missions they complete rely on semi-dependable wi-fi.

He still does the hard yards. He gets up close and personal with his victims.

If only she hadn't walked into the Lutetia and said those words and mentioned Room 11. If only Olivia Finn hadn't come across on the Eurostar. If only Josephine Benoit had not remembered.

All of this didn't need to happen.

But they did, and it must. The world cannot know the truth about what happened in Room 11 of the Hôtel Lutetia eighty years ago or about Sophie Leclerc and Josephine Benoit. The people must die, and the secret must die with them.

That is what the client is banking on.

René thinks of the instructions and the client waiting for confirmation. He hears the final bars of 'Waterloo' in his head, humming them for luck. There is a new ABBA show in London with avatars, apparently, and he'll reward himself with tickets when this job is done. But it must be done right first.

One favour for another.

It's time to move.

22

OLIVIA

Paris, to me, is always an evening city.
Young lovers drinking wine or strolling along the Seine, old lovers sitting on their balconies and basking in those memories, nervous singletons using Citymapper to find the small bar on the side street and seeing their blind date turn, smile at them, and feeling that flutter in their stomachs.

There is no wi-fi in the apartment and I want to catch up on emails and admin. Edward returns just before eight p.m. with some food from the local supermarché and tells me there's a café nearby with free internet. He promises to stock the fridge and stay with Gran while I'm gone. I want a bit of fresh air and to check everything is okay with TJ and Kyle. I also want to do some digging on Sophie Leclerc and figure out what I can.

I leave the apartment and step into the streets of Montparnasse. The city is full of tourists and families. I find the café Edward recommended nearby. It's a proper Parisian haunt. I order a café crème even though I usually stop all caffeine at noon – no sleep tonight, then – type in the wi-fi password and check my laptop has enough battery.

I open the browser and log in to my email account. I draft

an email to the hospital and cancel my appointments for the next two days. There will be a backlash, I'm sure, but that is the least of my worries. Next, I message Kyle telling him that TJ has karate tomorrow and needs his kit washing. I also try FaceTiming TJ but he doesn't pick up. Perhaps the drama rehearsal has overrun, or he's boycotted it all because of the tights.

More realistically, he's probably playing on Kyle's Xbox while eating Haribo Supermix and inhaling Dr Pepper. Or is that unfair? Probably. Kyle was to blame for the whole *Fortnite* catastrophe last year, plus the time TJ found three cans of Red Bull in Kyle's fridge and drank the lot. A six-year-old boy is hyper enough. A six-year-old boy on energy drinks is supersonic.

I'll try TJ again later. It's late and I'm getting tired after a long day. I can't wait to sink into bed in Gran's spare room, even if the bed is a sleeping bag and a blow-up mattress. I google the Lutetia hotel instead and click on a link for the BBC website. There is a podcast called 'Witness History' with an episode titled 'The Paris hotel that hosted Holocaust survivors'. There's a short article about how the Lutetia became the home for thousands of concentration camp survivors in 1945.

There's also a black-and-white photo that shows four men covered with dust and mud. They are wearing striped clothes from the concentration camps. There is a newspaper on the table and flowers alongside four mugs. The caption says: 'Concentration camp survivors in the Lutetia restaurant in 1945'.

I sit there and study the photo for a few minutes. I know the vague history of the hotel because of Gran's painting, but I've never stopped to dig much deeper and this photo makes it all so real. They were so young, and just like us. It seems too absurd to have actually happened. But it did. Holocaust survivors sitting in a grand Parisian hotel having just emerged from the most notorious event in human history. They are almost exactly where Gran and I were this morning, still dusty with the air of Auschwitz, eating bread and drinking water.

These are the first patients Louis treated as a medical student. This is where he honed his therapy skills, trying to repair minds damaged by so much trauma. I imagine him as a gangly, spotty seventeen-year-old and the stories he must have heard, then think of TJ in eleven years. My brain can't make the leap. Perhaps the greatest generation really were different.

I search for more on the Lutetia and the Second World War and then type the name 'Sophie Leclerc Paris 1945' into Google. But it's hopeless. There are too many results. For some reason, none of them are helpful, lots end up linking to the Netflix series *Emily in Paris* and a discussion about Lily Collins and her new houndstooth beret.

I knew it couldn't be that easy.

I go back to the photo of the Lutetia again and look at the four men sitting in the dining room. How do you continue after that? All these people in the photograph have stories of their own. Is Gran part of the narrative? They have parents, children, brothers, sisters, lovers, husbands, wives. If I'd been one of them, would I have killed someone to stay alive? If I found the people who betrayed my family and led us to the gas chambers, would I hesitate to take a life?

I'm sure I wouldn't. None of us know what we are really capable of in the right circumstances. I'm still not sure whether there's anything in what Gran is saying or not. The psychotherapist in me is always curious about recovered memories.

But now, having seen that photo, I think I understand why

the memory could be so jumbled. The trauma of it all was so huge that no one could remember it fully. Everyone repressed something. Could the entire history of my family be totally different to what I thought? Did Gran repress those memories because it was just too painful to remember? Is Louis, even now, trying to protect her from what she did or who she really was back then?

I'm still staring at the photo when I get a new message from Edward. I expect it to be something trivial about where Gran keeps her cleaning products or how to get the temperamental kitchen tap to work. He will be whipping up a standout ratatouille or stocking up the spice cupboard.

But it's none of those things.

The message simply says: *Olivia help E.*

23

OLIVIA

I read the message once, then again.
I call Edward and get no answer. I read the text again.
Something isn't right.

I close my laptop and zip up my rucksack and rush through the door and onto the street again. It is even busier now. So many people stand between me and the apartment. Getting a taxi will be too slow. I need to find the quickest way back through Montparnasse without losing my way.

I start running and, two wrong turns later, I finally reach the street outside Gran's apartment. I know the area, but I never usually navigate it at night, and Paris is busier than I remember it. I'm no longer the teenager with my headphones walking back from an evening class while listening to Avril Lavigne and thinking about lectures the next day. Perhaps I'm being overly cautious and my lack of sleep is putting my senses on high alert.

But I look at Edward's enigmatic message again. Could it be nothing? Or could it be serious? Did someone stop him typing out the full message?

Is Gran in danger?

I want to make sure. If only Gran had wi-fi in her apartment or a half-decent phone signal.

I climb the stairs and reach the apartment door. It is shut, just as I remember.

No panic. Or not yet.

I open the door with my spare key. Surely, I will soon discover this is a false alarm. Edward's voice will echo from the kitchen. He'll have that ratatouille waiting for me and perhaps a glass of red wine and I'll indulge in more fantasies about reformed men, the bad boy turning into a domestic god.

But I say nothing. Instead, I hear a male voice speaking rushed, slangy French. I shut the door softly. I do nothing but listen to the voice.

There are no other signs of anything unusual. No footprints.

Olivia help E.

'Edward?'

I say his name again, louder, then once more for luck. But he doesn't answer. The other voice keeps talking.

It's not a person, I realise, but the radio.

The wireless, as Gran or Louis would call it. Gran always used to listen while she worked, company for those long, lonely painting sessions. My memories of Gran are full of those smells and sounds: her perfume, the low hum of the radio, the old tunes she would sing to herself while getting dressed.

'Edward? It's Olivia . . .'

Still nothing. Until, finally, there's a groaning sound. Louder, now. I follow the noise through to the main room and see the radio still playing, sound coming from the speakers and Edward lying on the floor.

I see the blood before I see him.

His shirt and his face are already mangled. For a moment, it seems like it's happening all over again. I can see Mum's lifeless body at the kitchen table, the pill bottle beside her, the cupboard door open, instantly knowing that she was dead. That trauma shaped the person I am today. I've carried the secret of what I did, and didn't do that day, ever since.

I can't go through that a second time. I must be conjuring this from the past into the present.

He looks at me and groans.

Not Mum, this time, but Edward.

'Help,' he says. 'Olivia . . . *help.*'

24

OLIVIA

I don't understand at first.
 I drop my bag and try to stop the bleeding. But he pushes me away.
 'Help. *Help.*'
 I focus, clear my mind of flashbacks to Mum's death all those years ago, and see that Edward's pointing at the kitchen door, the hallway and Gran's bedroom beyond that. There is a trail of blood leading up to the kitchen door. Shadows dance across the floor. I hear a scratching sound, as if the intruder is still here. If they came for Gran and Edward, perhaps they have come for me too.
 'Edward . . . what happened? Who did this to you?'
 'Help . . .'
 I wait another second. Then, reluctantly, I leave Edward and run to Gran's bedroom. I turn the handle but the door is jammed from the inside.
 I try budging it with my shoulder and it still won't give. I try again. Eventually, I realise a shoulder won't do it. I stand back and prepare myself for the pain and kick as hard as possible until the old lock snaps and the door opens.

The bedroom is small, just a single bed, a wardrobe and a small dressing table. The curtains are closed but Gran is lying there. No, Gran. Please dear God no.

This cannot be happening. Anything but this.

Please.

Not again. Not like Mum.

'Gran . . .'

It doesn't look like she's breathing. I check her pulse, apply basic CPR. I do everything you're supposed to do.

No, no, no, no, no. Before I even reach the body, help her in whatever way I can, I know it's no use. I've seen what death looks like. It is unmistakable. I keep on with the CPR, wishing her better, but it's no use.

The bedroom window is open. There is a pillow beside her. Did the intruder attack Edward, smother Gran, lock her bedroom door and then leave through the window? Is that the sound I heard? How long did it take before she stopped fidgeting? Was she in agony or did it feel like a nightmare where she just never woke up? How the hell did this happen?

I look around the bedroom at the dressing table, wardrobe, the make-up box.

I don't remember the rest. I am back in the kitchen again opening all the cupboards until I find Gran's medical kit. I go over to Edward and help him up onto a chair. He slumps into it.

I crouch in front of him. I am still in total shock. All this has happened so fast. I have my phone and start to dial the emergency services. We need an ambulance, police, something. Should I try more CPR on Gran, or is that just cruel? I've heard the horror stories of ribs being broken and Gran was fragile enough anyway.

'Edward,' I say. 'What happened? Who did this?'

He looks towards the sink. I get him a glass of water. He swallows and his voice is croaky.

'Josephine,' he says. 'Is she dead?'

I can't bring myself to say it. I won't make it true. She was my everything. Without Gran, I am on my own. I simply can't think of a world without Gran in it.

This must be a terrible mistake. Something about what happened this morning triggered this. I have no doubt now. But can she really have been murdered because of her past as Sophie Leclerc and what happened in Room 11 of the Lutetia hotel? Could it really be a genuine recovered memory and not just a senior moment?

Sophie Leclerc or Josephine Benoit – which woman am I related to?

Which one have I called Gran all of my life?

'Who else knows about the Lutetia this morning?' says Edward.

My fingers still hover over the phone. I try to think. 'No one. Her, you, me . . .'

'The captain from the DNPJ,' he says. 'He must have told someone about what Josephine confessed to.'

'Why?'

Edward takes another drink. 'They knew what they were after. They knew the layout of the apartment. This wasn't some amateur burglary or armed intruder.'

'Why would a captain in the DNPJ care about an eighty-year-old murder?'

'He wouldn't,' says Edward. 'But the murder must be connected to something else.'

Edward is about to say more when there is a new sound

outside. The radio is still on in the background. I'm about to press the button to dial the emergency services and tell them to come to the apartment in Montparnasse.

Then I stop.

I wonder if I'm imagining it at first. I haven't called them yet. I look out of the voile curtains, though, and see the flashing blue lights below.

Gran is dead and her killer has fled.

But, somehow, the police have already arrived.

25

THE LUTETIA

1945

SOPHIE

Sophie Leclerc tries to concentrate. She must listen carefully. 'The government has ordered you all to be housed at the Hôtel Lutetia,' says the Red Cross worker, standing at the front of the bus. 'You will be held for three days to be checked and interviewed. You are not allowed to leave the hotel before that time. If you try, you will be arrested. Everyone will receive a police interview. The police will be looking for collaborators passing themselves off as deportees and you will be assessed by a doctor to check you pose no threat on your release.'

Sophie tries to recall the events of the day. She remembers arriving at Gare d'Orsay then following the other survivors to the transport. This all feels like a dream somehow. She will wake up and be back at the camp again.

'Any questions?'

The bus is silent. No one has the energy to think. Sophie looks out through the grimy bus window and sees the dregs of Paris. It is nothing like the city she left behind. She turns away from the window and closes her eyes. Eventually, the rickety bus reaches Saint-Germain-des-Prés and stops outside 45 Boulevard Raspail. Sophie opens her eyes and looks up.

The Hôtel Lutetia. Yes, it really is like arriving home. She has celebrated birthdays here. She used to come here with Louis, back when life was full of hope and romance. It was her father's favourite place and they would spend hours talking in the magnificent dining hall. She once imagined the Lutetia would be where she had the reception for her wedding, and that she and Louis would take their first dance as newlyweds in the grand ballroom. She can picture it now, even down to the detailing on the dress she was going to wear. But that all seems so distant now. She is no longer that innocent young girl with big dreams. She is a camp survivor.

She will never dance with her new husband in the grand ballroom with those friends and family for a simple reason. Most of them are dead.

Sophie realises, against all the odds, that she has survived. She wonders if Louis has too. In fact, that's the only thing that's kept her going. He is the last hope from the old world. Did he make it or is he buried somewhere in the battlefields of Europe? She prays more than anything that Louis is still alive. He dreamed of going into medicine, with a focus on the mind. Perhaps he will be one of the medical students treating survivors at the hotel.

The outside of the Lutetia is full of Parisians. Many of them are holding up signs with photos and names written in capitals along the bottom. There are people of all ages waiting to see if their loved ones return. As the bus stops, all eyes turn towards them. Some small portion of her wonders if Louis could be here, waiting for her, the ultimate romantic gesture. He will emerge from the crowd and sweep her into his arms and steal her away from this place.

But there is no Louis. She looks for that matinee idol smile, those dreamy blue eyes, tall and strong, the dark hair swept back, a cigarette dangling from plump lips. He dressed beautifully, but even the dressiest clothes seemed so casual on him. The memories probably don't match the reality now. They have all changed. He is still a teenager, like her. They are both so young, but have seen so much. The war has aged them by decades.

None of them can ever go back to how things used to be.

As she gets off the bus, Sophie knows she is not the person she used to be.

The war has changed them all.

26

THE LUTETIA

1945

SOPHIE

'You can enter now! One at a time! No pushing!' shouts the Red Cross worker.

Sophie is already struggling with the flashbacks, those memories of Drancy and the trains that took them from Paris to Auschwitz. She hates the crowds and the memories they bring back. She sees her father at Auschwitz being put into a different line from her and the last look he ever gave her and how soon he was lost in the crush. She didn't even get to say goodbye.

She still doesn't know what happened to him. Or rather she does, but she has no proof. It's like he just disappeared from the world. The memories, though, consume her. She feels like she might erupt at any moment and lash out violently at those around her. She doesn't just feel angry, but deadly. She has seen too much death and has lost control of her impulses. One wrong look and she wants to strike.

She has such memories. Sometimes the memories seem real, and she can't tell the difference between what she remembers and what is happening around her.

That will be her downfall, she thinks. She will confuse her memories with the present and act out to protect herself and end up killing an innocent person.

It is her worst fear.

The queue moves slowly. Sophie breathes, steadies herself. She looks round at the faces to see if she recognises anyone. Her head is shaved. Her body is dirty. She has lost so much weight it's difficult to stand. More than that, she has lost her soul. Her essence.

She no longer feels like Sophie Leclerc. She doesn't recognise the girl she used to be when she was last in Paris and walking back from school with Josephine as they talked about marriage, their futures, how wonderful adult life would be. Josephine was an only child who wanted a large family. Sophie was also an only child and wanted the same thing. That is what her future was meant to look like. She had her life all planned out.

Now her mind is filled with terrible scenes. When she sleeps, all she sees are bodies, the dreaded selections, all those split-second decisions she made in the camp that kept her alive. The memories are too much. More than anything, she wants to forget.

The entrance queue shuffles forward. Sophie eventually gets to the front. She sees why it is taking so long now. Each new arrival is being led aside by a nurse and into a separate room. Slowly, they return and the next person is let in.

It is about ten minutes later that she reaches the front of the queue. There is a man from the Red Cross who says, 'Name?'

'Leclerc,' she says, finding the strength to speak again. She looks at the man, knowing he must be her own age or thereabouts. 'Sophie Leclerc.'

'Age?'

She can barely remember now. There are no papers or official records any more. The war destroyed everything.

'Sixteen,' she says.

'Any infections or chronic illness?'

'No.'

The Red Cross worker nods abruptly. 'Proceed to the nurse,' he says. 'Welcome to the Lutetia.'

27

THE LUTETIA

1945

SOPHIE

When she dared to think of it, Sophie always imagined the return from the camps would be like a return to the normal world.

She would be back in the arms of Louis. They would marry, as they always planned, and move to a gorgeous chateau outside Paris and soon there'd be the patter of tiny feet and idyllic summers with their growing family. She can taste the picnics, hear the laughter, feel the warmth of Louis's hand on her skin.

But the city has lost its romance. She sees the same deadness in the eyes of the officials as she saw at the camp. They are still prisoners here. Above all, Sophie wants to be touched. She would do anything for a smile. Her father was the only person who smiled every time she walked into a room. Is it too much for someone to show some kindness to her here?

'You will be sprayed with DDT, which is a white powder, first,' says the nurse, adopting a similar tone to the others, 'and then deloused. After that, you will be assigned a room number. I repeat that if you attempt to leave before your police interview and psychiatric examination you will be detained. Do you understand?'

'Yes.'

Sophie is about to ask a question. But she doesn't have time. The nurse begins and looks bored. The whole thing feels humiliating. Sophie wants a bath and a fresh set of clothes but that doesn't seem to be an option. When did she stop being human in the eyes of others? Is it when she lost her hair, or had her clothes taken from her? Is it because she still carries the dirt and stink of the camps?

Sophie closes her eyes and does what she did at Auschwitz. She detaches from events and retreats into her own mind. She survives by imagining Louis standing beside her, nuzzling playfully into her neck.

When the spraying is finally over, she is ordered out of the medical room and handed the keys for Room 11 on the first floor. She's told she will be sharing with another survivor who has already arrived.

She needs food and water and doesn't have the energy for much else. This is her prison for the next three days. The police will question each of them and find out who is genuine and who is a collaborator. Paris is still full of traitors, people who allowed the Nazis to occupy the city and betrayed their neighbours. Many of those collaborators are now pretending to be victims in order to avoid any reprisals.

Surely, though, if he's alive, Louis will come and find her here. According to the gossip on the bus, this hotel is where all survivors from the camps are being taken. He might even be nearby at this moment, smoking a cigarette and counting down the seconds until they're reunited. The other explanation is too awful to think about. Sophie refuses to believe that Louis is buried in the rubble somewhere, or stuck in an unmarked grave. She is alive, so he must be too. Sophie has lost her father; she can't lose Louis as well.

She takes her key. There are restaurants, bars, suites, hundreds of rooms, thousands of people – the Lutetia is so vast and it seems as if all of Paris is here. She pushes through the crowd of people and finds the staircase and walks up until she reaches the first floor and Room 11. Even the halls of the hotel seem wider than she remembers, and behind each door is another story just as tragic as her own.

She turns the key and opens the door and sees the shadow of someone else inside. This will be her new roommate.

She is still thinking about those summer walks along the Left Bank with Josephine, so she almost doesn't recognise the figure at first.

There is something different about this woman, a flicker from the past. She thinks of Louis again, of the parties at this hotel, all those long hot summer evenings after class when the three of them were inseparable.

Sophie doesn't understand, her eyes blurring with the effect of the DDT. She rubs them, which makes things worse, then looks again and sees a smudgy face up ahead. It is a woman of a similar age with high cheekbones.

No, it can't be. Sophie knows she is imagining things. It is the hunger, the dehydration, the general exhaustion. They looked so alike before the war that people often thought they were sisters. Now, with their heads shaved and both wearing the same soiled rags, they are identical.

She knows the other person in Room 11. The woman who was once her best friend in all the world, and the person who then betrayed her.

She is looking into the eyes of . . . Josephine.

28

THE LUTETIA

1945

JOSEPHINE

Sophie.

It can't be.

Sophie Leclerc is dead. She died after being deported to Auschwitz. She must have done. Almost no one survived, and certainly not women. She is gone, a memory, the ghost of a friend who no longer exists.

And yet here she is. Sophie is standing opposite her.

They are reunited as roommates in Room 11 of the Lutetia.

Josephine has planned her escape for days. Being known as a collaborator in Paris means living with a permanent death sentence and constantly trying to outrun the mob hunting down traitors.

They have no idea, of course, why she really did it. She fraternised with Nazi officers, and even slept with some of them in this very hotel. But it wasn't because she was a whore, or just to try and stay alive – not that staying alive wasn't a good reason. She was doing what was necessary to help win the war. Not that any of them will believe that now. The Resistance leaders who could vouch for her were shot just before the liberation. The other women who saw her with the Nazi officers have already denounced her.

She is trapped. She did a brave thing, and now fate is punishing her for it. This is what war is like. It is lethal, dangerous and, most of all, unfair.

She didn't sleep last night and made sure she arrived at Gare d'Orsay early, hiding herself away until the first train back from the camps arrived. Then, once the station was flooded with survivors, she slipped out and joined them, melting into the crowd and praying no one noticed the deception.

She stood in line with the others – stinking, exhausted – as they queued for the transport that would take them to the Lutetia hotel. She was always a good actor. At school she was the star in the annual plays and even started acting professionally in those early years of the war. She was born to inhabit the lives of other people, to dress as them and pretend to be like them, copying mannerisms and voices. She once dreamed of moving to Hollywood and becoming a real star, taking a stage name and living in Beverly Hills and sipping cocktails.

Now she is still performing. But there will be no Hollywood, no happy ending. Everyone in this wretched city is looking out for themselves. To survive, this will have to be the performance of a lifetime.

She waited for someone to rumble her, to figure out she wasn't on the trains or in the camps. But there were too many survivors for everyone to be individually checked. They boarded the buses like animals on Noah's Ark, two by two, until the bus departed and Josephine was driven through the city she had never left, each moment getting her closer to the hotel and her own reinvention.

Surviving the war, the Occupation and the Nazis was a game; now surviving the liberation is one too. All she has to do is get through the next three days, pass the police interview and psychiatric exam and get the official stamp of approval. Everyone who collaborated with the Nazis is now rewriting their own stories. She pretended to collaborate in order to help the Resistance, but for most people that makes no difference. She looked, sounded and acted like a traitor to her own people and that is enough. If she pulls this deception off, she will turn into a concentration camp survivor.

It is her last and only hope of staying alive.

She's already had a few near misses. Bands of men are trying to hunt down collaborators, particularly women, and she has been moving from house to house and sleeping in doorways and streets. But the city isn't safe for her out there. The French men want to restore their own power and honour by blaming the womenfolk and publicly humiliating them. Pretending to be a camp survivor is the final option for her. If this fails, Josephine doesn't know what she'll do.

Or rather she does. She will die, either by her own hand or someone else's.

She arrived on the very first bus. The processing by the Red Cross went smoothly and she was given the key to Room 11. But, from the minute she came inside the hotel lobby, she could feel the shadow of death return. With every step, she sensed danger. She saw the glassy eyes of the survivors, the hollow expressions, these ghosts in striped clothes wandering through the hallways.

Any one of them could murder her as easily as breathing.

She has heard enough stories to know that being innocent did not necessarily mean survival in the camps. For some, the way to get through each of the selections – sent left to death, right to hard labour – was to become a kapo, a camp policeman, a cook, even a doctor. These fellow guests could be dangerous, having already made impossible choices to survive. They might not hesitate to make more.

Everywhere she looks, death stalks the corridors. It's there in the terrible wailing sounds coming from the rooms, the ceaseless pacing of survivors who can't get used to beds and chairs again, the mute paranoia of people who expect random executions at any moment and flinch at the sight of others.

And now this.

Sophie.

Josephine knows Sophie so well that even seeing her from a distance is enough. Sophie was the sister she never had. Despite how similar they looked they were always so different. Josephine was the extrovert, the showgirl, the flirt and tease, desperate to finish schoolwork and get on with real life.

Sophie was introverted like her father, always reading books. That's what made Louis fall in love with her. Sophie was beautiful and clever. Josephine was pretty and worldly. Sophie, Louis once said, was a born wife, whereas Josephine was a born mistress.

Josephine's palms are wet. Breath chokes in her lungs. She wonders if Sophie has met Louis again. Josephine's tried so hard to look convincing. Her hair is shaved off. She hasn't eaten a full meal for weeks. She hasn't used soap or water either and is disgusted by the smell of her own body. Getting the right clothes was more difficult. But she found some rags that were dirty enough to be convincing.

The plan was going so well. She was processed, deloused, sprayed, given her room key. She was acting like a survivor. And now this.

Sophie knows that Josephine was the one who betrayed her. Josephine told one of her Nazi lovers that she knew where Sophie and her father were hiding. She was being followed, her work for the Resistance could have been exposed, and she made the call to sacrifice Sophie and save herself.

She isn't proud of it, but she would do it again if she had to.

Sophie Leclerc was never meant to be here.

Sophie was meant to be dead.

DAY TWO

29

OLIVIA

NOW

It is past midnight, my second day in Paris, when I find myself back in the lobby of the Lutetia hotel. It looks much the same as yesterday. There is a night manager behind reception and the lobby is empty. The bars and restaurants are closed and all the guests have gone to bed. There is a cleaner mopping the floors with headphones on and moving in time to music.

Back then, Gran was still alive and I was worrying about the school run. As I reach the reception desk, Gran is dead and everything I know about her has a giant question mark next to it. I feel sick with grief and my eyes sting from crying. I have a horrible ache in my stomach. I don't even know for sure if the most important woman in my life was really called Sophie or Josephine and whether or not she was a murderer. But I do know someone killed her.

I want to rewind the last twenty-four hours and start all over again. I can't process what has just happened. It's like someone has smashed my life to pieces and then scattered those pieces to the wind. I am still here, but Gran is gone.

'Bonsoir, madame,' says the night manager.

I'm tired. I'm still in shock from the last few hours, ever

since I saw those police lights outside. It was followed by police footsteps rushing up towards the apartment and three fist-slams against the door.

'Police! Ouvre la porte!'

As I stand at the reception desk, I keep having flashbacks to Gran's apartment. Captain Vidal looms in the doorway. He hands Edward a piece of paper. I am ignored. Edward is still hurt from the attack, and living off painkillers, and struggling to stay standing.

'Nous avons un mandate pour fouiller cet appartement.'

Edward takes the document and reads. Blood is still fresh on his face from the attack, but the painkillers are numbing it and he can still function. He looks up, shaking his head. 'C'est absurde. J'ai besoin de parler à mes avocats.'

'Monsieur, veuillez vous écarter.'

Edward reluctantly steps aside. Vidal enters now.

'What's going on?' I say.

Vidal ignores me and turns to the uniformed officers behind him. 'Cherchez la chambre, la cuisine et la pièce de rechange. Ne dérangez aucune prevue.'

The other officers push through, the younger one from the hotel deliberately bumping into me. That must be revenge for the coffee run earlier. Vidal supervises them while Edward and I stand in the doorway.

'What's happening?'

Edward speaks in a whisper. But he sounds nervous. 'I can't afford police attention, Liv. How the hell did they arrive here immediately? What's going on?'

I think of the secrets we all have, and the one I'm still hiding. The secret that pushed Tom away. None of us are innocent here. I don't like this any more than he does.

'Tell them what you saw and that will be the end of it.'

'I was out of it, Liv. I was in the kitchen and then I woke up on the floor. The bastard must have knocked me out cold. I told you. Whoever he was knew exactly what he was doing. This wasn't some amateur burglary. Not that that will stop these bastards trying to pin the whole thing on me. They'll use anything to knock the de Villefort family down to size, just like the fucking trial.'

There is a shout from the bedroom. I don't need to guess what they've just found. Gran's body is lying there with the pillow beside her. Vidal follows the noise, so do the uniforms searching the rest of the apartment.

'Seriously,' says Edward again. 'I can't be dealing with this, Liv. I knew it was a mistake to come back. I should have stayed in New York.'

I look at him and see how scared he is. I'm sure he hasn't told me everything. I wonder what other dodgy things Edward de Villefort has got up to in the twenty years since I last saw him. Once a playboy, always a playboy. It sounds like the rumours of a drugs bust all those years ago must be real. Perhaps Edward was dealing? I remind myself not to trust him. He might be handsome, but handsome men are usually the worst. Just because I liked him as a teenager doesn't mean I can trust him as an adult.

'Madame . . . are you okay?'

I look up and see the night manager staring at me.

Focus, focus, focus. I'm no longer in Gran's apartment in Montparnasse. It is several hours later and I'm now standing alone in the lobby of the Hôtel Lutetia. I am looking for a bed for the night. I'm also coming back to where all this started. Somewhere in these walls is the truth about Sophie, Josephine,

Gran and my family's past. I don't know how, but I must find it.

'I need a room,' I say. 'A single room, just me. The cheapest one you have.'

'Of course, madame,' says the manager. He brings something up on his computer screen.

I can't stay at Gran's any longer. It's now officially a crime scene. The whole thing is cordoned off by police tape. Edward offered me a bed at his father's apartment at Quai Voltaire where his famous consulting room is, but that place has too many memories of its own for me and, anyway, I want my own space. I could try and get a bed in any Paris hotel, I suppose, but something draws me here to the Lutetia.

This is base camp. I want to walk the corridors and feel the atmosphere of the place. I can only solve the mystery of Gran and figure out whether she was really Sophie or Josephine by stepping into her shoes and imagining myself in this hotel eighty years ago. I want to stand in the lobby and look at the *Memory* portrait and figure out why all this has happened and what it means.

'Do you have any preference on which floor?' asks the manager.

'Yes,' I say. 'I'd like Room 11 on the first floor if it's available.'

The night manager nods. He asks to see my passport. He produces a key card and something to sign, then says, 'Enjoy your stay at the Lutetia.'

Gran must have heard those words too when she first arrived in 1945. Now, as I prepare to retrace her steps, it's as if she joins me here, another presence by my side. I see a young Gran, the woman I never knew, dressed in rags with no luggage but the scars of everything she'd just been through.

A Murder in Paris

It is the two of us, bound by our genetic memory over two generations, walking across the lobby of the same hotel together. She follows me towards the bank of lifts, sees me press for the first floor, and then waits with me as the lift slides upwards and pings at our destination. I'm not sure if I'm looking at Sophie or Josephine, but all I know is that it is Gran as I have never seen her before.

The first floor is dark, moody, bathed in low lighting, filled with mirrors and shiny surfaces that look like something from a video game. I keep walking along the carpeted floor until I find the door for Room 11 and take out my key card and press it against the scanner and wait for the light to go green.

Gran does the same, but all those years ago, without the low lighting or the mirrors, without the electronic key card, but walking the same corridor in the same space with her metal key which she slides into the lock and turns.

I can barely believe that Gran is dead. She feels more alive to me than ever. As I brace myself and prepare to walk into Room 11, I feel Gran take my hand, reaching out across the decades, her palm hot against mine.

Her knuckles are interlocked against my own, and I know that we are still in this together. Part of her still lives in me, the two of us against the world, just as we always have been.

I cross the threshold and step back into the past.

30

OLIVIA

The Lutetia is much fancier than any other hotel I've stayed in. People think that because Gran was famous we're all rolling in money. If only that were true. When she was just starting out, Gran painted *Memory* and it was bought by the Lutetia to hang in its lobby. She was pleased at the time. She could put food on the table, afford to look after Mum, pay her rent and buy painting materials. She had no financial advisor to tell her not to. When, or if, the painting is ever sold, the hotel will benefit, not me.

I'm used to small rooms in budget hotels with a kettle, complimentary tea-bags and outrageous mini-bar prices. I'm maxing out my credit card right now, but this is an exception. It's not every day that your grandmother has a recovered memory, throws your entire family history up in the air and ends up dead only hours later.

The room is gorgeous. The view onto the Left Bank is even better. I sit on the bed and feel overwhelmed by all this. It's so slick now, so smart, that it's hard to think that Gran once sat here in this very room. I am walking in her footsteps. She might not have had a rainfall shower, Carrara marble in the en-suite bathroom, tinted oak flooring or Murano glass wall lights, but the rest is the same. The street outside, the shape of the building, the city around it all – in the long history of Paris, the gap between me and Gran is the blink of an eye. We're two people looking at each other through the mists of time.

That brings the emotion back. I don't try and wipe the tears away. I reach out and touch the walls and know that, beneath the wallpaper and hidden in the fabric of the building, Gran's handprint is there too.

Now she is gone I want to hold on to every last trace of her. We take our loved ones for granted while they're alive. It's only when they're gone that we realise how loved we were and what a gap is left behind.

I feel now like I could cry oceans and never run out of tears. I want her back. I'd sell my soul for one more conversation with her. It's only been a few hours but it's already a wound that will never properly close or heal.

I feel restless, too. How did the police arrive at the apartment so quickly? Was Gran really experiencing a repressed memory from her own past or was she just getting confused because of her memory issues? Did she mix up her own painting with her own life and imagine that she was the woman in the portrait sitting in Room 11 of the Lutetia?

I hate not knowing. But it's even more than that. If I solve the mystery of Gran's past, will I also solve my own mystery? Am I the granddaughter of Josephine Benoit or Sophie Leclerc? Am I descended from a concentration camp survivor and a murderer? What if everything I've been told about my family's past is wrong?

And one other thought chills me. I know what I did that day all those years ago with Mum. I thought it was something wrong deep inside me. But what if it was inherited? What if I got that part of me from Gran?

For now, though, I can't keep my eyes open much longer. I'm not sure the last time I slept, but my battery is flat. For the first time since coming in from a student all-nighter, I'm too tired to even take my clothes off, wash my face or brush my teeth. I have no energy for anything apart from collapsing onto the bed.

Captain Vidal told me that he will interview me and Edward tomorrow, or actually today. That will have to wait. My body is going on strike. It's long past midnight and I've been up since before seven. I need sleep in the same way my body needs air.

I close my eyes and, as I lie there on the bed, I see Gran again. There is someone else in this room with me, the same woman who was also in the elevator, along the corridor, my companion here.

But it isn't the Gran I knew, it is her younger self. She is dressed in stripes with a shaved head. She is sitting on the end of the bed. She is the woman from the portrait downstairs hanging in the lobby as a memory of the past.

Here in Room 11 of the Lutetia hotel, she is calling to me.

31

OLIVIA

My iPhone is dead and I haven't set an alarm. I wake up expecting it to be half-six and thinking about making scrambled eggs on toast for TJ's breakfast. Then I see the TV and 'Welcome to Lutetia Hôtel' at the top. The hotel clock says it's already gone nine. And I realise now where I am and what happened yesterday. The woman I saw sitting at the end of my bed has vanished too.

It is just me in this room now.

I shower and let more tears melt into the rainfall effect from the showerhead. I find the change of clothes I packed yesterday morning, put my phone on charge and go for breakfast. Apart from the bite of the brownie on the Eurostar, I haven't eaten since the night before I got the phone call and I'm hungry. I miss Gran, but I also miss Tom too. One day we were on the road to a serious relationship, and the next he vanished and ghosted me and it's been a year since I set eyes on him. No matter how much I try, I still can't figure out what he wanted from me. I also can't fully let him go. There was no note or explanation. He was the patient who became a partner and ended up as a stranger. It turns out that I never really knew him at all.

It seems rude to think about food right after a loved one has died. But that's the funny thing about death. I remember the morning after finding Mum with the pill bottle, the one that was usually locked away out of reach, and the postman still arriving, the news still playing, the world carrying on, even a police officer whistling to himself – nothing had changed, yet everything had changed.

Today, if anything, will be worse than yesterday. Captain Vidal will interview me as a significant witness. I will have to relive all the trauma of Gran's death. Day two in Paris will be facing the terrible things that happened on day one. And I can't do that on an empty stomach.

There are four places to eat and drink at the Lutetia: the Brasserie Lutetia, the Bar Josephine (named after another Josephine, but, yes, not ideal and still triggering), Le Saint-Germain and Bar Aristide. Breakfast is served in the brasserie at street level on the corner of Boulevard Raspail and Rue de Sèvres.

Did Gran ever come here before the war? She must have done. I imagine her drinking here as a guest, then returning as a Holocaust survivor. How does anyone deal with that kind of change?

There is a buffet with pastries, bread, fruit salad and yoghurt. The à la carte menu has any type of egg, smoked salmon, French crepes, pancakes and Belgian waffles. I usually skip breakfast at home and only eat after midday. One of my work colleagues gave me a book about intermittent fasting and I said goodbye to my morning almond croissant from the Pret across the road from the hospital. My mood has taken a nosedive ever since. This morning, though, I need all the carbs I can get and stock up on cucumber-based detox juice, wholegrain toast and a mixed herb omelette washed down with a spiced pumpkin latte. It sounds much healthier than it tastes.

Soon enough my energy levels are back. I check my emails and texts and see a message from Edward asking where I'm staying. I reply and he says Captain Vidal will arrive at the hotel to question me at eleven o' clock.

That gives me a bit of time. Whatever happens, there is zero chance I'll be returning to London anytime soon. Gran is dead and I was in her apartment around the time of her murder. I will be kept here for as long as the police need me. Given how slowly the wheels of French justice turn, that could be a very long time indeed.

I text Kyle to see how TJ's drama rehearsal went last night and to check he's got everything for karate tonight. He'll be in class by now so I finish the rest of my breakfast and then head back up to the room. I stop by the *Memory* portrait again and spend a few minutes looking at it and then get tutted at by tourists who want to see it for themselves.

Back in my room, I connect to the Lutetia guest wi-fi and spend the next hour seeing if there's any news of Gran's death online. But nothing comes up. The death of an artist is usually announced by their agent or art dealer. Gran, though, never liked handing over commission to a dealer and never had an agent either. She couldn't stand being managed by anyone. That probably means I have to do it. I'm a memory expert, though, not a public relations specialist. How do you announce a death exactly?

That can wait for now. Next, I see if I can find out anything more about both Josephine Benoit and Sophie Leclerc. There must be birth certificates and other records. Perhaps I can piece together Gran's story that way. I click on a website called 'Family Search' and scroll through both names but there are too many results.

I realise again how little I really know about Gran. Do you know which town your grandparents were born in? Could you name the hospital? Do you know their middle names, blood types, birthdays? I should have asked her when I had the chance. I was too wrapped up in my own issues.

I'm still tapping away when the phone goes. It is reception saying that Captain Vidal is waiting for me downstairs. I've lost track of time. I know what it's like to be under suspicion. I remember giving evidence during Louis's trial last year and second-guessing my own answers. Will Vidal interview me here or somewhere more official? Should I try and find a lawyer or will that make me look guilty?

I take the stairs rather than the lift. Sophie, or Gran, or whoever was with me last night is no longer here, and I feel trapped in the present now, completely on my own.

I see Vidal standing by the reception desk. He looks even less friendly than he did yesterday. He sees me and nods.

'Bonjour, Dr Finn,' he says, pointing to the main door. 'This way please. The car is waiting outside.'

I follow his instructions and walk out onto the Left Bank and my mind goes back to a year ago. I remember the last time I got caught up in the legal system. Back then, Tom was still in my future. Gran could still remember day-to-day things. Paris was still a refuge.

I wish I could go back.

32

OLIVIA

THEN

I don't usually buy newspapers. When I'm in the office I have a cheeky lunchtime scroll through the *Daily Mail*'s sidebar of shame to see which celeb has been caught with their designer pants down. But today is still the Christmas holiday and so I get TJ into his thick coat and we make the trek from Fisherman's Cottage to the little corner shop. I've bribed him with the promise of a Twix for good behaviour. I haven't bought a hard copy paper in years or a Twix, come to think of it, and I don't usually approve. But it's Christmas and, well, no one wants to be Scrooge at this time of year.

The village always seems to stay the same. There's the pub, the church, the bowling green and lots of adorable cottages with curtains twitching and eyes everywhere. The lawyer for the upcoming defamation trial says there's a mention of me in one of the tabloids and so I buy a copy and the Twix for TJ. We stop off at the coffee shop next door. TJ eats his Twix without being caught by the waitress and I read the piece while sipping a latte and wondering how frothy milk can possibly be that calorific.

It's a slow news time between Christmas and New Year and the paper's rehashed a story about France's very own #MeToo moment and the trial of my mentor, Louis de Villefort, who is also Gran's oldest friend. He has always been a colourful and controversial personality, and one of the most renowned psychotherapists in France. Now a former patient called Ingrid Fox has come forward with an historic allegation. She has written an article for *Le Monde* claiming that, twenty years ago, Louis abused his position as her therapist, isolated her from her family, tried to coercively control her and implanted false memories of childhood abuse from her parents. Louis has sued for defamation and argued that it is a classic case of 'transference', where a patient puts their problems onto the therapist, and that Ms Fox is trying to secure a very big payday by threatening to cancel him and ruin his reputation with allegations from two decades ago. He claims she has asked for millions to settle, which he has refused, and is determined to clear his name.

When the allegations first emerged, I wrestled with them. But I was also one of Louis's patients at the same time as Ingrid Fox. I knew what my own experience had been during those sessions at Quai Voltaire and believed Louis. Looking ahead to the trial, the article says I am a family friend of Louis and calls me 'a memory expert who has promoted the controversial use of "recovered memories" and is also the granddaughter of Parisian artist Josephine Benoit'. It's hard to imagine a male memory expert being described in their role as a grandson rather than a professional, but I'm on holiday and I decide to let the micro-aggression slide.

I skim the rest of the paper and then leave it behind in the café for someone else. This one won't go in the clippings folder. We walk back to Fisherman's Cottage. This is where I come to unwind and make beans on toast with TJ and drink lots of hot chocolate while watching re-runs of *Midsomer Murders*. It's in the middle of nowhere so a few days is usually enough before we both get bored and head back to the bright lights of the city.

'Muuuuuuuuum . . .'

I think calming thoughts. It is just a phase, as Gran always says. He will grow out of it. I will one day look back and almost miss the days of TJ's weird pronunciations. I'll long for the way he giggles when an empty ketchup bottle makes a funny sound or his obsession with mock-Australian accents after years watching *Bluey*.

'Uh-huh.'

'Why can't I speak French?'

I laugh. 'Because it takes a long time to learn a language.'

'But I thought I am French.'

'I'm half-French, so technically you're a quarter-French.'

'Then why do I have to learn French? If I'm a quarter-French, shouldn't I already know it?'

I smile. His questions are wonderfully daft sometimes. 'That's not quite how it works, buster.'

'But you speak French.'

'Yes.'

'Did you learn it?'

'Well . . .'

No, is the truth. I spoke French because I sat with Gran as she painted and we talked together or listened to the radio. I spent all my holidays as a child in Paris when Mum was busy working, or more accurately sitting in pubs in Soho. I can't remember a time when I didn't know French. Perhaps TJ has a point.

'If you live in a country then you learn a language without realising it. If you don't live in that country then you have to try harder. Do you want to live in France?'

TJ is only small so France to him is not the land of croissants, patisseries, the Moulin Rouge and the language of love. The only thing he knows about France is that Kylian Mbappé is their captain and scores lots of goals and that he quite fancies a PSG top for his next birthday with 'TJ 10' on the back.

'Do I have to?' he says.

'No.'

'Okay.'

I feel his hand nestle into mine and have one of those rare but special moments where it feels like my heart might burst. Only a second ago he was this small bundle in my arms and now he's talking like a real human. I'm always amazed how much he knows and also how little. He can sound so sensible and then put two and two together and get three hundred. But he says things with such certainty it's hard to disagree.

We get back to Fisherman's Cottage and I rustle up a late breakfast. TJ loves nothing more than sitting with me in this remote cottage with the sound of the sea and the waves. He dips his toast into his fried egg and mops up the beans while I make a bacon and egg sandwich and squish it until the yolk slurps out of the sides. In London we'll be back to kefir yoghurt, blueberries, kimchi and daily kombucha. TJ will also be back to limited screentime, homework and books that expand his mind. But the rules don't apply here.

I stack the dishwasher and make two hot chocolates and pray the dodgy wi-fi allows us to get the all-day *Midsomer Murders* channel. TJ thinks that Midsomer is like Fisherman's Cottage and constantly asks why more bodies aren't discovered on the Norfolk coast. As I sit down and watch DCI Barnaby solve crimes, I can't help thinking of my sessions with Louis after Mum died, walking up those stairs to his consulting room at Quai Voltaire, just as Ingrid Fox must have done, and how messy real life is compared to TV. Back when Louis was still running his clinic, he helped patients recover memories of trauma in their past. It was difficult, and often distressing, work. Many of the patients couldn't handle the memories, and either quit or blamed Louis. People always think therapy is soft, fluffy and healing. Often therapy can be dangerous. We might not always like what we remember.

The article in the paper annoys me though. Not all recovered memories are controversial. Sometimes remembering bad things from the past is the only way to make them better in the present.

'Muuuuuuuuum . . .'

I look at TJ and then the TV. DCI Barnaby has just returned home to his wife Joyce which is usually where Barnaby has his lightbulb moment and finds the missing clue that solves the murder. I scoop my hand through TJ's hair and snuggle him tighter. I know he won't let me do that for much longer. I must stop worrying about the trial and enjoy what I have in front of me. This is close to perfect – messy, frustrating, exasperating, real, but perfect.

'Uh-huh.'

'I think you're like DCI Barnaby,' says TJ. 'You help people.'

'Do you think so?'

TJ nods and then adds, 'But you don't have a Joyce.'

I smile. I don't. I wish I did. Joyce is the anchor in DCI Barnaby's life. She listens to his problems, doesn't always agree with him, but is on his side no matter what. She is also blindingly experimental in the kitchen. We all need a Joyce in our lives, a constant presence with a comforting touch on the shoulder or a wink for good luck.

My boy is wiser than he looks.

33

OLIVIA

NOW

I force myself back to the present. I can't change what happened a year ago.

I must stay in the here and now.

I hoped the interview would take place at the Lutetia. But it looks like I'm being given the official treatment. And that makes me worried. Captain Vidal works for the Criminal Brigade of the Paris Division of the DNPJ. It's nicknamed 'la Crim' or 'the 36' because its headquarters are based at 36 rue du Bastion. But any unit called 'la Crim' isn't big on putting people at their ease.

I sit in the back of the police car and watch Paris through the tinted car windows and know the other people on the streets can't see me. I feel like a guilty secret being removed from view. Perhaps that's exactly what I am.

We arrive at rue du Bastion and I'm taken to a small interview room. I'm not technically under arrest – I'm here as a witness not a suspect – but it does feel that way. Vidal makes me wait for twenty minutes and then enters and sits down opposite. A female officer sits beside him with a notepad. I know from police dramas that this is the moment when I should demand to see a lawyer. But the French justice system is very different to the English one. I'm not sure exactly what my rights are. I never planned on being in this situation. I try and think if I know any decent Parisian lawyers.

Having been an expert witness in court, I know the first rule is not to annoy the cops unless I have to. I'm glad I carb-loaded at breakfast this morning. I'm missing TJ and want nothing more than to drive to Fisherman's Cottage and watch old episodes of *Grey's Anatomy* and have a duvet day with my good friends Ben and Jerry.

But Gran is dead. I'm in an interview room with 'la Crim'. And my son is hundreds of miles away in London. The Norfolk coast and a world before Tom, the trial and the death of Ingrid Fox seems like a distant dream.

Captain Vidal is in a proper suit this morning with a tie and newly ironed shirt. He has shaved as well which makes him look less like a UFC wrestler and more like a physics teacher who also coaches the school boxing team. I saw him yesterday with puffy eyes and sleep-dishevelled hair. Now he means business.

'Thank you for coming here to answer some questions, Dr Finn,' he begins. 'Let me say once again that I am sorry for your loss.'

'Thank you,' I say. 'I'm not entirely sure why this couldn't have been done at the Lutetia. But I'm happy to help in any way I can.'

He doesn't acknowledge my comment. 'Further to our meeting yesterday, Dr Finn, and to the distressing incident last night in Montparnasse, we have looked into your grandmother's claims. We have a hard-copy record from the government archives.'

This is it then. The police will have access to records I can't get. Will this rewrite the story of my family? Did Gran recover a memory yesterday which she has repressed for decades? Was she really Sophie or Josephine?

'They don't add a huge amount,' says Vidal. 'We already knew that both Sophie and Josephine were held for three days to be interviewed by police and evaluated by medical and psychiatric teams. However, we have uncovered another record that shows Sophie Leclerc was arrested in 1943 and taken to Drancy and then transported to Auschwitz.'

Just those two words fill me with horror: Drancy, Auschwitz. If Gran was Sophie, and was that figure on the bed last night, then how do I ever come to terms with what she must have been through?

After spending the night in Room 11 of the Lutetia, I've felt Gran speaking to me. She wants me to uncover the mystery of her past and find out the truth about her recovered memory. She needs me to find out who wanted her dead and why. What secret did Gran know that had to be covered up all these decades later? I can only understand it completely when I have found the answers to those questions.

'And what about Josephine Benoit?'

'We are still looking into that. But we have no record of her at Drancy so far.'

Did Gran live the lie so convincingly that she ended up believing it? Did she kill the real Josephine, as she claimed, and steal her identity? Or did she have some kind of psychological meltdown at the Lutetia all those years ago which meant she wiped the truth from her mind?

'If we consider the possibility that your grandmother's confession could have been correct,' says Vidal, 'we must also consider whether or not it's a potential motive for her murder yesterday evening. We are still waiting on post-mortem results to confirm the cause of death, but murder by suffocation is our working assumption at this stage.'

What happened last night only seems real now. Murder. When a detective sits opposite you and says that, there is no escape hatch. Gran was killed. In her past life, under a different name, it's possible she may have killed someone too.

I woke up yesterday morning worried about TJ wearing tights in the school play and whether he was secretly developing an energy drink addiction. Now I'm being asked about who could have murdered Gran in her sleep and hearing about Auschwitz and Drancy.

It's like the time I walked home from school wondering if Mum would smell the cigarette smoke on my clothes only to find the front door unlocked and our dog, Elton, barking in the kitchen. That is how life goes. There are long periods of nothing, then life happens in moments that change everything.

'Who would want to kill an old woman?' I say. 'Why would her confession about Sophie Leclerc mean she had to die?'

'That,' says Vidal, 'is what I intend to find out.'

34

OLIVIA

Captain Vidal sounds like he might be on my side. But he also works for the French state. I wonder how high this could go and how the police could possibly have arrived at the crime scene so quickly. I also remember Vidal mentioning that his own father was a police officer at the Lutetia when the Holocaust survivors returned.

Is he trying to find the truth or just brush it under the carpet for both personal and professional reasons? Is there something about what happened at the Lutetia which needs to stay hidden, perhaps even involving his own dad? Could this be a set-up and an inside job?

'What could Gran possibly know that would cause this?' I say. 'Tell me that and I'll believe you.'

Vidal doesn't react. 'All of us still live in the shadow of the Second World War,' he says. 'The last people who survived the war are now dying out. There are still scores to be settled, and secrets kept, even all these years later. When people think about the Second World War it's always Churchill and Hitler and D-Day. No one talks about the Occupation of Paris or what happened during the liberation. Those memories have been forgotten. Neighbour against neighbour, who collaborated and who claimed to have resisted, the false and real members of the Resistance, the way scores were settled in 1945 before order was finally restored. It is a memory Paris still has never fully addressed. All the French citizens deported to the camps by their own countrymen. Even today, after so many years, you will find a hundred motives on the streets of Paris that link back to those terrible events in those dark, dark days. Memories of the Occupation are like an iceberg. Most of them are below the surface. But they are no less deadly because they can't be seen.'

'Who gave you the tip-off that she was dead?' I ask. 'How did you arrive at her apartment so quickly?'

Vidal ignores me. 'That is not your concern.'

'Did it ever occur to you that the person who tipped you off was also the person responsible for my grandmother's death?'

'Dr Finn, it is my job to ask the questions.'

'If Gran did murder the real Josephine Benoit at the Lutetia, then surely the police would have looked into it at the time? A body would have been found at the hotel? This would have come out before now?'

'The Lutetia saw thousands of survivors return to Paris,' he says. 'The city was in chaos. The summer of 1945 was the last chance to seek natural justice before the world decided to forget the past and move on. Tell me, what do you know about the *épuration sauvage?*'

Épuration sauvage. Yes, I know that phrase. It means 'the wild purge'.

I've seen the photos and watched the old news footage on YouTube. I know about the women with their shaved heads being paraded through the streets of Paris and the tens of thousands of suspected collaborators executed without trial, even though some tried to insist that they'd actually been working with the Resistance all along. I've watched the films about the Parisian men hunting traitors and the tables being turned once the city was back in French hands.

'Around ten thousand people were killed during the *épuration sauvage*,' Vidal says. 'The real total is probably much higher. Paris was awash with bodies at exactly this moment in 1945. Sadly, few people would have noticed one more added to that number. The real Josephine Benoit, if that is who your grandmother murdered, may well have been written off as a "horizontal collaborator".'

I know that phrase too. That's what they called women who had any form of relationship with Nazi officers stationed in Paris. It was men who collaborated and gave the orders to deport over seventy thousand French citizens to concentration camps. And yet, somehow, women were the ones shamed after the war was over. Horizontal collaboration is just another term for slut-shaming.

'That still doesn't explain why someone would wait until now to murder Gran,' I say. 'What was it about her confession that got them so scared? Why did the name Sophie Leclerc cause someone to act like this?'

'Let's start with your movements yesterday. What happened after you left the Lutetia hotel with your grandmother?'

It's a leap in questioning, and that leap scares me. I thought I was here as a witness not a suspect.

'We got a taxi back to her apartment,' I say. 'I made her a cup of tea. Edward de Villefort turned up and helped me with Gran. I sat with Gran for most of the afternoon and evening, then Edward returned to give me a break. I left the apartment to use the free wi-fi in a café nearby and got a text from Edward asking for help. I rushed back but didn't make it in time. The café has security cameras. I'm sure you can check my alibi and, anyway . . . you saw the rest.'

'So you left Edward de Villefort alone with your grandmother for how long?'

I think of Edward's panic last night and his fear about getting involved with the police. I'm careful in how I reply. 'About an hour or so. He sat with her to make sure she was okay.'

'Does your grandmother have cameras inside her apartment?'

'She didn't have wi-fi, captain. Cameras were way beyond her.'

'So Edward de Villefort,' says Vidal, 'had more than enough time when he was alone in the apartment to carry out the murder himself?'

'Theoretically, yes,' I say. 'But I can't see what motive Edward would have. And it doesn't explain the fact he got injured.'

Vidal shrugs as if it's the simplest thing in the world. 'Monsieur de Villefort could fake an injury to remove himself from suspicion and stage the drama on your return. He left the apartment and then said he would come back? That would give him time to plan the murder out, yes?'

'It still doesn't explain how the police arrived so soon,' I say.

'As I said, madame, that is my business not yours.' Vidal looks at his notes. 'I presume you're aware of why Edward de Villefort fled Paris all those years ago?'

'Yesterday was the first time I saw Edward for decades,' I say. 'I literally haven't set eyes on the man since I was a teenager. I haven't been keeping tabs on him since. So, no, I'm not aware of why he left Paris.'

'I see,' says Vidal.

The truth is I was blindsided by Edward appearing yesterday.

But the Edward I knew dressed like a member of NSYNC and acted like an extra in *American Pie*. He says he's gone clean and is living off broccoli and flaxseeds, but that could be another lie, just like he lied all those years ago about having feelings for me. I believed him then only to hear he was on the red-eye to JFK the next day without even a message to say goodbye.

I'm all grown up now. Edward is a charmer. And charmers are usually deceptive.

But murder?

That thought troubles me.

Did I let a killer into Gran's apartment?

35

OLIVIA

THEN

Goodbye Fisherman's Cottage, hello London. TJ is back to school, I am back at work, and we are surrounded by cars, sirens and all the worst bits of living in a city. I can feel the pollution in my throat. It's a giant ball of phlegm that no nasal spray known to humanity can cure.

I'm getting used to my routine again and all the post-holiday catch-ups. I thought Fisherman's Cottage was a nice, scenic escape. But I've been outdone. Two of the other therapists at the Memory Unit went for Christmas sunshine to Qatar, another of the assistants was visiting her sister in Australia and another decided to have a safari in Kenya. Endless episodes of *Midsomer Murders* are tame by comparison. Kyle could never see the charm of the Norfolk coastline either. Even now, he's always threatening to whisk TJ off snorkelling or skiing. When I had my therapy sessions with Louis, he always told me it's not helpful to compare. But I'm human and I do and sod being helpful.

I wish it was Christmas again. When I was little, holidays with Gran felt very grown up. We spent hours sitting in cafés as she smoked Gauloises and asked me questions about school, boyfriends, life and love. I was cheeky and fearless and couldn't care less about Gran's art. She liked that about me. I didn't want her approval but just her love.

I wiggle my mouse to life and look at the calendar on my iMac. There are more meetings about the Memory Unit's role within the 'hospital ecosystem', whatever that means, a financial briefing and something about updated protocols for the gender-neutral toilets on the fourth floor.

I look at the rest of my inbox and see a new patient inquiry. The man's name is Tom Lomas. He says he will pay privately. I google it but there are millions of people with the same name and I can't find anything useful. He is a paying client. I'll take the appointment and hope he's not just sniffing for some gossip on the trial.

It is only a matter of weeks until the trial now. The French legal system is complex, and I don't entirely understand it all, but my job is to be a character witness for Louis. Ingrid Fox's lawyers will ask if Louis ever tried to coercively control me twenty years ago or manipulate me, taking advantage of a teenager. They will try and show that the claims in Ingrid's articles weren't defamatory and were based on repeated patterns of behaviour.

Did he ever turn me against my parents? (No, Mum did that all on her own.)

Did he implant false memories of trauma in my past? (Again, no, the trauma was real and very much my fault.)

But I have to be all over the detail about my sessions, even though they were twenty years ago, and make sure I don't slip up.

I start tapping out a reply to Tom Lomas.

I'm longing for Christmas all over again.

36

MYLES

NOW

The incident at the Lutetia wasn't enough to justify travelling to Paris.

But a murder is.

Or at least that's how Myles has spun it in his email to the Met's finance team. He tells them that his presence has been requested by the French police – another mild exaggeration, but deniable – and is now waiting for approval.

He finishes reading an article on recovered memories and then heads down to the canteen and gets his second espresso of the day. He pays via Apple Watch, downs the espresso in one and is briefly tempted by a packet of custard creams. But the crumbs will only mess up his waistcoat of choice for today, a classic single-breasted herringbone. He puts the custard creams back and picks up a Pink Lady apple instead. His personal trainer would most definitely approve.

Myles returns to his office. All the open-plan desks are messy with coffee cups, piles of paper and leftover cartons from last night's Chinese, the smell of chicken chow mein wafting through the place. But his office is always immaculate. He clears his inbox every day without fail and never lets a piece of paper stay on his desk for more than twelve hours. He cleans his keyboard once a week with an antibacterial wipe and always has a window open to keep some natural air circulating. A tidy desk means a tidy mind.

He's been this way ever since childhood. It was his only defence against the chaos. There was always a new place, new faces, constant change. He learned to control his own space. That's what kept him sane. His sister Laura is the opposite, happy to embrace the chaos. Her place is always full of shoes, homework, bags, PE kit and leftover food on plates. His home is immaculate. He wonders how he'll ever cope with having kids.

It's over an hour later when the email from the Met finance team pings into his inbox and he finally has approval to travel to Paris. Better late than never. He debates flying, but the Eurostar across the Channel is quicker and cheaper. He buys the ticket on his police credit card and keeps the receipt. He informs Captain Vidal of his ETA and then looks at the budget he has for hotels. The Met finance team are tight at the best of times. Soon they'll be telling detectives to take a sleeping bag and a packed lunch. Or to swim the Channel to save on transport costs. The best he can hope for is a two-for-one sandwich meal deal at the station and a bed with clean sheets.

Myles packs the Ingrid Fox case file then the burner phone he always carries with him containing all the new digital evidence – definitely not an official police item – and orders an Uber to take him to St Pancras. In the car, he reads through the Ingrid Fox case file again from the trial last year. He has read it so many times he can almost repeat it word for word. Olivia Finn's testimony was crucial to the civil trial, as was her relationship with Louis and the de Villefort family and the daily therapy sessions she had with Louis in the 2000s.

He imagines Olivia stepping into that consulting room in Quai Voltaire, and sitting on the famous couch where so many big names had been before her, and then telling Louis her greatest secrets and watching him at work. When Myles is finished with the file, he continues listening to the new evidence on his burner phone. There are hours and hours, here. If this ever got into the hands of professional standards, then he would be royally screwed. But he's careful. He has to be.

The waiting area for the Eurostar service from St Pancras to Gare du Nord is packed with families and tourists. Myles takes another sip of water and wishes it was something stronger. He checks his work email and sees confirmation from Captain Vidal about his arrival and meeting in Paris later today.

Myles and Vidal came into contact with each other when Ingrid Fox's body was found. The most obvious suspect was Louis de Villefort or a member of his family. After all, Ingrid had publicly accused Louis of coercive control and emotional abuse during therapy, and Louis has sued her for defamation in the French courts.

But Louis was now in his nineties and had cast-iron alibis for the time of Ingrid's death. Edward de Villefort also had an alibi, and the small matter of being in New York at the time. If Ingrid's death was murder, then who could have done it? Attention turned to Ingrid's adopted family and the possibility that the memories that had surfaced during Ingrid's therapy sessions might have been true. Maybe a family member silenced her as she realised her accusations against Louis were a screen memory for her own adopted family? Stranger things had happened.

Ever since, Myles and Vidal have run the joint case together displaying full Anglo-French unity, which consists of occasional emails and gruff updates over voicemail. But this could be something. It involves a lot of the key players from the trial. Myles is stretching the limits of his role as the lead detective on the case, but he'll gladly take a bollocking back at the station. He's doing this for Ingrid.

He joins the crowd heading towards the train and finds his seat. Despite the emails and calls, he has never actually met Vidal in person. A few more hours, thinks Myles. The last time he was in Paris was for that other extra-curricular work and he prays again that he didn't make any mistakes or leave a trail behind.

He tries to get some sleep as the train approaches the border crossing into mainland France. He finds everything scrambling in his head until he dreams about standing opposite Louis de Villefort as Ingrid accuses him of abusing his position as a therapist.

He rubs his eyes and shakes off the dream. He would kill for an Americano with oat milk and some lunch. He can already feel his cravings for opera cake, sugar puffs, millefeuille, macarons, and Paris-Brest return. He will have to be careful or undo his hard work in the gym. He's always been a foodie, another thing he could control, and loves nothing more than getting his apron on and trying something new in the kitchen. Maybe it's a good thing Met expenses don't stretch to a three-course lunch.

He continues listening to the files on his burner phone. He thinks of how many boundaries he pushed last year and how out of character it was. But he owed Ingrid. He had to do everything he could to help her.

Perhaps, together, he and Vidal can finally crack the case. They can figure out the truth about Josephine Benoit's recovered memory.

And finally get a lead on the tragic death of Ingrid Fox.

37

OLIVIA

The interview room grows hotter. I try not to appear uncomfortable. But that's like trying not to think of a pink elephant.

Vidal looks more calculating now. 'Edward de Villefort was the only person in the apartment with your grandmother, and you also called Louis de Villefort after you heard about your grandmother's episode, and Charlotte Fouquet. Why are you so reliant on the de Villefort family and their staff?'

'It's not a crime, as far as I'm aware. How is this relevant to Gran's death?'

'Louis de Villefort is your mentor and also used to be your long-time psychotherapist, is he not? And for your grandmother, too, in the past? That sounds like a conflict of interest, surely?'

'I admit it's unusual,' I say. 'But so are my own personal circumstances. I grew up never knowing my father. My mother had lots of problems and ended up taking her own life. I was a teenager and got into a bad way with substance abuse and alcohol. I came to Paris in the 2000s to stay with Gran after Mum died and, together, Gran and Louis pieced me back together. To be honest, I owe them everything.'

'That's why you became a psychotherapist too?'

'Yes. Louis helped me recover memories about Mum's death, and to deal with them, and that's what I now do with my patients.'

'Do you still have therapy sessions with Louis now?'

'Not since he retired over ten years ago. But the bond between a patient and their therapist can be very precious,' I say. 'They know you better than anyone else. Louis was one of the pioneers of psychotherapy after the war. I sometimes call Louis and talk, but nothing formal.'

'If anyone was aware of your grandmother's past as Sophie Leclerc, then it would be Louis himself? As her former therapist, he would have known her secrets? He was, according to my notes, stationed at the Lutetia at the same time your grandmother claims to have stayed there?'

'Yes. That might be where the confusion comes from. She's mixed up things Louis told her with her own life. It's known as "memory borrowing".'

'It's really possible to borrow someone else's memory and think it's your own?'

'Our memories are complex things, captain. The reason the memories need to be recovered is that we forget them in the first place. We can't deal with the trauma and so the brain self-deletes the memory as a coping mechanism. It's possible that Gran wiped her past from her mind and that only her short-term memory loss caused it to spring up again. At the Memory Unit in London, I've seen patients like that. Dementia often means patients recall events from the past but forget things happening in the present. That could be the case with Gran.'

I've never known the full story of Gran and Louis's

relationship, only that they knew each other when they were young and remained close ever since. If Gran was at the Lutetia, I wonder what happened between them.

Vidal looks down at his notes. It feels like he is about to make another leap, and that scares me.

'Let's talk about the trial last year,' he says, 'and the case of Ingrid Fox.'

38

OLIVIA

I'm still not sure how any of this connects to Gran's death. It feels more like this police officer has a vendetta against me. Maybe this is all a stitch-up. The French police want to attack the de Villefort family and they are using Gran's death, and my visit here, to do that. Or perhaps Vidal has a specific reason from his own dad's past.

'What specifically about the trial?' I ask.

'Did Louis ever discuss Ingrid Fox with you when she was a patient of his? And did he pressure you to testify at the defamation trial?'

'No. Louis is my mentor,' I say. 'As a psychotherapist, he pioneered our understanding of the role memory plays in our lives. He never discussed any confidential patient information with me. Nor did he pressure me to do anything. I'm his friend, and I wanted the truth to come out.'

'And, no doubt, you are fully aware of the criticism of Louis's methods?'

'Yes.'

'Do you agree with those criticisms?'

Since setting up his clinic at Quai Voltaire, Louis has been accused of many things. Helping patients recover memories from their past is hugely controversial. People say that he turns patients against their families, helps women leave their – often violent – husbands, even encourages people who lived through the Occupation to remember uncomfortable truths about Paris under the Nazis, and generally makes a nuisance for the families of patients who go to him for treatment. It's made him deeply unpopular in some quarters.

'No.'

I think of the secrets in my own life now. I remember finding out that Kyle was sexting his new woman and those Brazilian ju-jitsu classes were more hands-on than he was telling me. There is the shock, the denial, the anger, then realising that it all makes a twisted kind of sense. Sometimes I wish I'd never seen the texts and the whole thing could be brushed under the carpet. In a less trivial example, perhaps that's how those French collaborators felt. They are old, now, wanting to die in peace, desperate that those memories from the war are never recovered.

'What did you mean,' asks Vidal, 'when you said about the truth coming out?'

I sigh. 'Treating difficult patients is part of the job of a psychotherapist. My own patients have accused me of stealing from them, gaslighting them, planting false memories, having affairs with their partners, trying to take their children away from them, the list goes on. Ninety-nine per cent of our patients have a good experience and around one per cent react badly to treatment. Unfortunately, those one per cent grab all the headlines and cause the most issues. They don't want to confront the truth, so they accuse the therapist instead. We call it transference. It's one of the dangers of therapy.'

'Did you do any of the things those patients accused you of?'

Again, the question feels oddly personal and not connected to Gran. What is this man after? 'No, of course not. They also accused the receptionist at the Memory Unit of trying to kill them, and thought the biscuits in the waiting room were laced with cyanide. We are talking about people with severe problems, captain.'

'Patients like Ingrid Fox?'

'She had lifelong issues from her time in care, suffering from depression and anxiety, and had used alcohol and drugs as coping mechanisms. Louis had a name, and lots of money, and she saw an opportunity. She got her day in court.'

'And that remains your view of the accusations against Louis de Villefort?'

'I think Ingrid Fox's accusations were most likely screen memories protecting her from facing the truth. Louis didn't do those things, but her father – or adopted father – probably did. That's what Louis tried to help her confront. That's what she couldn't cope with, or her adopted family couldn't cope with. And that might be why she either killed herself or was killed by a third party.'

'That's what you said during the trial,' says Vidal. 'And you stand by that?'

I try not to get angry. I can't pretend that what happened to Ingrid doesn't still affect me.

I see her eyes staring at me, just like they did in that courtroom.

Even now, she is accusing me.

'Yes,' I say. 'I do.'

39

OLIVIA

THEN

The first meeting about Louis's trial is with a high-powered law firm in Lincoln's Inn Fields.

I wait in the plush lobby and then meet the French senior partner and his associate who are both over in London for the week. The meeting room is wood-panelled. Water is poured from decanters. The senior partner has a signet ring and his suit is beautifully tailored, while his associate doesn't wear a tie and looks as if he's just left school.

'Ahead of the defamation trial,' says the senior partner, 'we wanted to go over some more of the background to the claims against Louis and what sort of questions you might be asked.' His hair swishes like an advert for shampoo and I can smell his expensive aftershave on the air. How are French lawyers so much more debonair than British ones?

I know some of the details, but mainly what I've read online. Louis hasn't told me much directly, other than saying the allegations are not true and he is sad that his long and distinguished career has been tarnished by historic claims from twenty years ago. He claims his work as a psychotherapist has involved patients making accusations against some high-profile people, and now the French establishment is trying to get its revenge by publicly humiliating him.

The easy route out of this would be to ignore Ingrid Fox's claims. There is not enough evidence for a criminal trial and, so far, there is just an article written by Ingrid for *Le Monde*. But Louis is stubborn. His reputation is everything. If he doesn't clear his name, then other former patients with a grudge could invent false claims and try to get a payout. Louis wants his day in court. He didn't fight in the Resistance, treat Holocaust survivors in the Lutetia and build the most famous therapy clinic in Paris only to see his reputation trashed right at the end.

I listen carefully as the senior partner fills me in.

Ingrid Fox, fifty-two, is a dual UK–French national like me and began seeing Louis as a patient at his consulting room in Quai Voltaire in 2004. Ingrid grew up in care before being fostered, and always had problems with persistent anxiety issues. She spent many years trying to get sober. Standard hospital tests hadn't come up with anything and she wanted psychological treatment. During a long spell of psychotherapy, Ingrid began to recover repressed memories of her foster parent's violent physical abuse against her during her childhood. After many sessions, Ingrid was able to describe in vivid detail the methods of abuse. There was an attic, a belt and shiny black shoes on a creaky attic ladder.

The catch, of course, was that her father was no ordinary foster parent. He was a former French judge married to an English wife, a visiting law professor at various international universities and a famed philanthropist well known for fostering vulnerable young people. As Ingrid began cutting them out of her life, and making accusations of childhood abuse, her foster father used his deep pockets to launch a campaign against Louis and his psychotherapy methods. It didn't work. Once her foster father died, however, Ingrid seemed to have a change of heart. She reconciled with some other members of her foster family. She slowly rebuilt relationships. And, after many years of healing, she claimed to have realised that Louis had implanted false memories and pushed her to make the accusations.

Those are the claims she has gone public with in *Le Monde*. And those are what Louis claims have defamed his reputation as a psychotherapist.

'The court case itself,' says the partner, 'is about whether Louis abused his role as a psychotherapist during the years he treated Mademoiselle Fox. However, the broader debate is whether it's possible to recover memories from the past.'

'That's where I come in.'

'Yes and no. Again, strictly speaking, you are being called as a character witness to talk about what Louis is like as a therapist and your experience with him. But, given you work at the Memory Unit here in London, your knowledge of recovered memories could be useful too.'

'What is your strategy to prove the claims in the article are false?'

The senior partner looks pained. 'It's simple. Louis was doing his job in helping surface Ingrid's repressed memories of abuse. Her foster family knew the truth about what the foster father had done. After he died, they manipulated Ingrid back into the fold and persuaded her that the recovered memories never happened and the real abuser in all this was Louis.'

We sit in silence for a moment. In my mind, I am eighteen again and lying on the couch in the consulting room with my life falling to pieces. I always felt safe in that room with Louis.

A Murder in Paris

In all the hours, and the hundreds of daily sessions, it felt like talking to a beloved grandparent.

'Do you know what you will say as a witness?' asks the associate.

'I spent years in therapy with Louis,' I say, 'and it saved my life. His pioneering memory techniques have helped thousands of patients over the years. Without him, I would be shooting up in an alley somewhere, or drying out in rehab for the fifth time. He helped me recover memories around my mother's death and confront them head on.'

The senior partner and his associate look relieved.

'And you will say all this at the trial?' asks the senior partner. 'Just like that?'

My phone vibrates in my pocket. It's probably TJ's childminder saying she can't find the Nutella he's demanding, or Kyle bailing from the school run next week. My life seems to go from the profound to the ridiculous in a matter of seconds.

I don't look at the message immediately. It can wait. I think of Louis now, instead, long since retired and standing in his magnificent apartment in the 7th arrondissement looking out over the Seine and towards the Louvre and seeing his life's work crumble around him, cancelled by a world he once helped save.

'Yes,' I say. 'I'll tell the truth. Louis always told me that the truth will set you free.'

'Good,' says the senior partner, signalling the meeting is over. 'Let's hope he was right.'

40

OLIVIA

NOW

I'm not sure how much time passes. Vidal leaves the room with his assistant and I sit waiting again. Eventually, Vidal returns and says that I am free to go. He also repeats his warning about not leaving Paris and the DNPJ being in touch with further questions.

I am escorted out of 36 rue du Bastion. I take a taxi back to the Lutetia and the drive feels like the last day of school with its sudden taste of freedom. I have a brief urge to flee to Gare du Nord and never look back, but Vidal's warning rings in my ear.

When I get back to the hotel, I stop in the lobby and stare at Gran's *Memory* painting again. I look deep into the eyes of the woman sitting in the hotel room and almost beg her to speak through the painting and tell me the answer. Who are you? Are you Sophie or Josephine? What happened in Room 11 of this hotel? Which one of you survived?

There are more tourists, and I have to step aside again. It's mine, I want to say, not yours. My gran painted it, and you have no right to be here. But, of course, they do. It is public property. The artist might be dead but the painting lives on.

I go up to my room, instead, and try to get my head together.

A Murder in Paris

It still feels weird to call this my room. I'll always think of Room 11 as Gran's room. It feels haunted by her.

I think of Tom again and the questions from Vidal. I've been hurting so much since Tom vanished that it doesn't feel like anything else could compare. But now this. I have thought about Tom and his disappearance every minute of every day since he ghosted me. I've even blamed myself for breaking the rules around therapy and having a relationship with a patient. I wonder if this is what growing older is like. Life stops being free and easy and becomes weighed down with regrets, problems, always looking in the rear view mirror. What happened to hope and possibility?

No, that blame game is silly. I was let down by Tom, just like I was let down by Edward and Kyle. They were different in many ways, but they were also charmers with more style than substance and did a runner when things got tough.

They are men, I hear Mum saying, as she fills the house with cigarette smoke and stumbles drunkenly towards me. Men always let you down, Olivia.

I'm jolted out of my thoughts as the phone rings. I put all those regrets about the men in my life to one side. It is the reception downstairs. They tell me a guest is waiting in the lobby.

Edward de Villefort has arrived.

41

THE LUTETIA

1945

JOSEPHINE

'It's you,' says Sophie.

It's such an ordinary thing to say. But what else can she say? They should still be arm in arm, as they trip into the Lutetia as it used to be and drink café au laits and talk about Josephine's latest romance and Sophie's plans to marry Louis.

How can they be here, in the same hotel, as enemies? What possible sins have they committed in a past life to deserve this?

The emotion overwhelms her. There is shock, sadness, despair, all mingled together. Sophie was her best friend. They have known each other since childhood. They shared everything together. Sophie is the sister she never had.

Josephine wants to run across the room and hug her, hear that everything is all right and things can go back to how they used to be. But she also knows that can never happen. Josephine betrayed Sophie. She gave up her best friend to protect herself from suspicion and keep working for the Resistance. She sacrificed one person for the greater good.

Shame engulfs Josephine now. It was an impossible situation, but she also did a terrible thing, like so many people in wartime. She had to make a choice, and she made the only one she could. Didn't she?

She feels all this – a huge tidal wave of emotion – but knows she can't show it. She must keep focused. Everyone in this hotel is like that. They are traumatised, and unable to deal with what has happened. They walk around glassy-eyed and emotionless, like skeletons learning how to live again.

Josephine doesn't often let herself think like that. Pity is a crime, as her aunt always said. She wishes she'd been less trusting of her own side. She still believed in ideals like bravery, courage and sacrifice for your country. She thought the mob in Paris would celebrate what she had done for the Resistance and shower her with praise. She hadn't realised that would only be for the men. No matter what she said, or the justifications she gave, they saw her as a Nazi whore. They didn't care that she'd been gaining vital secrets that would help win the war. She was a woman with no honour or principles and must be treated like the other collaborators.

'I can't believe you're here,' says Josephine. The voice is right, the height too, there can be no doubt that Sophie is alive and standing in this room. 'They've put everyone who arrived today on the first floor. We must have missed each other at Gare d'Orsay by a whisker.'

There are no words to express what has happened to them. They stare at each other in silence. That dark time was so dark that it has changed them forever. They saw things and did things that can never be undone. Josephine has heard stories about the camps. She tries to imagine what Sophie has seen and how much fury she will have for the friend who put her there.

Sophie doesn't react. The soft features from before are harder. 'We're to be roommates then?'

'Yes. This is your space as much as mine.'

Josephine remembers this place well. The Old Lutetia, as she now thinks of it, was full of elegant and impossibly beautiful women in ballgowns, dashing gentlemen in formal dress and a piano playing in the lobby. She sees those ghosts from a past life lounging on banquettes and sipping coffee. It's hard to believe that world once existed.

This New Lutetia, though, is not like that. It's overshadowed by the Cherche-Midi prison opposite the Boulevard Raspail and the cries that spill into the street. The German prisoners of war are held there. Everyone is suspicious of guests in other rooms. According to the rumour mill, no one dares to sleep too soundly in case they are attacked in the night. The war is over, but it doesn't feel like that here.

The physical war might be over. But the war in people's heads is just beginning. It has traumatised them all.

Sophie must know that Josephine was the one who betrayed her. Josephine was the only one who knew where Sophie and her father were hiding. But Josephine must stick to her story and make Sophie believe she is a camp survivor. It will require another performance, the best of the lot, but Josephine is sure her plan can still work. She is an actor, after all.

'I remember when we came here for the last time,' says Josephine now. She sits on her bed and tries to smile at Sophie. 'Your father arranged it as a surprise and the look on your face was priceless. We were still girls and it was the most wonderful evening. Who would imagine being reunited like this?'

Sophie's guard falls. She was always sentimental about the past but, particularly, her father. Her reaction suggests her father must have died in the camps. But Sophie always needed her father, relied on his solidness and safety.

'Two friends in Paris before the war, now two survivors after the war,' says Josephine. 'It's like fate has brought us together again. I used to dream that you were still alive, Sophie, and we would meet again after the war was over. I prayed for it.'

Sophie is getting emotional now. Tears fill her eyes and she sits down on the other bed. They used to do this, staying up late and talking until the sun began to rise.

'I'm so tired and so confused,' she says, her voice cracking with emotion. The façade drops slightly, and Sophie's face creases with sadness. 'Our life used to be so good. When I was in the camps, I thought of when we were at school together or you coming home for tea with my father. It seemed impossible to have once lived that life.'

Josephine watches Sophie carefully. Sophie is still badly malnourished. Her skin is riddled with sores and marks. She is so vulnerable, yet still fighting on, and Josephine feels like every line on Sophie's face, and each stuttering breath, is another reminder of the terrible betrayal, the line Josephine crossed, the moment she stopped being a good person and became – forever afterwards – stuck in this moral grey area.

Sophie brushes away her tears. 'They told us some collaborators are pretending to be survivors to escape punishment. The shamed women of Paris are being left on roadsides to die like whores.'

'And they deserve it,' says Josephine, silencing her own conscience. 'I would shave them myself and spit on them if I got the chance. They don't deserve to live. They betrayed us. How can you defend them, Sophie? They deserve to be punished. You must see that?'

The last flicker of doubt in Sophie's eyes goes now. Really, she is too trusting. Josephine always used to take advantage of Sophie's good nature. Josephine has been able to play her like this since they were little, just like she played the Nazi officers.

'What really happened?' says Sophie. 'Father and I were in Paris, and the next day we were arrested and taken to Drancy. You were the last person I talked to. I always thought you were the one who betrayed us. You were the only one who knew where we were.'

'Everyone here was denounced by someone.' Josephine pauses for dramatic effect. 'I never said anything. I swear on my life. But, if I were you, I would think the same. All I can ask, dear Sophie, is that you trust me as your friend. I would never do that to you. I loved you then and I love you now.'

It's not that Josephine enjoys these games, but it's the same tactic she's always used with men. She gets into their heads, curls them round her little finger, until they can't tell what day of the week it is or which way's north.

There is a wail from next door, and the sound of someone pacing up and down the hallway. Sophie looks even more terrified of the Lutetia than Josephine is. This hotel may look like a palace hotel, the Old Lutetia, that place of ballgowns and glamour, but it is a warzone and neither of them are safe.

'You're back in Paris now,' says Josephine. 'If you pass the police interview and the psychiatric exam, you'll be free. We both will be.'

Sophie's lips tremble. 'No, I'll never be free.'

'Why not?'

'I have these memories . . . I can't remember everything, but I remember enough. I remember all the terrible things I did to survive in the camp. Surely you have the same?'

Josephine tries not to react. She hates this, but she must look after herself. She wants to know what Sophie is hiding, what things she did in the camps. They could be useful later. Those secrets might help her survive.

'Tell me,' says Josephine. She strokes Sophie's shoulder like she always used to. 'Tell me about the memories, Sophie. Your secrets are safe with me.'

42

OLIVIA

NOW

Can I trust Edward?
Part of me does. But that's mainly because of the past. I trusted him when we were young and it's hard to shake the habit. Now, though, I have no idea who the adult Edward is, just like I have no idea about the younger Gran.

It's becoming a theme. Do we ever really know anybody, even those closest to us?

I take the stairs down to the lobby of the Lutetia. I feel Gran's footsteps walking in front of me again, as if I'm following her through these halls and time blurs between 2025 and 1945, and she is slowly leading me towards the answer.

I see Edward sitting in Bar Josephine. Of course he is. Apart from the name, it's also the most fashionable bit of the Lutetia. I was about to say hip or trendy, but that's like Mum saying groovy and still thinking the Bee Gees and disco are where it's at. Soon I'll be adding 'the' to things: The YouTube, The TikTok. TJ will get progressively savvier, and I will get infinitely less, the doomed millennial with her ankle socks. As I look through the clear glass walls into the bar, though, Edward seems eternally young. Perhaps that's because he doesn't have kids. We'll all be living in a colony on Mars and Edward de Villefort will still look like he's just finished school.

The Bar Josephine has floor-to-ceiling art frescos and there is live jazz most nights. I'm surprised it's open then check the time and realise it's already afternoon. I spent more time in my room than I realised. I haven't eaten anything since my omelette and toast for breakfast this morning.

I join Edward at the bar and, for some reason, have the old fluttery feeling. Edward was always one of those people who seem to dress in the dark while always looking fashionable. A morning inside a Paris police station has only enhanced his rugged good looks, despite the injury to his face. Edward has spent a lifetime getting away with things thanks to that smile. He doesn't look at me immediately, and I've forgotten this side of him. My memory of him has edited out the bad bits. But he always could be grumpy, like a teenager in a sulk. I wonder what he's like with patients.

I read the drinks menu. There's a cocktail with Bacardi rum, coconut oil, French toast, lapsang and liquorice named 'Resistance'. I order it and the name gets his attention.

'Ha ha, very funny, Liv,' he says.

I half-smile. Even that seems wrong given what happened yesterday. 'What are you drinking?'

'Belvedere,' says Edward. He drains the last of the glass. 'Pour me another.'

'And I thought you'd given up the booze and gone all virtuous on me?'

'That was before I came back to this city and all its ghosts.'

'I love Paris.'

'You weren't born here. You didn't grow up overshadowed by its history. All the tourists think Paris is the city of love. But it can be a city of darkness and secrets too. So many secrets.' He pauses, realising how he sounds. 'I've arranged for Charlotte Fouquet to meet us here later on. She might be able to help us with your grandmother's confession as well.'

I look at him and think of Captain Vidal's theory about the murder. Did Edward inflict the injury on himself? Was the text and the scene at the flat all staged for my benefit? The more I think about it, the more nervous I get. This whole case feels like a trap, somehow, a web I'm being caught in.

My cocktail is served and, as I sip, I realise that I don't know what Edward is really capable of. This man has returned to Paris after two decades away. Now Gran is dead. I have been interviewed by the police. And a repressed memory from the past threatens to change my present and my future.

No, Edward cannot be trusted. Nor can Captain Vidal, or anyone else for that matter. Edward is the link between so much that has happened over the last twenty-four hours. I must be on my guard.

I trusted Tom too much, and I can't make the same mistake again.

For all I know, I could be sitting next to a murderer.

43

OLIVIA

THEN

Today I meet Tom for the first time.

I'm almost late for the session at the hospital. TJ doesn't want to go to school and I end up bribing him with promises of Haribo Supermix just to get him into the car. Haribo is the new Twix in our house now. His favourite sugary food changes from week to week. This year we've had Curly Wurlies, Freddos, Twirls and Jelly Tots. My son is a diva when it comes to his rider. It's a struggle to keep up.

When we arrive at the school gates – only three minutes late today – TJ stays in the car slightly longer than usual and, for a moment, I remember all those damp school mornings when I also wanted to run away. I remember the bullies in the corridors and how much I longed for school to be over and the rest of life to begin. He also has double games and he really doesn't like one helping of games never mind two. I want to turn the car around and tell him school's out for today.

Instead, I play our usual game.

'Would you rather . . . ?'

His face lights up.

'. . . be eaten by a dinosaur or hugged by a racoon?'

TJ makes a disgusted face and laughs and says, 'Eaten by a dinosaur.'

'Controversial decision.'

'Because their belly is so big, I could get out the other side.'

'Fair point.'

TJ doesn't like me hugging him in public any more, even in the car. But I do a quick check and no one is watching and so I give him a mini-hug which he pretends to hate but actually enjoys. Then he gets out of the car and I watch him walk inside.

'Have a good day, buster. Love you loads.'

He also hates me calling him 'buster'. But it slips out sometimes and I did give birth to him, so there's not a huge amount he can do about it. I feel the usual worry as I wait for other kids to talk to him. Does TJ have lots of friends? He never mentions many. He's become quieter recently. It's Kyle's fault, I'm sure. Kyle only knows how to talk to men his own age. He can be sarcastic with TJ, putting him down, laughing when he gets something wrong, that stupid male competitiveness that makes every sleepover turn into a I-am-the-alpha contest. Kyle says his dad did the same with him and, well . . . look how that turned out.

I speed away from the school gates and arrive at the Memory Unit with lots of apologies and see Tom in the waiting room. The Unit gets all sorts of patients. Tom is early forties, tall and thin with glasses and scruffy hair that he ruffles as a nervous tic. He wears a blue shirt tucked in neatly, dark chinos and scuffed Chelsea boots. The chair is too small for him. He has one of those messenger bags with a loose strap, which makes him look like he's a new kid at school with a packed lunch wrapped in cellophane. I like him before he's even opened his mouth.

I do the meet and greet and lead him to my office. I take

personal details, ask him if he's ever had psychotherapy before – no, is the answer – and then get him to tell me why he booked the appointment. How can I help?

'I'm ex-military,' he says. 'I always thought the touchy-feely stuff wasn't for me. Still do, really. But I've been having memories, recently. It's not PTSD, at least not according to the internet. I'm haunted by missions from the past. I'm not sleeping well and I think it's because of these memories. It's taking a toll on my job, my relationships, everything really. And I need some help with it. I looked up the Memory Unit online.'

I take notes. 'What about your family? Are you married? Children?'

'My partner and I split up. We were together for six years. She claimed I'd checked out of the relationship which was probably fair. We tried for kids but it never happened for us. The problem was me, and I think she couldn't get past that. It hurt for a long time, but I don't blame her, or not as much as I used to. It was just sad all round.'

'Did the memory issues start after the split or before?'

'After, I think. It's hard to know. The memories have been creeping up on me for a while now. I've been drinking more heavily, binge eating, smoking fifty a day, anything to distract myself. But it's not working.'

'Why do you think it's not PTSD?'

'I checked online. And I know friends who suffer from it. I don't get flashbacks or nightmares or distressing images or anything like that. I did things in the Marines that I remembered in a certain way. Now I wonder if my memory is playing tricks on me. I remember the first time I killed someone, and every time I see a news story about a murder it triggers me, and I can't move past it.'

'It sounds like a midlife crisis.'

Tom scratches his cheek. 'They didn't list that as a medical condition online. But I haven't started dating women half my age or buying a Harley yet . . . though give it time.'

'Insomnia can be a symptom of PTSD. I wouldn't rule it out at this stage. The two most common memory problems are PTSD and dementia. Have you been forgetting things lately?'

'No.'

'And is it just those old missions that bring you to the Memory Unit today?'

'I also read some of the articles you've written,' says Tom. 'You get what I'm talking about. All those patients you've helped with your recovered memory techniques, healing their addictions. That's what I need. I thought you'd understand.'

There is something so genuine and vulnerable in the way he says it. I'm not used to men being open like this with me. 'That's certainly true. Do you have any idea what this trauma in your past might be?'

'I did things during my service, like we all did. My mind has locked it away so it doesn't hurt me. It's there, though, and I don't think I'll get over this until I confront it. I thought I was okay with taking another life, it's what we're trained to do, but as I get older I'm . . . not so sure any more.'

It's grim subject matter, but I really do like this man. We've only been talking for about twenty minutes. But it's like that moment when you meet someone from a dating app in real life and you can tell from a first glimpse if there's something to work with or not. You walk into the pub ready for your life to change; or figure out how to fake that all-important emergency phone call.

'I think I can help you,' I say. 'I do have one condition, though, before we begin therapy.'

'Which is?'

'You must always tell me the truth,' I say. 'It's the only way we can make any progress. As a psychotherapist, whatever you tell me will never leave this room. That's a promise. But it has to be the truth and nothing but the truth.'

'It will be,' he says, smiling at me now. 'Scout's honour.'

And, in that moment, I believe him.

44

OLIVIA

NOW

I stop thinking about that first meeting with Tom. Edward and I finish our drinks and move from Bar Josephine to a corner table in Le Saint-Germain. The salon is fashionable without chasing style, if that makes sense. It is light and airy and there's a prismatic ceiling of purple, green and blue that looks like a stained-glass window hung the wrong way round. It doesn't offer cocktails with names that would embarrass anyone over sixty.

The hotel refurb is so shiny that it's hard to think of what the place used to look like. This glow-up has scrubbed out the stains and marks, like deep-cleaning a house once the kids have left home. But the secrets of the past are still here. They linger, taunting me.

Edward is also hungry after his interview and orders a Wagyu beef cheeseburger with truffle. I go for a baby lettuce salad. I think I overdid it at breakfast. When the waiter leaves, Edward scans the other guests and then says, 'You were interviewed by Vidal alone, right?'

'Yes.'

'What did he ask you?'

I don't trust Edward, but I need to make him trust me. I can't be too hostile with him. He must still believe we are old friends picking up where we left off. I keep my voice casual and say, 'It was mainly about you, actually. He made me go through the timeline of events and picked up on the fact that you were left alone with Gran for an hour last night.'

'Just as I predicted, then. The blame game begins.'

'Possibly.'

Edward looks angry, and even grumpier. 'I was the one almost killed, Liv. I was this close to being a victim too. I just came in contact with a killer. Any sympathy for that? I should be getting counselling, not defending myself. I hope you told him that was all bollocks?'

I don't respond. I'm seeing a different side of Edward now. He sounds defensive. He is in a difficult spot and the kind, smiley, domestic god from the apartment yesterday is a distant dream. I don't know what he got up to during twenty years as a single party boy in Manhattan. But I can guess.

'Vidal also mentioned you leaving for New York twenty years ago,' I say. 'What really happened, Ed? Why do the police think you could be a suspect in a murder inquiry? Yesterday you wanted me to tell you everything. Now you're holding out on me. You were genuinely worried in the apartment yesterday. What danger are you in?'

'Use your imagination.'

'What does that mean?'

'A lot of Parisians aren't exactly fans of the de Villefort family. They don't like my dad, and they certainly don't like nepo babies like me. Why else do you think those accusations emerged against Dad last year? It was revenge. Dad has pissed off lots of people by encouraging patients to remember bad things in their past. Many people in this city hate his guts and mine too.'

I can see the sense of injustice in his eyes.

'If your dad wanted to avoid the publicity of the trial, then he could have just left it alone, not sued for defamation.'

'Trust me, his enemies would have loved that.'

'Not suing for defamation doesn't mean he's guilty.'

'Legally? No. But reputationally? Of course it does. Dad didn't fight in the Resistance and save this country from the Nazis just to take the easy route out. He refused to have his life's work ruined by a former patient who decided to blame her therapist rather than her foster father for what happened in the past. Dad has always been a fighter. Without his reputation, he's got nothing.'

I know that much, at least. Louis is one of those people who believes the little things always matter. He pays his way, keeps his word, arrives on time and tells the truth. Despite his flamboyant reputation in the glory days of the 1980s and 1990s, he is still a hero of the wartime generation.

Edward takes another bite of his burger. 'Someone did this, and it wasn't me. For God's sake, I had a very close escape myself. The real question is: who would want to kill your grandmother? And what's the motive at the heart of all this? That's what we need to concentrate on.'

It hasn't been the two of us like this for so long. The last time was just before he went off to college and I never saw him again. Even now, part of me will always be the girl with braces sitting in a room in Quai Voltaire listening to him talk grandly about life. Gran might have been an artist. But I was still a girl from Redbridge who had to get herself ready for school each day and cope with the aftermath of Mum's death. Until yesterday, I thought I would never see this man again. I can't believe I'm sitting in Paris with Gran dead and talking about who might have killed her with Edward de Villefort.

'You want to get back to your son in London,' says Edward. 'I want this to be over as much as you do so I can fly back to New York. We both know that neither of us had any involvement in your grandmother's death. I've never been a saint, Liv, but I don't make a habit of killing old women. It's clear something about the recovered memory and your gran's confession set all this in motion.'

'And you're sure we can trust Charlotte?'

'She works with my father and he trusts her, that should be enough. She's the only option we have.'

'Did your father ever say anything about his sessions with Gran in the past, before he retired?' I ask. 'Do you know if he ever kept notes or files in his consulting room? Maybe Gran mentioned something during a session back in the day?'

Edward goes quiet. 'You know he doesn't talk about patients with me. It's against his principles. And, whatever else you might say, Dad has always been a man of principle.'

'Sometimes things get messy with patients. All sorts of boundaries end up being crossed.'

'Are you speaking from personal experience?'

I see myself walking into the waiting room at the Memory Unit and seeing Tom for the first time and how quickly I fell for him. I had a relationship with a patient and broke all the rules. I was terrified it might come out during my testimony at the trial. I've tried to justify it to myself, but there are no excuses.

I crossed the line. It's so easy to do. I never thought I would until it happened.

'We all have our secrets,' I say.

Edward takes another bite of his burger. He looks tired with the world.

'Yes,' he says. 'I suppose we do.'

45

RENÉ

It's not that he enjoys killing. Or not really. It's a skill, like any other. René always remembers those kids at school who were good with numbers or fluent in five foreign languages. He was a failure for so long that finding any sort of talent was a special moment.

Murdering the old woman was like putting her to sleep. He would gladly have killed the other man but the woman was the problem and so she was the one who had to die. That's what his client wanted and that's what his client got.

The rest was simple. He tipped off the police and then avoided the cameras, changed clothes and chucked the equipment. There was no forensic route back to him.

He is in the apartment now with Pink Floyd playing from the speakers. It's always ABBA before a job, Pink Floyd afterwards. René wonders how long the rest will take. The autopsy will be fast-tracked. But that's not René's problem. The old woman is dead. Dr Finn is stuck in Paris and holed up at the Lutetia. His work, for the moment at least, is done.

René continues reading until one of the burner phones starts ringing. He pauses Pink Floyd just as 'Money' gets going. He sees the number and clears his throat. This is the one person who can make his palms sweat.

The client.

'I have another job for you,' says the voice with its usual heavy disguise.

He thinks of the scene at the apartment and Edward de Villefort. Perhaps it's the ex-military strain in him, but René could never stand nepo babies like Edward de Villefort snorting their way through life and always being bailed out. He'd have marched them all to the guillotine himself.

René listens to the instructions for the new job and makes a mental note.

It's true, he doesn't enjoy killing or not really. It's just what he's good at. How he finds a role in the world. And the money isn't bad, despite what Pink Floyd might say.

He repeats the name of the next two targets.

'I'll confirm once it's done,' he says.

The line goes dead.

He's still just a soldier obeying orders.

46

MYLES

It's already evening by the time the Eurostar arrives at Gare du Nord.

Myles hates the pushing and shoving as everyone races to get off the train. He stays seated for a bit longer, allowing the other passengers to barge their way through before he collects his bag and falls into line with the stragglers.

He thinks about Ingrid Fox again and her accusations against Louis de Villefort and that terrible night when her body was found. He went to see her body and got the details from police colleagues. Some days he still can't quite believe it.

Ingrid is dead. And he could have stopped it. He broke enough rules to help her. Then, just before she was about to give evidence, the very worst happened. He should have somehow done more.

Myles considered going to therapy at one point but was always worried about losing his security clearance for the police if a mental health issue showed up on his medical record. He did the classic male thing of bottling it all up, which was dangerous. Instead, his therapy was shining his shoes each morning, brushing his waistcoats, tidying his office and being overly conscientious at work. He didn't see a shrink but did deep-clean the kitchen on a bimonthly basis.

He would like a day, though, where everything doesn't have to be tidy. He is tired of the demons in his head, and the toll his childhood troubles have taken on his private life. Most cops his age are married with kids. Myles is still on his own. He grew up without seeing a healthy, working parental relationship, and part of him still isn't quite sure whether such things exist.

Reading through Ingrid's case, and listening to the files on his phone, isn't easy. Recovering memories is difficult work. It's like being a detective in your own head. Ingrid was never the same after her therapy sessions in Paris all those years ago. It's like her mind was broken into small pieces but couldn't be put back together again.

He steps off the Eurostar and walks towards the barriers leading to the exit. The 5G works again and he checks his emails. He doesn't want to end up with unread emails in his inbox and break the end-of-day rule. He will put aside some time tonight for a mammoth deleting session. That will keep the demons at bay, for another twenty-four hours at least. After that, he'll have to do it all over again. His quest for order and control never ends.

Captain Vidal has sent a car to drive him from Gare du Nord to 36 rue du Bastion. As the streets of Paris flicker outside and the car pulls up at DNPJ headquarters, Myles looks out across the Seine flowing like a ribbon through this magical city. Whatever secrets are hidden here, he will find them.

He failed Ingrid once.

He won't fail her again.

47

OLIVIA

THEN

I'm in my office pretending to work.
Really, I'm scrolling through information about Tom. I'm cyber-stalking but in a non-sleazy way. Yes, he is attractive. Admittedly I like him. He has a handsome face. We're both only human and there's nothing wrong with a bit of window-shopping, is there?

I haven't made any moves and nor has he. That doesn't mean I haven't thought about it. I've imagined seeing that smile with a wine glass in hand at an expensive restaurant or waking up sleepily on the pillow next to mine. I imagine our hands getting closer across the table until the tip of my finger brushes his and that ripple of attraction is acknowledged, not with any sense of surprise, just inevitability.

But I'm daydreaming. That's a bad habit for a psychotherapist. I'm looking to find something wrong with him. He is too good to be true. Even his name is too neat. 'Tom' is nice and approachable, while 'Lomas' sounds mysterious. I've heard about these private Facebook groups called Are We Dating the Same Guy? It started in New York, apparently, and there are now a hundred and fifty groups with over three million members. You send round a photo of a guy you want checking out, ask if there's 'any tea' and see if armies of other women reply with horror stories.

I've done that with Tom and nothing happened. He has a clean bill of health from the AWDTSG community. That's something, at least.

I click off my cyber-stalking and go back to preparing for my appearance at the trial. Louis's legal team have sent through some background on how the prosecution will try and attack me. There is the original article in *Le Monde*. Then there is all the other coverage about the trial and the 'Memory Wars' in the 1980s and 1990s when patients in therapy started 'recovering' lost memories about terrible abuses in their past. The idea of recovering repressed memories spread all around the world and made recovered memory therapy a hot topic.

I know that the trial will be a big moment too. I will have to defend myself. I've helped people get out of bad marriages, escape abusive partners, ditch drug habits, stop drinking, turn their lives around and look forward to a brighter future. Some of that involves recovering traumatic memories in the past and I am proud of my work. But the same question will still be asked: are recovered memories true? Can people really repress traumatic events in their past?

I know they can, but I just can't say why. After all, that's what Louis did in my own life. I was at rock bottom, dropping out of school, in 'situationships' with bad men – not that I knew that word then – and spiralling into a drug addiction that threatened to put me in prison. Most of that time is a blur, but Louis told me that I was only weeks away from going out the same way Mum did. I couldn't cope with the trauma of finding Mum next to that bottle of pills and the secret about what I really did – or more accurately didn't do – that day.

Gran took me in and Louis treated me. Slowly, he helped me come to terms with my own emotions. Louis gave me the tools to rebuild my life and put one foot in front of the other. He said my addiction issues were because I'd repressed the truth about that day and I could only get better by recovering the real memory and facing it head on.

I spend a few more hours on trial preparation. Then I email Tom about our next appointment. He replies immediately confirming our next session.

Am I making a mistake? Or could he be genuine?

I suppose there's only one way to find out.

48

OLIVIA

NOW

I've spoken to Charlotte Fouquet many times over the years but haven't met her in person since I was a teenager. I feel like I know her, but I couldn't pick her out of a crowd. But her voice, and her surname, give me a pretty good idea what to expect. And when she arrives at the Lutetia and joins us in the Saint-Germain salon, I am not wrong.

Charlotte is dressed in a Chanel suit and sits with the poise of a black-and-white movie star. She is in her fifties, at a guess, though she could pass for a decade younger. I imagine her dealing with Louis's big-name patients in the past with the utmost discretion and poise, making sure no one catches them coming in the private VIP entrance and ushering them up to the consulting room at Quai Voltaire.

It's after seven-thirty and the hotel is on the evening shift. Rich, perfumed people head to Bar Josephine for pre-dinner drinks and then down to the Brasserie Lutetia for their meal. Charlotte Fouquet might be the chief aide to the de Villefort family, but she is definitely the sort of fixer and assistant who doesn't like the spotlight. She is the backroom phone-as-a-weapon type. Charlotte reminds me of those elegant French women I always admired with their stylish blend of cigarettes, couture and revolution.

Tom always claimed to find French fashion too dressy and I have a horrible feeling that's why he went for me. I'm an English dresser pining after French style. That's what he saw the first time he entered the Memory Unit. Maybe that's what TJ will inherit, despite my best efforts to dress him like Prince George.

'I see it's finally happened then,' says Charlotte, as she takes a seat and arranges herself. 'I've been predicting this day for so long. The ghosts of the past have come back to haunt us. The ghosts of this hotel, too.'

I need to stay close to Charlotte and Edward. But I'm treating everything they say with suspicion. 'Predicting what exactly?'

Charlotte waits while water is poured. She takes a sip, composing herself. 'Murder, of course. What else?'

The casual way she says it shocks me. 'You thought Gran would be murdered?'

'If not her, then Louis himself.' Charlotte watches Edward and I sense him confirming that I am allowed to hear this. 'Josephine and Louis emerged from the darkest days in French history,' she says. 'The memory of that trauma and those secrets are like a shadow that hovers over everything here in Paris. Louis has spent his life recovering those memories in his consulting room. It is a dark, dangerous subject and one many people in the French state don't wish to revisit. It's more than enough motive for murder.'

'But the Second World War was eighty years ago. Surely there can't be many more secrets to come out.'

'It is still within living memory. The only secrets left are the big ones. The mysteries that never went away. Your grandmother knew that and so does Louis. So did many of the patients who lay on that couch. That's why I feared for her, and still fear for him. And so it's proved.'

There is something typically French and elusive to the way she says it. But there are so many questions I want to ask. I almost don't know where to begin. I'm starting to see all my childhood memories of Gran in a new way.

When I was falling in love with Edward at Quai Voltaire, what were Gran and Louis talking about? Were they actually whispering about things that happened in this hotel? Is that why Gran became a hermit and shunned all publicity? I can see them both strolling through the garden area outside the apartment deep in conversation, arguing even, and the fear on both their faces, talking about something secret and forbidden.

'So what's your theory?' I ask. 'Why has all this happened?'

'I don't know,' says Charlotte. 'But I have many questions that have been going through my mind over the last twenty-four hours. As you know, Louis's patient list over the years includes many of the most powerful and best-connected people. Is there some possible connection here? Maybe, maybe not. There have been so many secrets revealed in the safety of Louis's therapy room.'

I struggle to keep the irritation from my voice. Charlotte is patronising me in the same way as Vidal earlier. I liked her on the phone, but I'm not exactly warming to her in person. She's a bit too theatrical for me.

'If you know anything more,' I say, 'then please tell me. My grandmother is dead. I deserve to know.'

Charlotte doesn't shrink. 'Very well, Olivia,' she says. 'But I must warn you.'

'Of what?'

'Of the dangers of finding out the truth.'

'I'm a psychotherapist,' I say. 'My life is spent finding out the truth.'

Charlotte pauses and stares at me. 'Not like this,' she says. 'No, my dear . . . this kind of truth can get you killed.'

Coffee is served. It's agony as the waiter pours then leaves for another table.

Charlotte waits a moment, then says, 'Olivia, did your grandmother ever speak to you about recovering memories from her own wartime past?'

I glance towards the hotel lobby. So much has happened since Gran walked into this very building and started it all. Did she know what would happen then?

Even now, it's impossible to know if she was telling the truth about having once been Sophie Leclerc or if her memory loss was confusing her. Was she really Sophie or Josephine? Which one of them am I related to? Which one of them is TJ related to? Are we the descendants of a Holocaust survivor and a murderer or an old woman getting details from the past jumbled up in all the wrong ways?

'No,' I say. 'She never mentioned anything. The first I heard was when I got the call from the detective.'

'Captain Vidal, yes. He has quite the reputation too. What do you think of him?'

'I'm not sure. He mentioned that his father was a police officer here at the Lutetia when the survivors returned. I wondered if he has some personal motive in all this. Why?'

'He does, but the one I know about doesn't involve his father. Many years ago, Vidal was involved in a shootout here in Paris. He suffered badly from it. His police chief sent him to Louis to get treatment. Back at the clinic, we still have his patient file. He was investigated after the shooting, and there was a rumour about possible corruption in his unit. He was suspended for a substantial period of time before being cleared and allowed back on the force. He went through a very difficult time which Louis helped him come out of. Like so many patients, he owes so much to Louis. One of the reasons he takes recovered memories seriously is that he benefitted from it in his own life. By recovering the true memory of the shooting, he was able to heal.'

I try to take that in. Captain Vidal went to therapy with Louis? He was investigated for corruption and also suspended? That muddies the water further. He is not the squeaky-clean officer of the law, then. He is also a more complex figure than I thought. No wonder his questions in that interview room were so precise. He knows what it's like to recover traumatic memories from the past. But could he really be working with whoever wanted Gran dead?

None of us speak. I don't touch my coffee. I want to know if Charlotte has any new evidence or is just teasing me with rumours.

'Are you sure your grandmother's dementia symptoms caused the confession, or could she have been thinking clearly?' asks Charlotte. 'Was she really Sophie, or really Josephine?'

We now seem to be calling yesterday's episode 'the confession', as if it's an official term. The confession this. The confession that. It sounds like a new gameshow. Was Gran thinking clearly when she told me those things in her apartment?

I don't know. The mystery still gnaws at me.

Sophie or Josephine.

Who was she?

49

MYLES

It feels so late by the time he arrives. And the one thing Myles hates more than anything is being late. He's the sort of man who travels across West London as if it's the Pacific Crest Trail. If you recklessly assume the District line will be quick in the middle of rush hour, or the M25 free and easy on a bank holiday Friday, then all hell breaks loose. It's how he compartmentalised his life last year while doing all that stuff outside work. Being prepared never hurt anyone.

Myles walks into the large entrance of 36 rue du Bastion. The French police are notoriously abrupt and old-school. Myles undoes his top button and regrets shaving this morning. He looks like the classic British cop with his shoes shined and tie knotted while the French team discuss extravagant feats of lovemaking and the art of infidelity.

He approaches the front desk and shows his warrant card. 'Detective Inspector Myles Forsyth. Metropolitan Police, London. I'm here to see Captain Vidal. He's expecting me.'

There is a lot of tut-tutting, some shoulder-shrugging too. Myles doesn't really like going abroad. Yes, Paris is just a short hop and a skip across the Channel, but it's still foreign soil. He loves exploring other countries, but he doesn't like the lack of control that brings. He doesn't know the quickest route round the supermarket, what the signs mean or which metro lines to avoid at rush hour.

Here, in Paris, he is vulnerable again. That's the feeling he can't stand. All those old childhood feelings come back – being powerless, ordinary, at the mercy of other people. He shivers now and tries to get a grip. But it's deep-rooted, in his bones. It's the reason he went into police work in the first place. It sounds a bit psychopathic, but there we go. It is what it is.

Eventually, Myles goes through the security protocols. He is scanned, patted down and then escorted into the inner sanctum. They whir up several floors and emerge into a carpeted hallway with glass-doored sections and individual offices.

'DI Forsyth.'

The voice is gruff and deep. Vidal is bigger in person than Myles expects. There is some peppery stubble and, beneath the white shirt, what looks like a smoking patch. They have worked together on the Ingrid Fox case since her body was found last year and had some phone calls. But this is the first time Myles has put a face to a name. In person, Vidal looks more suited to a boxing gym than an interview room.

'Captain Vidal,' he says, shaking hands. 'It's good to finally meet in person. Thank you for staying late and seeing me at such short notice.'

'Of course. Please, sit down.'

They enter Vidal's office. He closes the door.

'Following your work on this, I thought you'd be interested by the developments here in Paris,' says Vidal. 'Especially after the events of last night and the murder of the woman we know as Josephine Benoit.'

'Yes,' says Myles. 'Very interested. Do you think it could be the same MO as the Fox murder?'

'We are waiting on the autopsy. I know your Home Office pathologist concluded there was a fifty-fifty chance of either suicide or murder in the Ingrid Fox death. Are you still personally convinced that Ms Fox was murdered?'

Myles nods. 'Until evidence suggests otherwise, yes. My problem is just how to prove it.'

50

OLIVIA

THEN

It's session two with Tom today.
I shouldn't really call him Tom. It sounds too intimate. I should call him Mr Lomas. But that seems dishonest. He is Tom to me.

'You said in our first session that memories haunt you,' I say. 'You mentioned memories from your service in the Marines. But I want to go back further and see if you can remember more about your father's influence. You said that he was a veteran?'

Tom looks a bit nervous here. 'My father?'

'Yes.'

'I mean, look, I think these memories are real. But perhaps they're not. How can you tell whether a memory is a recovered memory or a false one?'

'Let's start with a simple question,' I say. 'What is your earliest memory?'

He is more relaxed now. 'That's easy. I was almost two. I remember my little brother being born and visiting him and my mum in hospital.'

'Before you were two?'

'Yes.'

'You're certain?'

'Uh-huh, absolutely, clear as a bell. I can even remember the sound he made and how my mum looked in the hospital bed. That's the earliest memory I have.'

'I see.'

'You don't look convinced?'

There's that smile again. Kyle would never have said that. His simpler, ballsier, attack-the-day attitude was refreshing until it wasn't. Kyle ended our marriage because he could no longer see the 'upside' to continuing, once called love a 'loss-leader' on Valentine's Day and decided to pay for TJ's karate lessons because he considered his own son an 'asset worth investing in'. There's only so many times you can watch your other half doing bicep curls when carrying in the shopping bags before the magic fades.

I like seeing Tom in two dimensions here. He has no edges for me yet. He is neat and ordered, as usual. He is the sort of man who makes sure the duvet is tucked in at all four corners when making the bed. That's the problem with trying to stay professional. It's a great plan until his perfect smile and all-round gorgeousness punch the plan to smithereens. I don't want that third dimension yet. Or, perhaps, ever, when the tidiness becomes pedantic and the quest for order means colour co-ordinating his vinyl collection. I don't want Tom to become 3D yet. I like him in 2D for now.

'There are no right or wrong answers here.'

'So what's wrong with my earliest memory?'

'Nothing, except it's what's known as an "impossible memory".'

Tom looks confused. 'I take it that's not a good thing?'

'Studies show that human beings can't form memories that last into adulthood until they are about three and a half. Your brain wasn't developed enough to remember your brother being born when you were two. You may think that is your earliest memory but it's not.'

Tom is annoyed now. 'You can't tell me what I can and can't remember.'

'No. But I can separate what you think you remember from what your brain is capable of remembering.'

'If that memory is impossible, then where did it come from?'

'Memory borrowing, most likely. You stole someone else's memory.'

'I stole that memory from someone else when I was a two-year-old?'

'No. It wasn't your two-year-old self that stole the memory. It was probably your teenage self. A family member told you about the birth of your younger brother and, eventually, you thought it was your own original memory.'

Tom looks crushed. 'This one is different, though. I know it happened. If my memory is lying to me about that, what else is it lying about?'

'Our memories aren't like cameras that record events. We edit our memories every time we access them.'

'I thought you believe in recovered memories?'

And here we have it. He's definitely been reading stuff about me online. I guess that means he's interested, even if he does get the wrong end of the stick. This is my chance to correct him. It's also a mini-rehearsal for the trial.

'My job is to help my patients discover what their own minds have repressed so they can come to terms with trauma in their lives. By surfacing the repressed memory, they can confront it and, eventually, learn to cope with it and stop cycles of destructive behaviour used to mask the pain.'

Tom shifts in his seat. 'What about in my case?'

I pause. 'That depends how deep you're prepared to go,' I answer. 'You're a good candidate for recovered memory therapy. But I should warn you that some patients remember things they wish they hadn't. Are you ready for that?'

Tom swallows hard. He sighs, cracking his knuckles. My own words echo in the room, and I can hear Louis saying the same thing to me all those years ago.

I know what it's like to be haunted by something you've done. I've been in Tom's position. I understand that look of hesitation. The patient is so vulnerable here, and the therapist is so powerful. I sit and listen while the patient has to tell me their biggest fears and the memories that keep them awake at night. The power imbalance is huge.

'Yes,' he says, at last. 'Yes, I think I'm ready.'

51

MYLES

NOW

Myles listens carefully as Captain Vidal goes through the events of yesterday and today. He makes notes throughout: the Lutetia, Sophie Leclerc, Room 11, murder, memory issues, Edward de Villefort, then the incident at the apartment in Montparnasse.

As Vidal finishes, he says, 'As part of our joint operation into the Ingrid Fox case, you promised to share the further evidence you had?'

Myles spots a crease on his waistcoat and smooths it out. This bit will be delicate. He can't afford Vidal to raise any concerns with his superiors. He thinks about all the extra-curricular things he did last year, and how much trouble he'd be in if his bosses knew about the audio recordings on the burner phone. He must let Vidal into the secret but without suggesting that the evidence was obtained in an unorthodox manner.

He says, 'Part of the investigation into Ingrid Fox's death involves looking more deeply at questions around recovered memory techniques and the manipulation of vulnerable patients. It's possible that Ingrid Fox could have blown the lid on that more widely. If I do share the new evidence then you have to promise me that you won't ask how it was obtained.'

Vidal looks sceptical. 'I thought we were partners? Anglo-French agreement for once?'

'Which this is. But I also need some discretion.'

'On what exactly?'

'Evidence that sheds an entirely new light on the issue of recovered memories. Verbatim testimony from the key players themselves. The first concrete evidence about whether or not recovered memory therapy can really be relied upon. It's part of another operation the Met is running and, as I'm sure you can understand, it's, well . . . delicate.'

Vidal can't hide his interest now. 'How did you come across this new evidence?'

'I'm afraid I can't disclose that.'

Vidal sits back in his chair and strokes his chin. His hands are fidgety, as if looking for a cigarette. 'How reliable is this evidence?'

'Better than good,' says Myles. 'If handled correctly, this new evidence could be the breakthrough in getting justice for Ingrid Fox and dealing with cases concerning recovered memories in the future.'

Vidal leans forward. 'Very well. I'm all ears, DI Forsyth.'

52

THE LUTETIA

1945

SOPHIE

Sophie finds it difficult to cope with the emotion of seeing Josephine again. It is scrambling her mind. She's thought about this moment so many times and all the things she would do to the woman who betrayed her and her father.

But to have the living, breathing person in the same room as her is overwhelming. She feels so many different things, from pure hatred to total despair, and even flickers of the love and friendship they once had.

Most of all, she just feels sadness. They were both so pretty and free, two women with the world at their feet. Now their heads are shaved, their own clothes gone, and they meet in dirty rags. This wasn't what life was meant to be. She thinks of her father and the last time she ever saw him. She has cried all her tears, or most of them, but she will never get over the look on his face as they were separated at Auschwitz for the last time.

There was such nobility, but also terror, in his face. He could no longer protect his own daughter. He was being sent to die by people from his own country occupied by another, all for the crime of having some Jewish heritage in the distant past. Why did humans do this to each other?

Her father was so kind, thoughtful, but immense too, at least to her as a child, with his tall stature and deep, booming voice. Seeing him being dragged away by men young enough to be his sons will never leave her. It will be the last thing she thinks about before she dies, whenever that might be. It showed what people are really like, and once you've seen that you can never not see it. No one can go back to normal.

Those dark thoughts go through her mind again. She sees herself suffocating Josephine with a pillow. She could do it tonight, end the life of her betrayer.

No, she must not think like that. But it's difficult not to. She has seen so much death in the camps. She knows how easy it is to kill someone. And so she focuses her mind on other things. She tries to find the one ray of hope that still exists in the world.

Louis.

Sophie can't talk about the camps yet, especially not with Josephine. She leaves Room 11, instead, and goes down to the lobby again. She remembers when it was filled with the most famous faces in Paris. Now there are photos of survivors on the boards and groups of relatives desperately trying to see if their loved ones have returned.

Sophie finds a chair in the lobby. If Louis is alive then he will come and find her, she is sure of it. The Red Cross workers look at her oddly, but she doesn't move. She is only here for three days. If Louis is waiting for her, then she will wait for him, and somehow fate will bring them back together again. That is all she has to live for now. Her father is dead, she never knew her mother, she is an only child, and her best friend betrayed her. Louis is the only one left.

Hours go by as Sophie stays in the lobby scanning every male face that enters the hotel, desperate for it to be his.

When he finally does arrive, she almost doesn't recognise him. Louis was always slim and athletic but now is too thin. His cheekbones stick out like matchsticks. She remembers those moonlit strolls by the Seine, and the feeling of his hand on hers, and the way he would recite poetry to her as they dreamed of a future together, teenagers stuck in this city in the middle of wartime. He dressed in such beautiful clothes – the finest tailored shirts, the sharpest suits, hand-stitched shoes. He seemed effortlessly sophisticated even at school with his interest in psychiatry and the mind.

Now there is none of that old swagger beneath the mothy grey coat he wears, the worn shoes, his hair greasy and ragged. But the light in his eyes hasn't changed. He can still fill a room with his smile. There is a commanding look about his tall frame, the languid way he walks and that sense of authority. Yes, it really is Louis. Her Louis. The man she once hoped to call her husband. She has been through hell, and has somehow returned, and her love has come looking for her here, just as she always thought he would.

Suddenly the hunger and weakness feel almost overwhelming, until she wonders whether he will even recognise her. He fell in love with a different version of Sophie. That Sophie was reserved, academic, but witty and brave. What if he walks straight past? That would be the final humiliation. She has waited all this time to be reunited, and now she is hardly strong enough to call out his name.

But thankfully she doesn't have to. Louis scans the lobby and then, at last, he stops looking as he sees her. Their eyes meet across the din and chaos of the hotel entrance. Despite everything, there is a connection that time or fortune can't break.

Sophie hasn't cried for so long that she wonders if she is still capable of tears. But Louis's eyes glisten as he puts one foot in front of the other, dazed by her return, until he is pushing through the crowds. She stands, too shocked to speak, to feel even, just knowing that her last reason to survive has now been satisfied.

There are no words as Louis gently reaches out and holds her. Their foreheads press together, oblivious to everyone else around them in this grand palace hotel.

'Hello stranger,' he says, as he always did, this time taking an imaginary lick of her hair in his hands and curling it behind her ear.

'Hello stranger,' she replies. It was their code together, so much part of them that she can't remember when it started.

'I knew you'd be here. Somehow, I always knew.'

'And I knew you'd find me.'

The lobby of the hotel is full of noise. People are crying or shouting as they recognise a loved one; others are being given instructions by the Red Cross team; some weep as they look at the board and realise, slowly, that whoever they are searching for is never coming back.

It is chaos, but Sophie doesn't hear it. She thinks those dangerous thoughts again and all the terrible things she wants to do. She wants to make Josephine suffer like Sophie herself suffered. She will put the pillow over Josephine's face and not stop until her father has been avenged.

Matthew Blake

But she must not think like that any more.
Louis is here and she can hope again.
As her dear, sweet father would always remind her:
Two wrongs don't make a right.

53

THE LUTETIA

1945

SOPHIE

They sit in silence in the dining room with the other survivors, the Red Cross workers, the soldiers, a two-seater table by the window in this vast space, just one small story among hundreds of others. But the whole world is contained in each other's eyes. They slowly find words again.

'I thought you might not recognise me,' Sophie says. 'Without my hair, or clothes, I look like some kind of scarecrow.'

'Fate can take away material things,' says Louis, 'but it can't change the beauty of a person. I've been walking through this lobby every day since the camps were liberated and the buses started from Gare d'Orsay. I've been waiting for you to arrive.'

'How did you know I was still alive?'

'I didn't. All I had was hope. I would have come here every day for the rest of my life if it meant one more meeting with you, Sophie.'

Before she would have laughed at such talk – so dramatic, so serious, so adult – but now she savours it. She feels almost undone by Louis's words. The only male voices she's heard since being deported are shouts and orders. Hearing someone talk gently like that – lovingly, in fact – is too much. It reminds her of everything she's lost.

'What about you?' she says. 'I worried you would be caught in the Resistance round-ups? That you might have been captured during the last days of the war?'

'So did I,' says Louis. 'It was a very close-run thing. Some of my unit were taken by the Nazis just before the liberation. I had to go underground to survive. The only Resistance fighters who survived were the ones who did the same, cut off contact, made sure they couldn't be compromised, went underground.'

'Fate kept us both alive then,' she says.

He smiles and sips more coffee. 'I never used to believe in fate before. If this war taught me one thing, it's how little control we have over our own lives.'

Sophie thinks of all the selections at the camp. She sees the eyes of the guards making the decision over who to send to the gas chambers and who to keep alive. Some guards seemed to relish it. The prisoners ended up believing in fate. It was the only way to make sense of the world. Left to death, right to hard labour.

'What about your father?' asks Louis.

Sophie dips her head. Her father always loved Louis, the son he never had. 'My father died in the camps,' she says. 'Or at least I think he did. He was too ill to work. He was sent to the left during the very first selection when we arrived at Auschwitz. I never found out exactly what happened.'

'I'm so sorry, Sophie. He was a great man.'

Louis reaches across the table and Sophie slides her right hand into his, feeling the soft brush of his thumb over her gnarled skin. It is the first warm human touch she has had since leaving Paris. She has lost the connection in her brain. It will take months, years even, for human touch to feel good again.

'Where are you living now?' says Sophie.

'I'm back with my parents, for the next few months at least. I've started my degree at the Sorbonne.'

She nods. 'I have to stay here for two more days to get assessed by the doctors and the police.'

'And after that?'

'I don't even know if my father's home is still standing,' she says. 'It could be rubble by now.'

'Then you must come and stay with me,' says Louis.

'That would hardly be respectable. When you asked me before, I told you that I would only darken your door with a ring on my finger.'

'God didn't save us from the war, Sophie. Why should we follow his commands now?'

Again, before the war, she could be sceptical and ironic, laughing at talk of God or fate. Life was a theme park designed for her amusement. Now, though, it's changed. Sophie pauses. She is embarrassed to ask him, but she has no other choice. She feels like she is going mad. The memories are so intrusive.

'Are you still planning to specialise in psychiatry?'

'Yes. In fact, some of us medical students have been asked to fill in for shortages assessing returnees here.'

'So I can't get rid of you even if I wanted to?'

'No, Mademoiselle Leclerc, you cannot.'

She smiles, and it feels odd, and she becomes more serious. And she tells him. She worries Louis will judge her.

She describes the things she saw at the camps and the memories she's been left with. She tells him about the impulse to kill those who wronged her and the worry about what she might do here now she has her freedom. She has lost control of her mind. Most of all, she tells him about Josephine. When she was in the room with Josephine, Sophie felt like putting a pillow over Josephine's head and never letting go. She isn't left with bitterness, but fury.

'Josephine?' says Louis, suddenly. 'What is she doing here?'

Sophie has been so wrapped up in the reunion that she realises she hasn't told him. 'She's in Room 11 with me,' she says. 'She says she was sent to the camps.'

'I see.'

'I'm worried, Louis,' she says. 'I don't know how to go back to normal any more. I'm not sure I even know what normal is. I'm worried what I might do to Josephine. It's wrong, but I can't stop the thoughts in my head.'

He tightens his grip on her hand, still stroking her skin, his voice as deep and reassuring as her father's used to be.

'I'm here now,' he says. 'We're a team again, Sophie. Your problems are my problems. You don't have to fight them on your own any longer.'

They are the words she has longed to hear. The terror inside her – at who she is, what she has become – subsides a little. She wants to sit here looking into his eyes and feeling his touch forever. Reluctantly, however, she remembers what waits for her upstairs.

'Will I ever go back to normal?' she asks him. 'Will life ever be the same again?'

He keeps hold of her hand. 'Of course it will,' he says. 'I'll make sure of it.'

54

THE LUTETIA

1945

SOPHIE

Louis is needed back at the hospital. They agree to meet in the lobby of the Lutetia again tomorrow. It is growing late and Sophie is tired.

When she returns to Room 11, Josephine is asleep, or appears to be, and Sophie can't keep her eyes open any longer. She always used to be a delicate sleeper, disturbed by the slightest sound. Then, in the camps, she realised she could sleep through anything. Only the memories stop her sleeping now. She tries to think of Louis but that makes it even worse. Sophie knows what she did and can't undo.

It's what she might do next that she really fears.

She must get used to a proper bed again. She lies in Room 11 and the sounds of the hotel echo around her. The shouts continue, and the pacing outside grows louder. The new guests here haven't slept on mattresses for years. They are used to cold floors, deprived of any home comforts, and trying to readjust to hotel rooms will take time. So, for now, they pace up and down and cry in their half-sleep and fill the air with the names of the loved ones they lost and who will never come back.

One of the memories comes again. She is in the hut and one of the prisoners is begging Sophie to help end her life, anything other than enduring another day in the camp. Please, says the prisoner, please help me. Sophie sees herself standing over the prisoner and knowing that once she does this, she will never be the same person again. She is bending down, pressing harder and harder, putting the prisoner out of her misery.

Sophie snaps awake. It is still dark. She has been asleep for a few minutes. She looks across at the other bed. Josephine is still breathing, which means nothing has happened. The memories haven't become real again. Both of them are still alive.

She could do it now. Sophie could get up, walk across to Josephine's bed and smother her or strangle her in revenge for what she did to Sophie and her father.

And yet she still lies here. Her father's face comes to her, and his soft deep voice, and he tells her that forgiveness is the greatest gift. She feels him watching over her in this room, and that killing Josephine would disappoint him. But she also knows that her father's kindness and gentleness led him to be naïve sometimes. Others got away from Paris earlier. They didn't think so much of their neighbours and the good in people's hearts. They saved themselves. What if her father was wrong about all that? What if two wrongs can make a right?

Sophie always knew that Josephine never had the loving family background that she did. Sophie's mother died in childbirth, but she always had her father. Josephine's parents both died in a car crash and she was brought up by a stern aunt. Josephine never experienced real love and learned, instead, to manipulate people. She was always such a good actor, even in school. She dreamed of going to the West End in London, or Broadway in New York, and becoming Paris's latest actor to become a household name. Then the war happened. It destroyed all of their dreams. But it didn't take away Josephine's ability to inhabit a role.

More than anything, Sophie longs to believe in the goodness of another human being again. She is too much of her father's daughter not to. Is it possible to pick up the pieces of that old life, the dream she once had, and start over again?

She hopes so.

First, though, she must get better. The visions and anger must be treated. These terrible memories must stop and what happened in the past must be allowed to stay there. More than anything, though, she will have to learn what love really means again.

She thinks of Louis stroking her hand and the feeling of his skin on hers.

It will take time, but she can do it.

The camps took away so much.

The last thing she has left is her heart.

55

THE LUTETIA

1945

JOSEPHINE

It is the second day here in the hotel and the sounds stay the same. There are constant yells, cries, sobs.

The only change is the sound of boots in the hallway outside Room 11 and a scraping sound as a piece of paper is pushed under the door.

Josephine gets out of bed and crouches down to see what the piece of paper says. It is folded in half. She goes to the door, unfolds it and reads the message: 'BENOIT, JOSEPHINE: REPORT FOR POLICE INTERVIEW AT 1500'.

She shudders as she reads it a second time and thinks of the obstacle ahead. The police interview today will change everything. If she passes it, she will be free. If she doesn't, then she will be arrested and shamed and probably killed, left on the roadside somewhere as an example to others. The thought is too horrible to think about.

The door opens and Sophie walks in. She has been downstairs for breakfast. She sees Josephine holding the folded slip of paper.

'What's that?' she asks.

'I've been summoned for my police interview,' says Josephine, deciding that more lies will only catch her out. 'It's set for three o' clock this afternoon. Have you had any word yet?'

'No. But I think they do them alphabetically, or that's what some of them say downstairs. L is some way behind B in the alphabet.'

'Yes, I suppose it is. How was breakfast?'

'I still can't really cope with proper food. It feels like my stomach will never grow back to what it was.'

'I know. Hunger becomes a way of life, doesn't it? We'll both exist on bread and water for the rest of our lives.'

Sophie takes a seat on her bed. They have spent most of the last twenty-four hours just sleeping. They are so thin and have no energy. Sleep is the only thing they can do. Sophie yawns, even though it is morning time.

'I've been thinking more about what you said yesterday,' says Sophie. 'When you told me it wasn't you who betrayed me.'

Josephine doesn't sit on her bed. She stays standing and holding the note. 'Yes.'

'My problem is, I don't understand. I don't understand how you could betray your best friend. But I don't understand how the enemy could know where father and I were hiding. I keep going round the problem in my mind and can never find an answer. One doesn't make emotional sense, and the other doesn't make logical sense. I saw Louis yesterday and I said the same thing to him.'

'Louis was here?'

'Yes. He's a student at the Sorbonne now. Some of them have been sent here to treat survivors.'

Josephine relents and goes to sit on her bed. She places the note behind her. 'I know I'll never be able to convince you,' she says, choosing each word carefully. 'All I can do is show you that I'm the same friend you had before. And that I went through what you went through. I love you now, Sophie, as I always did love you before. Your friendship was always the most important thing in my life. I can't stand us sharing this room, being locked up together all day, and being enemies. Can you?'

Sophie looks at her. There is such a depth of torment in her eyes. 'My father died. He deserves justice.'

So perhaps that is what it will come down to, thinks Josephine. Either Sophie will kill Josephine, or Josephine must kill Sophie. Fate has placed them in Room 11 together but only one of them is destined to leave the room alive. Josephine knows she deserves to die. That would be justice. But what in this war has ever been just? She saved herself before, and she can do it again. Josephine worked for the Resistance to save thousands of lives; Sophie blames her for her own suffering and the loss of her father's life. There is no justice in any of it. Sophie has been through so much that perhaps it would be kinder to take her life and relieve her suffering.

'Get some sleep,' says Josephine. 'I'm going down for some coffee myself. I will check in on you later before my interview.'

Sophie nods and turns away and pretends to sleep. Josephine leaves Room 11 and walks down the staircase to the lobby of the hotel and enters the restaurant. She must not bump into Louis if he is here this morning. She eats alone then paces round the hotel trying to get some thinking time. It is claustrophobic being stuck in Room 11 all day.

She returns to the room eventually and sits watching Sophie sleep. She could do it now, of course. The pillows on her bed are calling her. She could take one, place it over Sophie's mouth, and then hold it down until Sophie is dead. Sophie is so weak that she wouldn't be able to struggle. No doubt Sophie has had the same thoughts. These two friends, turned enemies, are now sitting in a luxury hotel on the Left Bank wondering how to kill each other.

As she sits there, Josephine wants to tell Sophie that she didn't mean for any of this to happen. She still remembers the night of the betrayal. She was with one of the Nazi officers and returning to this very hotel. Part of the Nazi delegation in Paris stayed here, and this is where she came for their liaisons. It was afterwards, as they lay in bed smoking, that the Nazi officer started drunkenly taunting her.

'I had you followed last night,' said the officer. 'I saw you meeting someone. You never told me about her. My people tried to follow her afterwards, but she escaped them and scurried back to her hidey-hole. I presume you were only talking to her in order to pass the information to me? According to the Gestapo, we are being infiltrated with Resistance fighters. They sleep with us and steal our secrets. We've been ordered to be extra-vigilant and anyone with links to the Resistance will be arrested, tortured and sent to the camps.'

Josephine still sees the cold, deadly look in the officer's eyes. He had all the power. She had none. He would turn her in and watch her die as easily as he dispatches more French citizens to the camps. Yes, it is true that Josephine met Sophie last night. It was a reckless, foolish thing to do. Sophie had returned to where she and her father were hiding. The idea that the officer had Josephine watched terrifies her. That means she is under suspicion. If she doesn't play this right, then she could end up being arrested and never seen again.

'Of course,' she lies. 'Of course I was going to tell you.'

'Where is your friend hiding? She must have told you. Why wait to tell me until now?'

There is a split-second before Josephine does it. She thinks of it now as the last moment of her old life, of innocence, before she crossed the line and life changed. She repeats the address that Sophie told her. Nothing awful happens straight away. The officer continues smoking. Josephine dresses and leaves the Lutetia, as usual. She returns home and locks her bedroom door and huddles in a corner, cursing herself for what she's done. She hopes that the officer doesn't act on the information. But she is also scared for herself. If the Nazis suspect that the Resistance is using honeytraps, then her life is now in permanent danger. She is being watched. She can't trust anyone. And she has just betrayed her best friend to try and save herself.

The next day she found out that Sophie and her father had been arrested overnight and taken to Drancy, which was a temporary camp before prisoners were moved to Auschwitz. That was the last she ever heard.

Josephine has tried to justify her actions ever since. Paris was feverish back then, with everyone trading favours to survive. It was a desperate scramble to avoid being arrested and deported to a concentration camp. People were taken at random, almost, with even the most distant trace of Jewish ancestry a death sentence. Josephine was on the right side. She was working for the Resistance. Yes, betraying Sophie like that was wrong, but she was in a city that was falling apart, trying to survive in a world of anarchy, to make sure that the Nazis were defeated and Paris was liberated. Surely Sophie will understand that? Is there no world in which they could be friends again?

When the clock nears three, Josephine gets up and leaves

Room 11 and forgets her thoughts of suffocating Sophie. She concentrates instead on what lies ahead. She arrives in the lobby on time and is ushered into one of the old servant quarters. The French police officer looks bored, as if he's already done hundreds of these interviews today, and points lazily at the chair opposite. He wears a pair of heavy spectacles and polishes them on his jacket.

Josephine tells him her name and date of birth. The police officer shuffles papers and searches for another file.

'You claim to have come back to Paris from Auschwitz yesterday, is that correct?'

'Yes.'

'And before that?'

'I was here in Paris.'

The officer doesn't write any of this down. That unsettles her. She can feel the danger that she's in.

'What were you doing here in Paris?'

Josephine braces herself and then prepares to say the first truthful thing in a long time, but the only truth that matters to her.

'I was working undercover for the Resistance,' she says. 'I was fighting to liberate Paris.'

56

THE LUTETIA

1945

JOSEPHINE

There is silence, filled with the sound of other guests outside. Josephine doesn't blink or swallow.

'And yet your file contains no verification from other Resistance members? In what capacity were you employed by the Resistance?'

'On the file point, I don't deny that. But I wouldn't have been much use to the Resistance if I'd torn down flags and told everyone I was working for the end of Nazi rule. I was pretty, young and got access that other Resistance members didn't. I had a cover to maintain. That was my sacrifice. I did what I could to help the liberation.'

She is playing a dangerous game. But then she always has. This is how she gets through life. There is always a man she must use, and if she knows anything it is how to manipulate men. This officer will be no different. He's probably one of those strict law-and-order types who's never had a woman. If pushed, she can bend him to her wishes. There are some advantages to being the mistress type and not the wife.

The agony of this situation eats away at her. She slept with those officers, and betrayed her friends, in a higher cause. Why does she now get no credit? Why are men who did nothing allowed to get the glory, and women like her are not believed and shamed for their sacrifice?

'Can anyone else verify your membership of the Resistance?'

'We operated alone and through codenames, mostly. Those were my orders. A lot of the go-betweens I dealt with were rounded up and shot just before the liberation. I only managed to escape by the skin of my teeth. We never told each other our true identities so we wouldn't reveal them under torture. It was lonely work, but I wanted to do my bit. I knew I might be accused of collaboration once the war was over, but I was prepared to take that risk. All that mattered was getting the Nazis out of Paris.'

The officer keeps looking at the file. 'Do you know anyone at large in Paris, or inside this hotel, who did actively collaborate with the Nazis?'

Josephine watches him carefully and wonders what the right answer is. Men don't like women who snitch. Her strategy is to keep her head down and try not to be noticed. She must stick to it. Even this officer probably collaborated. It was the French police, on Nazi orders, who made the arrests and rounded up French Jews.

'Everyone must come to terms with their conscience in their own way,' she says. 'I wanted to help free Paris, not denounce my fellow citizens. I stand by that.'

He looks up. 'I see.'

He asks more questions, trying to trip her up, but she is careful. Then, finally, he tells her that the interview is over for the time being, though warns that she could be called back at any moment. He also tells her that she must pass the psychiatric examination next door before she can be released.

She dreads meeting the medical team. But, thankfully, Louis isn't here today. Afterwards, once the doctors have examined her, Josephine walks through the Lutetia and the crowds in the lobby.

She is so close to safety now. She served her country, but her country forgot about her. She can't risk being lumped in with the real collaborators. She did what she was told by Resistance leaders. Now she has been left on her own. She can never tell Sophie, of course. To do so would be to admit that Josephine is responsible for the death of Sophie's father. She wouldn't understand, anyway. Sophie would think that Josephine was claiming to have been in the Resistance as an excuse for her shameful behaviour.

Men are praised. Women are damned.

Two more days here, then the rest of her life can begin. She will forget some bits, remember others, and her memory of the war will put her in the best light possible.

Josephine reaches Room 11 and waits for a moment before going in. She thinks again about the name on her lips and about Sophie tossing and turning last night, and the things Sophie must have done to survive the selections.

Yes, she can use that if she has to.

Josephine survived the Nazis. She sacrificed her honour in the service of her country. She has lost everything and still, if needed, she would do the same again. The information she got from the Nazi officers and passed on to the Resistance network helped win the war. She is proud of that, at least. She did something to help France survive, even if that will never be acknowledged.

In her own way, Josephine Benoit is a survivor.

DAY THREE

57

OLIVIA

NOW

It's gone midnight and I'm back in Room 11 at the Lutetia. I still don't trust Edward. I should never have left him alone with Gran.

Charlotte teased a lot, but didn't have much substance to back it up. She said she'd return tomorrow with more potential evidence about the link between the trial and what's happened with Gran and threats towards Louis. But I'm not holding my breath.

I'm not a police officer and I don't have case files of evidence. I'm a therapist and therefore what I have are gut instinct and my knowledge of human behaviour. And I don't trust either of them. I can't back it up, or send a file to the prosecutor's office with evidence. But the more I see of Edward, the more broken and desperate he becomes. The domestic god was an illusion. He knows he will never be like his father, but still wants his father's approval. He is the sort of person who ruled the world in his twenties with his sex appeal and effortless good looks and it's been downhill ever since.

I arrive back in my room to find an envelope waiting for me. I tear it open, curious how anyone can know I'm here, when I see a beautiful handwritten note on watermarked writing paper. I recognise the writing and sit on the bed to read it.

> My dearest Olivia,
> I thought about calling you, but that seemed an inadequate way of saying how devastated I am to learn about the events at Montparnasse and the death of your beloved grandmother. I am of a generation where letters are still the most important and solemn way of communicating, so I am writing this in the consulting room where I treated your grandmother for so many years. Words will never express the depth of my sorrow at her death, nor the joy and friendship she brought to my life for so many decades. All of us are lucky if we meet a true friend who we can walk the journey of life with, and your grandmother was always a soulmate for me, as I hope I was for her. I know Edward is with you. My health is not what it was, but I hope to be well enough to see you in person very soon and share in the memories of your grandmother's life and the gift she gave to the world with her art. Speak soon, dearest Olivia, and know that I am thinking of you during this terribly difficult time as you grieve.
> With the deepest love and affection,
> Louis

I cry reading this. The gorgeous writing paper ends up damp with my tears. There is something so heartfelt about Louis's words. I wonder again how such a noble, courageous father can produce the opposite in his son. Edward has some good bits, but it's hard to find any depth to him. Louis, on the other hand, can encapsulate life in a sentence. Perhaps that's what comes from listening to so many thousands of patients over so many years. It makes you wiser than other people.

I think about Edward again. If I consider him as a suspect, then I need to figure out what his motive is. The facts are clear: he was alone in the apartment when Gran died. He was the closest to the scene of the crime. His word alone is the only evidence for an intruder. But why would he want to hurt Gran? She was a woman he knew so well as the son of Louis. What am I missing here?

I put the letter back in the envelope and place it under my pillow. I complete my usual night-time routine. I listen to Sleep Sound with Sienna Miller and the 'Ice in a Hot Spring' episode on Audible and then set my alarm as the yawns start.

But it's only as I snuggle into the sheets and bring the blanket high against my chin that I see her again at the end of the bed.

Just like the night before, Gran is watching over me.

58

OLIVIA

I sleep well and when I arrive at Place Vendôme, I see Charlotte is waiting for me alone. Charlotte has the glow of someone who rises at 4.15 a.m., meditates, exercises, breakfasts on chia seeds and cider vinegar, cycles into the office and then works at her standing desk complete with green tea and wobble board.

She explains that Edward is not feeling well and suggests taking a walk, and so we head out of Place Vendôme and away from the tourists and towards narrower, darker side streets. The new atmosphere feels ominous to me. We return to our conversation from yesterday. I wonder if Edward really is ill, or if he even knows that Charlotte is here and why she feels the need to come alone. Is there something she wants to tell me about Edward that she couldn't when he was sitting right beside her?

'I said I'd come back with more evidence to back up my claims. I can't give you the evidence directly but I can tell you what I know. Louis has treated many famous people in his consulting room over the years. His patient files contain more secrets than you can possibly imagine. That has made him a target. Many people would do anything to get their hands on that information.'

I remember how shocking Ingrid's claims were when they first went public. Louis was the ultimate establishment figure. France, unlike America or Britain, had taken a more relaxed attitude to the MeToo allegations. Of all the people to make an example of, why him and why now? Louis always felt like a chess piece in a bigger game.

'Blackmail, you mean?'

'Yes,' says Charlotte. 'That is the biggest risk. So many prominent figures have walked up the steps to the consulting rooms at Quai Voltaire and lain on that couch and poured out their problems. Those files are a goldmine. If someone ever got their hands on them, then lots of very important people would be very worried indeed.'

Before his retirement, being treated by Louis was like having an audience with the Pope or Beyoncé singing at your fiftieth birthday party. People paid lots of money to say they'd been in the famous Parisian consulting room and been treated by the father of psychotherapy himself. Not many blackmailers are interested in insurance brokers with daddy issues who live in Mile End. Big Hollywood movie stars confessing to cheating on their A-list partners, however, is a different story. Many of those patients have only got more famous since their sessions with Louis. The value of those files has risen too.

'Louis has always insisted that all patient files are hard copy and patient notes are done by hand,' I say, 'so they can never, ever be hacked. Surely the risk is minimal?'

'That's true,' says Charlotte. 'We also insist that all smartphones, digital watches and any other devices are put in a secure box while sessions take place. It's like Fort Knox, at least on my side of things.'

'Then what's the problem?'

'During a routine check a few months ago, a security company found several audio bugs planted in the landlines in Quai Voltaire, the ones Louis continued to use for his consultations with some former patients like your grandmother. It's unclear how long they have been there. It means that, in effect, Louis's ad hoc sessions could have been recorded.'

'Including Gran's sessions?'

'Yes.'

I am speechless. It is so simple, but also so devastating. Although Louis has retired from daily work as a therapist, he still does occasional phone calls with some high-profile patients who need or want his help. The thought of someone else having recordings of Gran speaking to Louis makes me feel ill.

'Why was it not swept for bugs before?' I ask.

'Louis is from the analogue generation. He hates mobiles and always uses a landline. We even thought that was safer than a cell phone that could be hacked into.'

'Then how could someone plant listening devices?'

'They had to get inside Quai Voltaire,' says Charlotte. 'We've been back over all the tradesmen, painters, delivery drivers, everyone we can think of. And we think we know who it was. I know you think I didn't have any concrete evidence for my theories yesterday. But Louis has authorised me to show this to you. This is why we fear there are threats against Louis and the de Villefort family.'

She takes her phone out of her pocket and holds up the screen. There is a still photo from a security camera showing a

forty-something man dressed in Chelsea boots arriving at Quai Voltaire.
   I stare at the photo and feel my heartbeat stop.
   I don't need to ask her who he is. I've seen that face before.
   I'm looking into the eyes of . . . Tom.

59

OLIVIA

THEN

It's my fourth session with Tom. Though when you're two vodka tonics down and the pub soundtrack is 'Love Songs from the 80s' can it still be called a 'session'?

It is late and the Memory Unit is closed for the night. We're getting a drink in a pub nearby. Yes, okay, it is a dangerous move. One of my colleagues could walk in and see us together and start asking questions. But the pub is noisy and we're hidden in a corner. Our conversation is drowned out by Tina Turner belting out 'What's Love Got to Do with It?'

Since my wild years as a teenager and going into therapy with Louis, I've always been the cautious one who does the right thing, drives at the speed limit and never gets a parking fine. My secret weighed heavily on me, and I tried to make up for it. Now, though, it's time to take a small risk again. I'm no longer that troubled student listening to Avril Lavigne and hoping that being in Paris will solve my problems. I'm a mum, a professional, and I don't have to play it so safe any longer.

Tom and I have become friendlier. It started when I told him about Gran. Tom can't get over the fact that Josephine Benoit is my grandmother. He never stops talking about her. It turns out he's a bit of an art buff and spends his weekends going round galleries in London. One thing led to another and I told him about the book I'm writing and my idea to call it *Memory Wars*. I had Tom down as a scruffy explorer type, but I'm discovering another side to him now.

Since then, it's been different. Not that anything physical has happened yet. But we've connected in that rare, can't-look-away, checking-your-phone-every-minute way. Unlike the bankers on Hinge, there have been no messages saying the first date 'had potential' but 'didn't have the spark needed' and they are 'actively considering other candidates'. I've printed out a few chapters of the manuscript for *Memory Wars* like he asked. It's the first time I've shown it to someone. I didn't think I'd feel this nervous.

He takes the pages and promises to read them when he gets home. I hate this sort of thing. I feel very exposed. I want him to like it, but I feel like I'm revealing part of myself and will get judged for it. It reminds me of our hospital awayday when we did a version of the *Great British Bake Off* and one of the nurses trounced us all with her flawless rum, plum and raisin cake. My fondant fancies never stood a chance.

He smiles at me. 'I promise I'll read it, but give me the elevator pitch first.'

I don't like to say I've rehearsed it, but I have. 'Our memories are like our Instagram feeds. We choose which photos to post, which filters to apply, and which ones to delete. That also means we can sometimes go into the trash folder and take a deleted photo back out and restore it. That's what I try to do with recovered memories.'

'That sounds scary.'

'Not really. You're doing it all the time. My memory of this drink, say, will be the smell of your aftershave and how blue your eyes are. I won't remember the bit you missed shaving or the breakfast stain on your shirt.'

Tom glances at his shirt front. He looks embarrassed. 'Supermarket own-brand muesli,' he says. 'The rock and roll breakfast cereal of choice. I thought I'd rubbed it off. It might increase my fibre intake, but it's a bloody nightmare to clean.'

I smile. It worked. It always does.

'What about false memories? How does anyone reach inside my head and implant something which isn't there?'

'They don't. They take something that is there already and tweak it just a little.'

'So if I kissed you now and we went back to my place, you would forget the muesli stain, the rushed shaving and the Tina Turner pub soundtrack and just remember how much you fancied me? Is that what you're trying to tell me, Dr Finn?'

I smile again. I hoped that Tom would say something like that. I haven't been subtle with my signals tonight, and it's good to know he has some sort of radar. I'm also tired of talking shop. Tom is no longer my patient, at least not officially. I made that a condition of having this drink with him tonight. It was a way of testing his interest in me.

I can't be Dr Finn and Liv. He has to choose one or the other. Thankfully he chose Liv.

I haven't felt like this for ages. I'm a therapist falling for a former patient and I know I shouldn't, but I am. It's a nice distraction from the upcoming trial. I feel so comfortable with Tom. The only person who knows my secret is Louis. But I could imagine telling Tom someday. I never felt as if I could tell Kyle. He would laugh it off, tell me to stop being such a diva, not get the emotion of it at all and the way in which my actions from that day have shaped me in so many ways.

I can't get too far ahead, but I'm already thinking about how I introduce him to TJ, and looking up articles about blended families. That's for the future, though. Now I want to live in the present. Soon the trial will start and life will get messy again.

I want to enjoy tonight.

This isn't my fourth session. This is my first date.

And, as he leans in to kiss me, I hope it's the start of many.

60

OLIVIA

NOW

Tom.

I can still remember that first kiss, the taste of him on my lips. I remember the waft of his aftershave, the slight bristle where he'd missed a spot shaving.

Now, though, I feel sick. I try not to make my reaction too obvious, but it's hard.

Everything that's happened over the last year flashes through my mind. I see Tom standing outside my house with flowers after I gave testimony at the trial. I hear him whispering to me from the opposite side of the bed and I remember the divots his head made on the pillow and the trips he took that he never talked about. I remember all those nagging worries about how elusive he was being and whether I would ever figure out what he was hiding from me and whether or not some mystery was good for a relationship.

I told this man my darkest secret. Was he lying to me all along?

I hand the photo back and say nothing. But my brain is in overdrive.

Tom planted bugs in the apartment of Louis de Villefort. He

is involved in this case. He arrived at the Memory Unit pretending to be a patient. He was using me all along.

I was such a fool to trust him.

'We think this man might have been hired by Ingrid Fox's legal team to try and gather dirt,' says Charlotte, 'and influence the trial. If they found evidence that could discredit Louis and his therapy methods, then Ingrid would win and Louis would be destroyed. Given the he-said, she-said nature of the trial, getting concrete audio evidence could also have been a game-changer.'

'I see,' I say, trying to keep some control of myself.

I don't say anything else. I'm still trying to get my head round the photo. Did Tom lie to me all the time? Did he ever really love me? Is this why he suddenly ghosted me and vanished into thin air? Was anything he told me true? Was it all just about the trial?

Was I really just another mark he was trying to get information out of? I showed him the pages from the *Memory Wars* book. I opened my heart to him.

Charlotte looks at me. 'And you're sure you have never seen this man before, Olivia? You have no idea who he could be?'

I think about when he stayed at my place and what he might have done while he was downstairs making the tea. He could have planted tracking devices on my phone, laptop and iPad. Even now, he could be monitoring my emails and my movements.

I really thought Tom was a different kind of guy. How could I have been so wrong?

I pretend to study the photo again then shake my head and pass the phone back to Charlotte. 'No, sorry, the face doesn't ring any bells.'

I feel completely shaken. I've had suspicions about Tom since he ghosted me. But I didn't imagine something like this.

I don't know what to say. It's as if my entire world has come crashing down.

Charlotte says, 'Edward asked me to tell you that his father has agreed to meet you this evening. He's attending a performance of *Madama Butterfly* at the opera house.'

'Will that be safe?'

'Edward said his father will meet you during the interval. He will see you at the Place de l'Opera at eight o' clock this evening, okay?'

I nod. I am still in shock at that photo of Tom.

'Louis also stressed that this evidence,' she says, holding up her phone, 'can't be shared with anyone. He's showing you because he trusts you. Until we figure it all out, this stays between us.'

61

OLIVIA

I hurry back to the Lutetia trying to get my thoughts together. But I'm still in shock. I enter the lobby and stop by the *Memory* portrait again and look straight into the eyes of the woman sitting in Room 11. Who are you? I ask. What secrets are you still hiding from me?

How can one incident from eighty years ago still cause so many problems so many decades later?

It's as I'm walking back to my room that I see a wedding party emerge from a private entrance by the stairwell in the hotel.

I can't stop thinking of those haunting photos online of the concentration camp survivors dressed in their rags and eating in the magnificent hotel ballroom. I've been trying to find it ever since. The hotel has been refurbished and the rooms have changed but the ballroom must now be used for private hire. I wait until the wedding party leaves and then sneak through the private entrance to see if I can find it.

I immediately know I'm in the right place. The ballroom matches the photos almost exactly. It must still have its original décor. I have read online about the Cristal Ballroom having its own entrance on the Boulevard Raspail and a private reception area. There are five large windows with beautiful champagne-coloured curtains along the right-hand wall which look out onto the hotel gardens. There are vintage crystal Lalique-style chandeliers and chairs designed by Jean-Michel Wilmotte and, despite the leftovers from the recent wedding reception, it feels like I am stepping back from 2025 to 1945.

Gran is with me again, still with her head shaved and wearing those stripy rags from Auschwitz. She is walking through this space, seeing the same things I am, and sitting at one of the tables with her small allowance of bread and water. Around her are fellow survivors from the camps, these French citizens who have seen horrors that will be permanently marked into history. Gran stops eating for a moment and looks up as if she sees me through time. At the same age I was living with Gran in Paris and trying to piece my life back together through daily therapy sessions with Louis at Quai Voltaire. I was a broken mess wondering what the future would hold and tragically in love with Edward.

I stay here in the ballroom of the Lutetia, totally transfixed as the past and present meet, until the spell is broken. The sound of a hoover starts and catering staff from the hotel try to shoo me away when they realise I'm not with the wedding. I leave now and go back to the stairs and up to the first floor. I wonder again whether TJ's children will look back at my life and see the world of 2002 – boybands, Britney Spears in *Crossroads*, the start of *American Idol* – as alien as Gran's world of wartime rations seems to me.

How does time pass that quickly?

Why do I still feel like my life is just starting?

I reach Room 11 and see that the bed has been turned down and the towels replaced. I still haven't been told that I'm allowed to leave Paris yet. I feel trapped in this hotel, and yet strangely I don't actually want to leave. Being here keeps me close to Gran in a weird way. Heading back to my semi-detached house in Redbridge would be to accept she is gone and that I won't see her again. Being here is like wrapping yourself in a loved one's old clothes, smelling their distinctive scent, holding on for as long as you can.

By mid-afternoon, I know TJ will be out of school and I eventually manage to get him on FaceTime. He looks puzzled at seeing me on a screen, but also slightly hyper too. There is a Hula Hoops variety pack right next to him and he munches away as he talks. He hates the BBQ beef flavour. But try and take a packet of salt and vinegar crisps out of his hand and be prepared for world war three.

'Where are you, Mummy?' he says, as he wriggles in his chair. TJ hasn't quite grasped the concept of looking at the camera on video calls, and he looks around as if trying to see where my voice is coming from. In the fridge? No. In the biscuit cupboard? Also no. Underneath the table? Maybe.

'I'm in Paris, buster,' I say. 'That's where I've been the last three days. I had to come to Paris to look after Gran.'

I wonder how I will tell him that Gran is dead. He knew her as an old woman who ruffled his hair and fed him sweets from a tin, but I don't know how much he can remember of her. The pandemic stopped us seeing her much. She was just the nice old lady, like the Queen, who smiled at TJ, but without being a daily part of his life.

'When are you coming home?'

'Soon, darling, very soon. I just have to clear a few more

things here and then I'll be right back and you can come home again. Is everything okay at Daddy's?'

He nods and then takes another handful of Hula Hoops and directs them precariously towards his mouth. One or two go in and most of the others scatter in every possible direction and fall to the floor.

I hear a woman's voice off camera and see TJ looking towards someone. Then he says, 'I have to go now, Mummy.'

And then I see the New Girlfriend's face as she scoops TJ into her arms and waves at the screen before ending the call. I try to remember if I've missed something in TJ's diary. I sound like his social planner. Drinks at the Ned, dinner at the River Cafe, an after-party at the Groucho. No, he had drama on the first night I was away and karate on the second night. But today? There is nothing. He could have stayed and talked to me all evening. She has ended the call out of nothing more than spite.

I can't stop thinking about New Girlfriend's gym-toned arms, the glimpse of the small dolphin tattoo on her right wrist, the ease with which she whisked my son up and how little TJ protested.

It's absurd, I know, and petty, but I feel rage building inside me.

I don't want to leave these memories of Gran. But soon I will have to get out of this hotel and get home to my boy.

62

OLIVIA

THEN

Today is the day of the trial. Not for the first time, I'm struggling with tech issues.

TJ has come down with flu and been in and out of hospital for the last few days. My testimony slot has also been moved, which means I've been allowed to appear before the court via video link rather than travelling to Paris in person. I've made a cup of strong coffee, eaten half a packet of chocolate biscuits, and tried every camera position for the best possible lighting. Now I'm sitting in front of my screen in a smart trouser suit waiting for the little circle of doom to stop spinning and the link to work.

While I wait, I keep wondering if anyone knows about me and Tom. Has someone found out that we slept together at his place? Did they see us kiss in the pub near the hospital? Could they report me for getting involved with a former patient?

This might be a defamation trial rather than a criminal one, but I still feel like I'm walking into the lion's den here. The case is heard, like all defamation cases in Paris, in 17ème chambre before a panel of three magistrates.

I don't want to lose my job. I also don't want to lose Tom.

He reminds me of Edward de Villefort, which is a name I rarely think about these days. Sure, Tom is much kinder, more sympathetic, less of a coke-snorting bad-ass than Edward was. But, then again, he grew up in Nether Wallop and had two dentists for parents, not a war hero father running the most renowned psychotherapy clinic in Paris.

The wait seems to go on forever. Finally, my computer connects and the staff at the court guide me through what will happen next. I imagine the scene in my mind: Louis dressed immaculately; Ingrid Fox attending each day; reporters sitting in the public gallery. I am given instructions, forced to wait a bit longer, then I'm beamed live into the courtroom. I just hope my French is good enough and I don't end up having to google obscure legal jargon. It feels weird doing this remotely, but then I think of TJ's fever last night and wonder if I'm catching it, and thank my lucky stars for the invention of the internet.

'Dr Finn,' begins the lawyer speaking rapid-fire French, 'you have known the defendant for your entire life, is that correct?'

'Yes,' I say, trying to lower my voice and make it sound more convincing. 'Monsieur de Villefort is a friend of my grandmother on my mum's side of the family.'

'And you were once his patient too, is that correct?'

'I was a patient at his clinic in Quai Voltaire when I was a teenager and studying at the Sorbonne.'

'How old were you when you started treatment with the defendant?'

'Eighteen.'

'How would you describe Monsieur de Villefort as a therapist?'

'He was the very best. He knew when to ask questions, when to listen. He was always sympathetic and kindly, but firm in trying to help his patients lead happier lives rather than disappear in the past.'

'Did he display any signs of coercive control or psychological abuse?'

'No, he did not. Quite the opposite, in fact.'

'How did you feel during those sessions? You, one on one, as a teenager with a man old enough to be your grandfather?'

'I felt completely comfortable. Louis was the person who helped me understand what my mother had done, and why her suicide wasn't an act of abandonment, and that she really did love me. Without that therapy, I'm not sure I would be here today.'

I pause and sip some water. I long for another chocolate biscuit too. This is even more stressful than I thought.

The lawyer waits, looking at her notes, and then asks, 'Dr Finn, do you believe it's possible for patients to recover memories of trauma in their past?'

This is the tricky part. I have to explain to them that it is possible to recover memories of trauma, and that Louis successfully surfaced awful truths about Ingrid's past and what her foster father did to her. And now Louis is the one being punished.

'Memory is a very delicate thing,' I say. 'But, in some circumstances, recovering memories can be a useful way to help patients deal with the original source of their trauma. It's not recommended for every patient, but it's up to the psychotherapist to use when appropriate.'

'Is that what happened to you during therapy?'

'Yes.'

'During your recovered memory therapy, did Monsieur de Villefort ever try to influence you or tell you to cut off contact with your family? Did he ever give you suggestions about what your recovered memory might be, or which bits might be true and which not?'

'On the contrary, he's always said my relationship with my grandmother was one of the greatest strengths in my life. He urged me to seek help from her when I needed it. Recovered memory therapy often involves hypnosis and other techniques, so the patient is vulnerable, I admit that. But I don't remember Monsieur de Villefort ever trying to influence me, no.'

'Have you ever heard of any other cases where Monsieur de Villefort has been accused of abusing his powerful role as a therapist?'

'Not that I can recall, no.'

'When seeing a patient, how can you tell if a recovered memory is factual or false?'

'It comes down to trust,' I say. 'Often my patients have repressed traumatic memories. They've developed coping mechanisms rather than dealing with the trauma. As the years go on, those coping mechanisms become more like handcuffs. By recovering the memory at the heart of that trauma, I help them realise that they don't need the coping mechanisms any more. They no longer need to be frightened of the memory. They don't have to repress it or mask it with drugs, alcohol, binge eating. It takes time, but often my patients can cure their addictions through recovered memory therapy.'

'So the judgement about whether a recovered memory is true or not is entirely down to the therapist themselves?'

I can sense the trap. 'To begin with, yes. Once it goes beyond the consulting room, however, the recovered memory must be backed up by other forms of evidence, especially if allegations are made and it proceeds to any form of trial. In this particular case, the recovered memory in question pointed towards Ms Fox's foster father as the perpetrator of the abuse. Unable to handle that fact, Ms Fox now seems to be transferring the blame for her foster father's actions to Monsieur de Villefort himself.'

There are a few more questions and then, just like that, it is over so quickly. The live link stops, and I am talking to one of the court staffers again. I still can't see the courtroom, but I imagine Louis sitting there and the sadness in his eyes, defending his reputation and his life's work. He fought to save Paris with the Resistance, and has helped thousands of the city's residents deal with trauma in their past, and has never refused to treat vulnerable patients despite the risks involved. This is the thanks he gets for it. The real predators, of which there are many, get away with their crimes, while the public witch-hunt goes after an old man who was once a hero.

I turn off my computer, make another cup of coffee and eat the last of the chocolate biscuits. I feel sadness, anger, and frustration. It all feels so unfair. Then I see a text from Tom asking me how it went and saying there's a surprise at the front door. I usually hate surprises.

But I can't help smiling as I open the front door. Tom is standing there with a bunch of red roses.

'Excuse the overblown romantic gesture,' he says. 'But, well, it turns out . . . actually I'm an overblown romantic. Who knew.'

I haven't let myself think this yet. But I might just love this man. Even that thought feels dangerous to me. What is life, though, without a little danger?

I step back and he walks inside.

I realise I never want him to leave.

63

OLIVIA

NOW

Despite all my childhood trips to Paris, I've never been to the opera house. The Palais Garnier is as much a part of this city as the Louvre or Notre Dame.

Gran was largely a recluse, so didn't enjoy going out to shows. Mum had no interest in opera and thought the tickets were too expensive and the drinks in the interval a mercenary racket which showed the wild contradictions of late capitalism.

We visited Gran every few months in Paris, but always ended up in the dusty cafés and bookshops that Mum liked, not the blingy tourist hangouts dripping with gold. And the opera house, as even I know, has its fair share of gold.

I always quite fancied a warm glass of fizz and some overpriced nibbles while watching grown adults in far too much make-up sing about love and death. But opera, like skiing, always seemed to be something families either did or didn't do. Our family didn't.

I don't have anything fancy to wear so I put on the one dress I packed and time my arrival just as the interval strikes. Edward is waiting for me in Place de l'Opéra and is back to his heir apparent role with a sharp suit and polished shoes.

He looks fine to me, and I bet the illness line earlier was an excuse. I don't trust him at all, but I also want to see Louis, and Edward is now acting like his father's gatekeeper.

He kisses me on both cheeks and then takes in the dress. 'You look stunning, Liv,' he says, 'if I'm still allowed to say that.'

'I'll allow it this once. You don't look too shabby yourself.'

'Shall we?'

When we reach the opera house, Edward gets the attendants to wave me through. I wonder if there's anywhere in Paris where the de Villefort family name doesn't get you access. No wonder Louis has so many famous patients, and no wonder others in the city want to bring them down.

As we walk inside, I have a similar feeling to when I stood in the ballroom this afternoon. Entering the Palais Garnier is like stepping into an underground labyrinth. I can already imagine the Phantom of the Opera haunting this space with its Palladian and baroque styles and the heavily marbled surround.

'My father is a major donor here,' says Edward, as if father–son get-togethers happen at the opera all the time. 'He's in the Empress's box tonight, which is by far the best seat in the house. This way.'

I'm still mesmerised by the grand staircase. There is white marble underfoot and red and green marble on the balustrade. The ceiling is rich and ornate and light comes from the female torchères at the pedestals on either side. We reach another floor and Edward walks up to one of the doors.

Slowly the majesty of the opera house itself emerges around me. The first sensation is visual. I have never seen so much red and gold. The ceiling is so over the top that the sheer dazzle of it is almost comical, just the right side of kitsch. Everything is too much, yet also fitting. It's hard to believe that just outside this place ordinary life continues. It's like entering a Disney castle, except each bit is real.

I am nervous too. Since Louis retired, I haven't seen much of him. Very occasionally we talk on the phone. But this man knows more about me than anyone, down to the secrets that have shaped my life, and is the closest to a father figure that I've ever had.

With Gran gone, he is the last rock in an uncertain world. I miss him. I hope that he misses me too.

'Dad,' says Edward, walking up to the seat at the front of the box and bending down to whisper. 'Olivia is here.'

64

OLIVIA

I approach the seat and see familiar white tufts of hair and a walking stick. The voice reaches me before I see his face. There is the precision I always remember from my childhood visits to Quai Voltaire with Gran. The voice is deep and comforting, as if it's been left to fully ripen.

'Forgive me, my dearest Olivia,' says the voice, 'but my legs aren't what they used to be. Please, please, have a seat beside me here. It seems so long since I set eyes on you. I only wish we didn't meet again under such unfortunate circumstances. I wanted to see you before now but, alas, my health wouldn't allow it. This is the first time my medical team have let me out of the house in days.'

I reach the seat now and, as I sit, I see how much Louis has aged since I last saw him. After the trial, he retreated fully behind the walls of his lavish apartment. I thought he might be completely broken. But there is still a twinkle in his eyes, and a smile beneath the wrinkled skin.

He has longish, thinning white hair, combed beautifully backwards until it tucks neatly behind each ear. He is smartly dressed, as ever. He wears a velvety jacket with a pocket square, some equally velvety slip-on loafers and then what looks like a bespoke shirt and trousers, each crease hugging his body shape exactly. He is rich enough to have an army of carers, but I wonder if they select his clothes each day. Apart from the general sense of age, Louis seems like he's been preserved in aspic. Perhaps once you've been in the Resistance, everything else seems like small fry. Either that or it's all those milk baths.

Edward sits to the left of Louis. I sit on the right. Louis keeps his hands resting on the top of his walking stick. The stick is as stylish as its owner, with a beechwood shaft and a Derby handle at the top in a marbled blend of gold, beige and dove-grey. It is the same stick he has used ever since I first knew him. I remember it resting in a special stand along with his hat and coat in the consulting room. Whatever else he might be, Louis has always been the best-dressed psychotherapist in town.

'So, dearest Olivia,' says Louis. He looks sad now, haunted by what has happened in the last few days. His voice is croaky, and catches slightly. 'Your grandmother has been taken from us. Charlotte Fouquet has filled you in on what's been going on behind the scenes. I think this is the first time I've laid eyes on you since you so kindly gave testimony at the trial.'

'Yes. That seems a long time ago now.'

'You risked your own reputation to help me, and I'll always be eternally grateful.'

'It was nothing,' I say. 'Certainly not compared to what you've done for me.'

Louis shakes his head, a lion ruffling his mane. 'I think I was probably your grandmother's only true friend. And, in some ways, she was mine. Not acquaintances, you understand, or colleagues. But friendship in the truest sense. Someone who can see into your soul. She was always fiercely private. But if anyone can claim to have seen through her, then perhaps I can. You got my letter at the hotel?'

'Yes. Thank you. It was beautiful.'

'I hoped the trial might be the end of the persecution against me. But, alas, it seems it was only the beginning. I was in the Resistance when most people collaborated, and I spent my life recovering memories of secrets that most people wanted to hide. My enemies have been trying to ruin the de Villefort name for years. Now, finally, they seem to be succeeding. I only hoped they would keep their focus on me. Your grandmother didn't deserve any of this.'

I see the guilt and grief in his eyes, and it breaks me. I reach out and touch his shoulder gently. 'None of this is your fault. We don't know that's why Gran was targeted. The police are still investigating.'

'Did Charlotte tell you about my phones being bugged before the trial and the man we think is behind it?'

I try not to give anything away. 'Yes.'

'A terrible business. I've treated thousands, even tens of thousands, of patients over the years, and I always vowed that what they said to me in the consulting room was sacred. If patients don't trust you as their therapist, then nothing truthful can ever emerge. To have that trust violated, even if I am long retired . . . it's the greatest possible betrayal.'

I see the photo of Tom now, and the terrible knowledge that I fell for his lies. I am partly responsible for this too. I should have seen through his act and alerted Louis. I wanted to believe love was real this time. If only I'd listened to my early doubts. He really was too good to be true.

'Who do you think is behind it all?' I ask. 'Who could the man in the photo be working for?'

'I don't know. Probably the same people who persuaded Ingrid Fox to go to the police and invent those lies about my therapy techniques. Her adopted father, for one. When you're my age, dearest Olivia, you have more enemies than friends. It could be any one of them.'

Louis glances at Edward. Then back at me. For the first time, I see genuine fear in his eyes. He looks so suave, stylish, elevated above the cares of the world. But not today.

'What do we do now?' I ask.

I try to remain calm. Without this man, I would have ended up in an alleyway somewhere, broken by Mum's death. I might not trust Edward, but I do believe in Louis. So did Gran. I have to believe we can get through this.

Louis looks tenderly at me. 'My dearest Olivia, we do what I've spent my whole life doing. We must try and find the truth.'

65

OLIVIA

I've been in Paris for three days now but this is the first time I've experienced the city that I remember as a girl. The Paris opera house is bursting with people in their black tie and dazzling gowns. The first half of *Madama Butterfly* has finished. There will be wine, food, conversation, then everyone will return and my moment with Louis will be over. I can almost imagine the Phantom of the Opera in his box haunting us all with his presence.

Louis says, 'Your grandmother was always hiding something. That's why she became so reclusive. As her therapist, and her friend, I failed in my treatment. I treated the symptoms, but never got close to the root cause.'

Louis looks sad, and I want to tell him that he did all he could. I think of the way Gran would hug me and kiss me and hold me close, the sharpness of her perfume and the smoothness of her skin. To me she was always just Gran. I loved her to pieces. My frustration was directed at Mum, mostly, which wasn't fair but perhaps inevitable when you're a teenager forced to watch a parent with addiction issues.

TJ won't have grandparents to spoil him on my side. He

will have Kyle's parents, though, and that thought doesn't fill me with joy. They will buy him Rolexes, dress him in Gucci, take him on holiday to meet women with too much make-up and too few clothes. It's all very *Love Island* and I dread the thought of him turning into Kyle 2.0.

'Did Gran ever talk to you about what happened during the war?' I say.

Louis jabs his cane against the floor, as if jolting a memory. 'You have to understand, my dear, that the Occupation is a trauma that Paris and France have never really come to terms with. Everyone prefers to forget what happened rather than remember. I knew bits, but not everything.'

'Everyone knows you were in the Resistance,' I say. 'Doesn't it annoy you when people try and conveniently forget like that?'

'Don't flatter me, my dear,' he says, as if it's the most boring topic imaginable. 'I did the little I could. I can hardly point the finger at others, though, when my own humble achievements have been made so much of. I was a teenager with the bravery of youth.'

'I'm sure you're just being modest.'

Louis gives me a twinkly smile. 'Well, as Edward will tell you, there's a first time for everything.'

'I still don't understand why your enemies would target Gran? Did she mention her worries about the Lutetia and being Sophie Leclerc during her therapy sessions? Could the person who planted the bugs have killed her because of that?'

Louis is serious again. 'I don't know. During the last few years, your grandmother's memory problems became worse. She was haunted by guilt. I was retired, so we no longer had in-person sessions, though on rare occasions I tried hypnosis and other techniques to help her, but her dementia symptoms were increasing and it was hopeless. We spoke mostly by phone and it was clear that her mind was going.'

'Do you think Gran could have stolen someone else's identity to survive?'

Louis flashes those darting eyes. 'In her mind, she was escaping the trauma of her own past. Perhaps, in light of today's events, she was actually making sure the truth could never find her. Could Josephine Benoit have been another mask for your grandmother to hide behind, the recluse in her apartment? Yes, psychologically speaking at least, it could. But it is still a mystery to me.'

I realise that I still haven't asked the most important question. I can see Louis is tiring. Soon Edward will step in and my chance will be over. The opera crowd will return, the house lights dim and I'll not get the chance to ask again.

'One more question,' I say. 'Then I promise we'll let you rest.'

Louis nods, used to his own frailty. 'I will answer as best I can.'

'You were at the Lutetia treating survivors. I get the sense you know something about Gran and what she did in that hotel that you don't want to tell me? That you're still protecting her, even in death?'

There is another tiny flicker in Louis's eyes. He looks so sad. 'My dear, you know better than anyone that the agreement between a therapist and a patient can't be broken, just like a client and their lawyer. I'm sure there are lots of things your grandmother told me in confidence which it isn't appropriate to tell you as her grandchild. Just as there are things in all of our lives which disappear in the mists of time, as they should. Do I know things about your grandmother that you don't? Of course. But, I assure you, nothing that affects this case. She deserves her dignity in death, just as we all do. You have to trust me on that.'

I don't disguise my disappointment. I know I shouldn't have asked, but I have a desperate hunger to know. But he is right. It's the one thing he taught me when I was training to be a psychotherapist. Always respect the patient. It's what made the trial and the false accusations so cruel. The modern age is one of oversharing. Every single thing we do is posted online for the world to see. Nothing is real unless it's documented on Insta. I admire Louis's old-fashioned sense of dignity.

'Your grandmother suffered terrible trauma at an early age,' he says. 'She was still able to love you as her grandchild, and be a good friend to me. Sometimes, not always, she found a way to dance despite the storm in her own mind. Whatever the truth about how she died, let's remember her like that. It's how she would have wanted it.'

I feel embarrassed by my question now. As a therapist, I should have known better. Louis would never willingly betray the secrets of his patients. He loved Gran too much to gossip about her failings or things she did in the war which will change my view of her. He wants to preserve the memories I have.

The second half performance is about to begin. People return to their seats. Louis leans towards me with a final thought.

'There is one place in Paris, however, that may be able to shed more light on your grandmother's past,' he says. 'It's late now but if you mention my name they might let you in. The state records are one thing, but the original files are quite another.'

'Where?' I ask.

'The ultimate place of memories,' he says. 'The Mémorial de la Shoah.'

66

OLIVIA

THEN

Are Tom and I now Instagram official? Well, not quite. That would give the game away. I'd be suspended for having a romantic relationship with a patient and possibly struck off too. They'd go through all my emails and texts and then the worst bits would come out during the hearing. There'd be some god-awful photo of me and a headline about a sex-obsessed therapist chasing a patient and the shame would force me to move to the Outer Hebrides and take up crofting.

So, for now, we're keeping our romance quiet. But we are a couple. We haven't done the I-love-yous yet, but we're in our thirties-slash-forties not holding hands at the back of the school hall. And after my testimony at Louis's trial, that is just as well. My name is now public property. That makes it good for book publicity, but bad for my work at the Memory Unit. The advance for *Memory Wars* has come through and we're planning a trip to Paris. Tom wants to go to Le Grand near the opera house. A cheeky Google shows lots of lavish furnishings and old-school Parisian glamour.

It's still weird going on a date with Tom though. I can't forget that he used to be my patient and that I know more about what's going through his mind than the average couple who've been dating for a few months. He stays over at mine when TJ's with Kyle, but we haven't talked about moving in together yet. Both of us just want to enjoy what we have and not rush things. We've both come out of marriages that didn't end well. We know life doesn't offer many happy-ever-afters. Why rush?

Tonight, we meet at a bar near London Bridge. He is as neat and tidy as ever, and also as elusive. He sips at a beer while I make do with gin and tonics. He never drinks to excess, and always remains in control. He's been away a lot recently. He won't say much about his job, he's always so cagey like that, but it's contract work with one of his buddies from the Marines, and his jet-setting lifestyle seems more exotic than my steady-as-she-goes psychotherapist one. I sit in the same office every day and listen to people's problems. He is out there in dangerous parts of the world helping people dodge bullets and bombs.

I spend the starter trying to get some info out of him, but he just mumbles into his soup, as usual, about corporate events and crowd control and makes it all sound much more boring than it probably is. He is always so ordered, in the way military people are trained to be, and never makes a fuss of stuff, which is another Marine thing. Even the way he dabs his napkin on his lips, straightens his collar and adjusts the cutlery on the table so the pieces are in line with each other gives me a sense of calm. I would go into battle with this man. He would have packed enough rations, ammo and calculated the optimum weather conditions.

By the time the mains arrive, he turns the spotlight onto me. I've always wanted a guy who listens. Kyle's idea of a conversation was a monologue on how underappreciated he was by me and wider society. And at least Tom's not like those guys showing me PowerPoint decks about stage three funding rounds or reading aloud their latest performance reviews. Tom listens to my answers and asks follow-up questions.

'Tell me honestly,' he says. 'What was it like giving evidence in the trial? I've got friends who've done stuff like that in military courts and, I swear, even the most macho ones end up with serious stage fright. Were you nervous?'

'No,' I say. 'That's like asking if you get nervous guarding some A-list pop star. I talk about memory and people's minds for a living.'

'How much of what you said was personal and how much professional?'

I'm annoyed by the question. 'I always base my opinion on facts. There's nothing personal in it. I'm a psychologist not a crystal ball reader.'

'There is, though,' he says. 'I mean, you were once in the position that Ingrid Fox was in. She sat on the same couch you did. You were treated by the same psychotherapist. There must be something personal in there. You had therapy with the same man at the same time in the 2000s. You literally walked in her shoes at Quai Voltaire.'

'My testimony, and my book, is based on the latest science. Psychotherapy isn't just feelings and emotions, you know. My job is to understand how the mind works, and doesn't work, and try and make it better.'

'Do you think Louis de Villefort will win the case?'

'I don't know,' I say. 'I wasn't sure if Louis would sue her for defamation. But he's stubborn and wants a public record of his innocence. I don't blame him. I'd want the same. It's complicated.'

We finish eating. The plates are cleared and we ask for the dessert menu. Louis's part of the trial is over, and now Ingrid is due to give her evidence.

Finally, he says, 'Not everything has to be complicated, you know. I'm no longer your patient. You're not my therapist. There are no rules against us now, as . . . partners. We don't have to skulk around like this, as if our relationship is a secret. I want you to know that you can confide in me, Liv. I'm your guy. I want us to be able to tell each other everything.'

That other worry about his true intentions fades away now. This is more like it. The word 'partners' lingers in the air and neither of us know what to do with it, but we also know we don't have to do anything at all. That's when I know this is the real deal. We trust each other enough not to need a five-point plan for where this is going. We can move one step at a time, fumbling our way through the darkness together.

Dessert arrives and we share one dish with two spoons. We sit in silence and don't need words. I wish every night was like this. I've already forgotten about his trips and what exactly his job is and why he doesn't tell me more. It keeps the mystery alive in our relationship. He is elusive, and I can't get a grip on him. My younger self would have hated that. I needed to know everything. But I'm more mature now. I get that people are private and don't want to make themselves vulnerable by telling someone everything. And that's fine, even if I do sometimes lie awake wondering what he's keeping from me.

I have him and he has me and that is what matters. I'm considering whether I want to tell him my secret, and cross that final bridge with him, when my phone goes and I see the news alert on the screen and suddenly all my thoughts of what happened in the past vanish.

'What is it?' says Tom, seeing my reaction. 'Liv?'

I try to keep my voice steady. But I can already feel the pain in my stomach.

'Ingrid Fox,' I say. 'Police have found a body.'

67

RENÉ

NOW

René continues his vigil near the Place de l'Opéra. He sees all the tourists in their shapeless holiday clothes taking selfies. Olivia Finn and Edward de Villefort arrived at the Palais Garnier but they weren't dressed for the opera. It's a meeting, René is sure, probably with Louis. Olivia has spent most of the day holed up in Room 11 at the Lutetia. The opera house is a smart move, and Louis will probably have one of the fanciest boxes too.

René checks to see if there have been any further messages. His client only sends messages through encrypted apps or disguised voice calls. Nothing can ever be traced back. All he's been told is to keep track of Olivia Finn. He doesn't know why, or for how long. But he charges by the hour and is happy to take the work.

Sitting in the car with the radio on and a Big Mac is about as good as his nights get. He flicks through his MyFitness app on his phone. It's a bore, but a necessary one. If he doesn't keep track then one Big Mac becomes a Double Big Mac with bacon, those small fries become a family-sized fries and the Coke Zero is suddenly a chocolate milkshake. It took him years to finally kick the booze. Now it's the fats and sugars that dance in front of him with their goddamn deliciousness.

It helps him to stop those memories about the past, the people he killed and the comrades who never came back. He keeps waiting, chewing, waiting and chewing, listening to bad pop music on the car radio and wishing he was young and starting over again.

Perhaps that's another reason why the stunt double or TV career would never have worked out. All those guys are jabbing themselves with Ozempic and throwing up four times a day so they look lean on camera. René is more of a traditional muscle man. One thousand five hundred calories a day is his idea of hell. He goes hard on the food, hard at the weights, and hopes a swift heart attack will take care of the rest.

As he continues to watch the opera house, René sees the old version of himself stumbling around the city all those years ago. He was just out of the Foreign Legion, dumped onto civvy street, resisting those tempting offers of mercenary work and trying to break into close protection work for proper VIPs. But his problem, like so many soldiers, was of the mind not the heart.

The flashbacks wouldn't stop. They were with him in bed, at work, at rest. There were flashbacks of the first kill, the first colleague killed, the first house full of bullet holes. The doctors called it PTSD. Deep down, though, it was a memory disorder. The flashbacks warped reality until the flashbacks became reality.

Why couldn't he just forget?

He tried booze and pills. But, in the end, he needed more. That's when he learned how to control his mind and compartmentalise. He was taught to place the bad memories into different spaces, like putting them into a safe and locking it.

The memory palace hack doesn't stop the flashbacks entirely but it helps. He often wishes he could return his brain to factory settings. But he's stuck with it.

If you don't control your memory, you don't control yourself.

Memory makes us who we are.

René looks at the Palais Garnier again. He reaches across to the front passenger seat and checks under the newspaper. He feels the cold outline of the Beretta M9. It's a toy weapon, really, compared with those he used in the army. But it will do.

He watches for another few minutes. Then, finally, he sees Olivia Finn step out with Edward de Villefort. They are leaving the opera house just as the second act starts. They see a taxi nearby and hail it.

René waits for another second, then edges out of his parking space and follows the taxi. He dials the number as he drives. The client is always prompt, picking up on the first ring.

'Yes?'

'I have eyes on,' he says.

'Good. Where are they heading?'

'I'm not sure. What are my orders?'

The voice is clinical, totally without emotion. 'The woman is the threat. Deal with her and then find the British cop and deal with him. The two foreigners. Only them. Anything else will create too much noise. We can't afford to let Vidal and the DNPJ stick their noses in.'

'Copy that.'

The call ends.

René continues following the taxi. Edward and Olivia head away down the Rue de Monceau. He follows the taxi to the last place that René expects.

Take out Dr Finn. Then find DI Forsyth and do the same.

Don't, under any circumstances, attract the attention of the fearsome Captain Vidal or the DNPJ.

He checks the Beretta and looks at the location again.

Seventeen Rue Geoffroy l'Asnier.

Up ahead is a large building. René searches for the location on his phone.

Memories, memories, memories. More damn memories.

The Mémorial de la Shoah.

Why have they ended up here?

68

THE LUTETIA

1945

SOPHIE

Sophie is nervous.
She takes a breath and prepares. She looks in the mirror and wonders how long it will take for her hair to grow back. Will her body ever return to normal? It seems silly to be vain now, but she wants to look good for Louis. She has no rouge or nice clothes, no lipstick or scent, and yet she splashes her face, does a sink wash, anything to make herself more like she used to be. Maybe that is a good sign. She has got her vanity back, or part of it, which means she has some self-worth too.

The war didn't take that, at least.

Louis is waiting in the lobby for her this time, rather than the other way round. He has a different coat on, long and black, and his hair is washed and his cheeks shaved. He looks less pale, as if seeing her yesterday has revived him. Despite the lack of food and nutrients, he still looks strong. It's hard to say exactly what the attraction is, but it's like their souls were meant for each other. She could meet him at any age, in any country, and it would be the same. Even after all this time, it's like picking up a conversation that's already started.

It is only the second day, but already they have their little routine. Guests aren't allowed to leave, but they can walk through the hotel and have visitors. The Lutetia is like an open prison. They find their table in the restaurant again and sip cheap coffee. Sophie could almost write off yesterday as a dream, but today Louis is even more real than before. She feared waking up this morning and finding he didn't exist.

The hotel is busy again today. The restaurant is filled with survivors. The smell of unwashed bodies is overwhelming and Sophie continues to sense danger everywhere. She will never get used to the noises and cries from the other rooms. Nobody here is well, in mind or body. Louis has his work cut out treating these survivors. Death still lingers in the air. But, despite all that, there is space for romance. It is not the golden, champagne-swilling luxury of the Old Lutetia, with its ballgowns and orchestras. She will take it, though. This is some reminder of what real life used to be.

After they have been together awhile, Louis says, 'Tell me more about these memories, Sophie. I hate to think of you suffering so much now, after everything you've been through.'

How does someone survive the camps unless they've sold their soul? How can any survivor start to tell someone what it was like in those places? She has told him some of what happened yesterday, but not all.

'I don't know how to begin,' says Sophie.

Josephine, and perhaps Louis, still think of her as the naïve, trusting, good-natured Sophie she used to be. The Sophie who saw the best in others, turned the other cheek, didn't gossip or trade rumours, always tried to be kind and to treat others in the way she wanted to be treated.

But that was before. She was arrested as a girl and is now a woman. Josephine was always more grown up and calculating. She never had the love of her parents. She schemed and plotted and strategised ever since she was little.

Her father warned her about Josephine. He said there was something missing at the heart of her. Sophie never believed him, convinced that Josephine was her greatest friend, until the day the fateful knock came and her world changed forever. She knew then that Josephine was the one who had betrayed her. Josephine was the only one who knew where Sophie and her father were hiding.

She wanted to believe in Josephine's goodness and, even now, she is sometimes taken in by her and the memories of how it used to be before the war ruined everything. But, always, she sees her father's face as he was dragged away from her. This man with his kindly eyes and crinkled face looking like a scared little boy again. No, she will never forgive Josephine for that.

But she is still too cowardly to take revenge. She has allowed her betrayer to lie in her bed and sleep peacefully.

'Take your time,' says Louis, reaching out his hand again to take hers. 'I've heard some of the stories from the camps with other patients I've treated. I won't judge. We can cure this together, dearest Sophie. All I need is for you to tell me everything that happened to you.'

69

THE LUTETIA

1945

SOPHIE

'I'm not sure if they are memories,' she says. 'True memories, or false ones, I mean. I can't remember if I did the things I remember or just witnessed them. It's all a blur in my head. How do I tell the difference?'

'That's natural. Trauma works like that. Just tell me in your own words.'

She lowers her voice until it's a whisper. 'My age helped me survive the selections. The guards would select people for death, and the others would be spared, until the next day. The older ones went first. Everyone was looking for a way to survive a few days longer. Some became capos, camp police, cooks. I was given a choice to cook for the commandant and his family. I knew if I refused, then I would be sent left rather than right the next time, and that would be it. I didn't want to die. So I did as I was told.'

She fears that Louis's grip will weaken and he will sit back in disgust. He is the Resistance fighter, after all, the brave hero who didn't collaborate. But his grip remains the same and she has never loved him more than this moment.

'All of us would make that choice,' says Louis. He reaches up and curls another imaginary strand of hair from her face. 'It's not even really a choice. We're built to survive, Sophie. Stop blaming yourself. No one emerges from this war having made all the right choices. Especially not me.'

And now the tears start. Like her vanity earlier, Sophie knows this is a good thing. She hasn't been able to cry for so long. At one point, as she arrived at Gare d'Orsay, she thought she might never feel emotion in the same way again.

'No,' she says. 'You were so brave. You and those others in the Resistance. You risked torture and death. You fought right to the end.'

'Because we were still free to fight,' he says. 'You were a prisoner. You can't make that comparison. None of us were in the camps. We didn't face selections or the same choices you did.'

Can she ever tell him about the other memories? She remembers being alone with the commandant when he would shut his study door while his children were out for a walk with their mother. She can still hear the lock turning on the door, the smell of tea in the fine china cup, the creak of his leather belt being unbuckled.

'That's the problem,' she says. 'I feel emotions I never knew I was capable of. During those selections, I did kill people, in a way. I avoided being selected for the gas chambers and made sure others were selected instead. I played the game like everyone else. I've got their blood on my hands, Louis, and it will never go away. I don't want to be Sophie Leclerc any more. I want to rub out the past and start again.'

'That is also an expected reaction,' says Louis, with his calm bedside manner. 'Wanting to escape from that identity is a normal psychological response.'

Sophie has always seen herself as strong and independent. Her heroes were the women who blazed their own trail and forged careers in cities like Paris, women who never needed others. But the camps made her desperate for human company. She longed for her father to put his arm round her and say everything was going to be all right. She dreamed of Louis's kisses during those moonlit walks through the city, or meeting her mother who died during childbirth. Anything was better than being alone.

'You're very understanding,' she says, finally mirroring his touch and stroking his hand, the first bit of affection she can manage. 'You always were.'

He smiles again, then his eyes grow more serious. 'And, speaking as a doctor, do these memories ever . . . become real again?'

She knows what he is asking. He has tapped into her deepest fear. That is why he is the medical student and she is the patient. He knows how people's minds work.

'Not yet,' she says. 'But they might do. When I'm in that room with Josephine, I don't feel in control of myself. My impulses overtake me. I think about standing over her and putting a pillow on her face and pressing down until she doesn't breathe again. Does that make me a terrible person?'

'No, no,' he says, still holding her hand. 'When you are out of here, I will treat you myself. We will banish these memories together. You can get better. But it will take time.'

It's as if he has seen her greatest fear and made it appear less scary. She thinks of last night and checking that Josephine was still breathing. When she passes through the crowds here in the hotel, she feels like she could murder anyone who steps in her way.

Louis checks his watch and starts collecting his things, ready to leave.

'You're going so soon?' she asks.

He bends down and kisses her forehead. 'I'm needed at the hospital. You have another day and a half to survive here. Then we can be together. Think of that. And remember what I said. You will get better, Sophie. I guarantee it.'

She wants to say 'I love you', but there is no time. Instead, she watches Louis walking away. They are still so young, just teenagers, but they act like people twice their age. That is what war does. Everything seems to accelerate. Sophie knows she and Louis have seen more than most people ever do. He turns as he reaches the door and blows her a kiss, and she smiles back, and then he is gone.

A day and a half, that is all she has left.

It is her final trial. She must pass her police interview and medical evaluation and not kill Josephine no matter how much she wants to. Then she and Louis will rebuild their shattered lives.

After that, everything will get better.

70

THE LUTETIA

1945

JOSEPHINE

It's a risk, but the injustice burns inside her.
Josephine has decided to tell someone. She refuses to be unfairly punished like this while other people get away with their crimes.

It is later, just after the evening meal, that she sees the police officer who interviewed her leave the dining hall and walk into the hotel gardens. There is space near the old staff entrance where people sometimes gather for a smoke. Josephine can see the light of the city and the sense of freedom. Only one more day and she will be out there again but, this time, with papers saying she is innocent. She is desperate for a cigarette and she walks beside him and turns, as if surprised.

The police officer looks different in the evening light. He almost reminds her of pre-war Paris. He looks dapper and his face is chiselled. He still wears those thick spectacles which he polishes on his uniform. She imagines this man dancing with her at the Lutetia before the war, both of them tipsy and laughing, with no knowledge about what was about to happen.

'Would you like one?' says the officer, offering his packet of cigarettes.

'Yes, thank you,' she says.

He shuffles a cigarette from the packet then bends to help her light it. She sees the name badge on his uniform: VIDAL.

'I imagine you're not meant to mingle with other hotel guests,' she says. In her mind, she isn't dressed in rags and without hair, but in a little black dress with a drink and the piano playing, like she always used to be, and the lights of Paris twinkle in the distance.

'This hotel is overcrowded and chaotic,' he says, 'just like everywhere else in this city. Half of London is bombed, most of Berlin is destroyed. Given the state of the world, I think we can get away with a bit of mingling, don't you?'

She laughs, and it feels good, and he smiles and takes another drag. There is a devilish side to him, almost a sense of danger, like some of the boyfriends she used to have.

'Everyone sees me as the bad guy,' he goes on. 'I'm the one who asks survivors whether they're lying. All I want to do is make sure the Nazis pay for what they did. And make French citizens who helped them pay for their crimes as well.'

'Do you think they will?'

'Oh, sure, a few Nazis will hang, some will be locked up, but only the big names. Everyone else will disappear and lie low. People are already trying to forget the Occupation. Everyone is pretending to be a member of the Resistance. No one wants to remember what really happened.'

'The men get away with their crimes,' she says, 'while the women are made to pay for them. That doesn't seem like justice to me.'

'No. I suppose it isn't.'

Josephine pauses. Anything is better than being one of those women left on the edge of Paris to die. The Lutetia is her last resort. She knows how near she is. Her fate is in the hands of people like this police officer. She has been let down by the men in the Resistance. She took on the most dangerous job, prostituted herself to collect vital secret information from Nazi officers, and then was left to fend for herself afterwards, forced into hiding because people saw her as a collaborator. She has gone through so much, but she can at least get her own back in one way.

She looks down at the rags she is wearing. She feels her stomach cramp with hunger. The officer continues to smoke.

'What about those people who collaborated during the war and now claim to be in the Resistance?' she asks. 'Do they get to escape, too?'

He finishes his cigarette and drops it to the ground, stamping it out with the sole of his shoe. His spectacles have steamed up and he cleans them. 'All collaborators are being rounded up as we speak, if they haven't been executed by their own people already. They will be tried and hanged, or made pariahs. Do you have the name of anyone who was a collaborator? Give it to me and, if I can find any evidence, they will be arrested.'

There is one name. The problem with the Resistance was the lack of central control. It was all split into units, with codenames, and everyone only knew things on a strict need-to-know basis, in case they were captured and tortured. That has been her problem all along. During the war, it was necessary for the Nazis and ordinary Parisians to think she was sleeping with the enemy. In reality, she was using it as cover. The better she did her job, the worse it became for her after the war was over.

She tells the police officer the name and watches his reaction. He nods, as if he's made a note in his head, and then says he has to return inside.

'If you're staying in Paris, then I hope we meet again,' she says. She flashes a last, fleeting smile, hinting at what might be when they are rid of this hotel, and now she has totally forgotten about her appearance. She is still young, beautiful, so far removed from a world of survivors and collaborators.

He nods again and lingers for another moment. He puts his thick spectacles back on. Josephine wonders if she reminds him of someone, a sweetheart who didn't make it through the war.

'Goodnight,' he says.

'Goodnight.'

Josephine continues to smoke. She thinks again about that fateful decision she made to sacrifice Sophie and her father in order to protect her own position. There is never a day when she doesn't think about what she did. She wonders if this is how it always will be. That trade-off will haunt her forevermore. She will never be able to go back to what it was like before. The war has made her into a different person.

She finishes her cigarette and heads back inside. She is so nearly there now. She has endured so much, overcome so many obstacles, been let down by so many people.

But she still has some fight left in her.

71

OLIVIA

NOW

Rue Geoffroy l'Asnier is a quiet street for such an important building. It's almost surprising to see how normal the Holocaust Museum looks. The Mémorial takes up most of the street, mixing the usual creamy façade that dominates the city with a bulky black front that looks respectful and serious.

We find the main entrance. I have heard so much about this place but never actually been inside. As Louis predicted, it is already shut for the night. But we ring the bell anyway and then Edward does his usual trick, explaining who he is, who his father is, until the staffer has no choice but to welcome us both in. I don't approve of blatant bribery, but this time I can let it slide.

As a memory expert, I've heard other people describe what it's like to come here. The entrance contains a memorial with the names of the seventy-six thousand French Jews who were deported by their own government to the concentration camps. It is memory carved into stone. I stand next to the wall of names and keep going until I find the letter 'L' and the name 'Leclerc, Sophie'. There have been so many profound moments over the past three days, but this hits me the hardest. What began with a confession in the lobby of the Lutetia hotel is made real here.

I just wish there was more time to take it in. Something in this space can help unlock the truth about what happened to Gran and the murder at the Lutetia eighty years ago. Edward is deep in conversation with the curator, a fifty-something woman with her coat on ready to go home for the day. She clearly recognises Edward and, checking her watch, offers to show us round after-hours.

'Let me guess,' I say, as we follow her lead, 'the de Villefort family funds the Mémorial too?'

Edward shrugs. 'Something like that.'

'Is there anything in Paris your family doesn't support financially?'

He smiles. 'Not if we can help it.'

I try and imagine the upkeep this place needs. My two-bed in Redbridge provides constant drama with its endlessly leaky pipes and creaky ceilings. This is in an entirely different league. Louis de Villefort comes from a long line of French aristocrats and is a very wealthy man. Edward will one day inherit the kingdom as his only son. If Louis donates enough for the best box at the opera house, then Edward can donate enough to save this place for the next generation. No wonder they let us in after-hours, and no wonder their enemies in this city will do anything to take them down.

'Please,' says the curator. 'This way.'

We follow her downstairs and into the most famous part of the Mémorial. This is the bit of the building I have read about online. The crypt is the centrepiece of the museum and a vast and overwhelming space. It is bare except for a star-shaped tomb in the middle made out of black marble containing the ashes of victims from all the camps.

There is a blue sign on my right. I crouch and read the words and realise why Louis told us to come here. This is the only place in Paris that might still have answers about the mystery of Gran's past. The flame in the middle of the marble star burns to honour the memory of the departed. The Book of Memories, meanwhile, is hidden behind the cabinets along the side walls and contains the names of the missing. On the other side of the crypt are the Police Files.

This really is the ultimate place of memories. It reminds me of standing in the lobby of the Lutetia and looking at the *Memory* portrait for the first time. So much of how we understand the world, and ourselves, comes from preserving these memories for the next generation.

Something in my past, the women who came before me, is drawing me to this flame. I think of Gran sitting in the Lutetia all those decades ago and walking with me as I make my own way through the hotel. I think of TJ and what I'm passing on to him. It's as if all my life has been leading to this spot.

'Here we are,' says the curator.

I turn and see Edward and the curator moving to a room behind me. This must be the file room. There are lots of boxes locked behind glass screens and yellow bits of paper in small folders like a very basic filing system.

'Which name was it again?'

'Leclerc,' says Edward. 'Sophie Leclerc.'

The curator works along until she finds the 'L' section. She opens the glass door and pulls out a box. She flicks through the box until she sees the victims with the surname 'Leclerc'. Finally, she takes out two files.

'Here we are. There is a file for "Leclerc, Jean-Baptiste" and for "Leclerc, Sophie". I presume these are what you're looking for?'

'Yes,' I say. 'Father and daughter, I presume.'

Jean-Baptiste Leclerc. He could be my great-grandfather. It feels so weird saying that.

'Let's see,' says the curator. 'The files don't say that much, I'm afraid. They just give the name of the camp and the dates. They haven't been digitised, so don't come up on official records, but we try and keep them safe here.'

We wait patiently. It seems wrong to demand she goes quicker.

Finally, the curator says, 'According to this, Jean-Baptiste and Sophie Leclerc were both held at Drancy internment camp for a period in 1943 before being deported to Auschwitz. It says Jean-Baptiste died at Auschwitz as soon as he arrived in November 1943.'

'And Sophie Leclerc?' I ask.

'According to this card, she died on the journey back to Paris from Auschwitz,' says the curator. 'She survived the camps, but died during the liberation, as so many did. Another tragedy of war.'

72

OLIVIA

The news lands like a dead weight. I wonder if I've misheard the curator. Sophie Leclerc died before reaching the Lutetia? No, that can't be right. I take the two cards in my hands. There are stains and rough edges. I see Sophie Leclerc's death date and all my assumptions from the last three days are suddenly thrown into the air again.

I feel so many emotions now. I imagine everything about me being put on a single card and feel almost overcome with sadness.

'I don't understand,' I say, showing the card to Edward. 'If Sophie Leclerc died before reaching the Lutetia, then how can Gran ever have been Sophie Leclerc?'

Edward takes the card. 'Perhaps this proves that she wasn't,' he says. 'You weren't sure whether your grandmother was saying those things because of her dementia or because they were actually true. Now you have your answer.'

The curator takes back the card. I still don't know what to think. Was Gran Sophie Leclerc or Josephine Benoit? Did she murder someone in Room 11 of the Lutetia hotel? Is the *Memory* painting autobiographical or not?

Edward looks at the curator. 'Can we definitely trust these cards?' he says. 'Is there any chance they might have got some things wrong?'

The curator looks slightly embarrassed. 'These files were put together in the chaos of the post-war period. There's always a chance, I suppose. But it's unlikely.'

I move away from Edward and the curator and across to the crypt again. It is such a profound space that I feel overcome by it. This place is called a memorial, so clearly it is all about memory. But I've never seen something that underlines how important memories are. I see that vision of Gran at the end of my bed in Room 11, following me down the hotel stairs, looking directly at me in the ballroom. I felt such a connection with her. Is this how my patients in therapy feel as we work on recovering their lost memories? Do they feel as uncertain, and confused, as I do now?

The historical memory is recorded here in black and white. The official card tells me that Sophie Leclerc died in transit in June 1945 before reaching the hotel. Gran was always Josephine Benoit. She didn't lead a double life. And yet, somehow, the confession at the Lutetia was still enough for her to be killed.

Why?

Edward comes down the stairs of the crypt and joins me. We both stand looking at the tomb and the flame and this living tribute to the dead.

'What are you thinking?' he asks me.

'I don't know,' I say. 'All I know is that, whoever she was, I miss her. My gran isn't the figure found on that bed, or some words on a card in a filing system. It's the daily acts of love she left behind.'

We stand in silence. I let those memories come. It's the chocolates she would leave on my pillow when I stayed with her, or how she would sit beside me reading when she knew I was sad, never intruding but just so I had some company. Or how she learned to text so she could message me before my university exams to wish me luck. That is the Gran I loved, and who loved me back. That love is what I remember and what leaves such a hole in my heart.

Edward slides his arm around me, tentatively at first before I lean into him and enjoy the presence of him here. I still don't trust him. He is still the only person who was at the crime scene when the murder took place. We only have his word that a third party killed Gran and that his wounds weren't self-inflicted.

But, right now, there are other things on my mind. We haven't touched like this since that night he left for New York, two star-crossed lovers who thought the world was an extension of themselves, who had so much growing up to do but still believed in what the future might hold. I'm tired of suspicion. I'm weary of searching for the truth about the past and seeing it slip out of my hands every time. I want to believe in what I had, even if I can't prove all the facts.

'Let's go, Liv,' he says, squeezing my shoulder. 'It's time. We've found what we came for, even if it's not the answer we wanted.'

I take one last look at the tomb and the flame. I pay my respects to all the stories collected in this place. Then I know we must leave the memories behind.

It's time to face the present again.

73

RENÉ

He's done it so many times before. It is almost muscle memory now.

And the client's instructions were clear.

The location isn't ideal. But the street leading up to the Mémorial de la Shoah is fairly deserted. The job can be done cleanly. Disappearing in a major city is relatively easy. The crush of people, the endless hiding places, the twisty detours – cities were made for disappearing, especially at this time of night. Darkness, once again, is his friend. He knows where to lose the weapon.

No, the escape isn't the worry. The worry is the job itself.

Which is why he leaves the car and pulls his cap further down and keeps the glasses over his eyes. The car has fake plates and will lead nowhere. The cap and glasses are crude, but enough to stop any cameras making a positive ID. The Beretta M9 is tucked into the back of his jeans.

With one target, he would do the usual double-tap. Standard special forces procedure to ensure the target does actually die. There isn't time for that here. Two shots will be too splashy. One shot, aiming at the broadest mass, is the way to go. But it means this is one time only, like an Olympic swimmer waiting four years for a shot at gold, or a gambler staking everything on the single roll of the dice.

Drop the target. Chuck the weapon. Vanish.

He must rely on muscle memory again from all that training, all those operations.

He has to hit the target.

Dr Olivia Finn.

Then he needs to find DI Myles Forsyth and take him out.

After that, he gets paid in crypto and lies low until the next job.

René takes a deep breath. He checks either side of him and waits for the heavy exit doors of the Mémorial to shut. He needs to see the target emerge into the lamplight.

Soon, very soon. He slowly reaches behind him for the Beretta.

It will be over in seconds. It's what the Foreign Legion taught him. He takes out his earbuds, finds the right song on his phone, and then listens to the comforting sound of 'Waterloo'.

His pulse slows, his heart rate steadies. This job, like the others, will be fine.

When it comes to killing, memory is the key to everything.

74

OLIVIA

THEN

It's a weekday morning when I get the call from Louis. I'm on leave from the Memory Unit, taking a few days of annual holiday. Since Ingrid Fox's death, there has been a strange waiting period. I still see patients. None of my colleagues mention the trial. Life seems to be going back to normal.

Tom brings me a cup of tea in bed. He is a two-sugars person, while I'm most definitely not. I have strong feelings when it comes to important things like mixing sweet and savoury. But Tom has snuck into my life just before the drawbridge comes up and I'm set in my singleton ways.

It feels weird to have him here in my bedroom in Redbridge, and yet also inevitable. This room has felt so cold and lonely by myself. Sometimes TJ runs in and squashes up with me on a weekend. Soon, though, he'll find me boring. I'll have to get a puppy or install a bedroom TV and watch *Midsomer Murders* all by myself.

This is a rare child-free day. It might be stressful having TJ's permanent energy in the house, but before long we'll be into adolescence and the hellscape of smartphones and socials.

At least I've avoided the 'sharenting' trap and never posted a photo of TJ online. Kyle and the New Girlfriend can't say the same. TJ can sue them for invading his privacy when he turns eighteen and I will gladly pay the legal bills.

I take my tea, look at the mug Tom picked and smile as I see the 'World's Okayest Husband' on the side. I bought it for Kyle as a joke when he started buggering off to his Brazilian ju-jitsu classes in a ridiculous pair of Lycra leggings twice a week. It ended up being a bit too on the money. It was over the chokeholds and joint locks that Kyle met a black belt called Kylie who looked a lot like Kylie Jenner, petite and brunette but without the billion-dollar cosmetics empire, and the joke over their names turned into the end of us and the start of them.

Tom takes care not to spill any tea and even has coasters for each mug. Kyle never made the tea. He was always in bed with his phone while I put the kettle on. Kyle couldn't have a shower without informing his sixteen thousand followers of the breaking news. There are entire holidays where he did nothing but take selfies and upload them. It really is possible to visit the Empire State Building and spend the entire time looking at LinkedIn.

TJ is with Kyle. Usually, I spend the day tidying up the house or, if I'm lucky, fitting in a lunch or a coffee and catching up with friends. It's a relief not to have an empty house or be waiting for the happy-family smiles of Kyle, TJ and the New Girlfriend. TJ has even talked about taking up ju-jitsu when he's older. God help us all.

After my testimony at the trial, the publishers have brought forward the date for *Memory Wars* to capitalise on public interest in recovered memories. I feel uneasy about that, but I also want to defend my own reputation. Louis hasn't got the public vindication he wanted, and now I've been dragged into a controversy over whether the pressure of the trial is what led to her death. It is a horrible mess all round. The only person who seems to have escaped scot-free is Ingrid's foster father who died without facing any justice for his actions. Everyone else has ended up being a victim.

The book is all done now and Tom is my first reader. Letting him read a work-in-progress while I'm sitting right beside him feels like a big step in our relationship. It started during our recent trip to Paris and our stay at Le Grand. Now we have our routine of sharing tea in bed while he reads the latest section.

It's silly, I know, but I want him to fall out of bed with astonishment at how good it is. I want him to be so engrossed with the power of the book that he loses all capacity for speech. But we have different love languages. I'm a words-of-affirmation type. Tom is an acts-of-service man. He might not say how brilliant the book is, but he can stack a dishwasher like no man I've ever met and he is a wizard with rinse aid. His light-bulb-changing skills are already legendary.

I expect him to ask about recovered memories. That's what most people are usually interested in. Is there some big trauma in your past that your mind has repressed? Does it explain your anxiety or sadness in the present day or why your relationships keep going wrong? If you surface that repressed memory, will the trauma destroy you, or could you get through the pain and come out stronger than ever before?

Instead, though, he asks about the other big thing in memory research: false memories. This is the even weirder one. Every time we recall a memory, we change the original, and all we have is the latest edited version of the memory. Over time, the memory that has been edited tens, hundreds, even thousands of times, has no connection with the original event. It could be your first kiss, the dying words of a loved one, a life-changing accident – your memory of it will be different from how it actually happened, just because you've remembered it so many times.

My book looks at how easy it is to implant false memories into others. People start believing things that never happened. That is next-level weird. It's too freaky for most readers. Tom, though, seems fascinated by it. I like the fact he's interested in what I do. In the book I argue that recovered memories can be helpful for patients in therapy and argue against the idea that all recovered memories are really implanted false memories. Bad things happen. Patients can remember them even years later. Victim-blaming is not okay. Therapists don't gaslight patients or make up wacky stuff. Why would we? Our job is to help people, not harm them. Writing off all recovered memories as false memories is just another way of silencing victims.

'If it's possible to implant false memories,' he asks, 'is it also possible to implant false emotions? Could you make someone fall in love with you?'

I smile, lean over and kiss him. 'Why, do you have someone in mind?'

He smiles again and kisses me more fully now. I want him to like the book, but I also want this more. I can feel the heat of his body as all thoughts of tea are soon left behind and the long, child-free morning stretches out before us.

It's only afterwards, as I listen to the shower running, that I realise how perfect this day feels and, once again, how much I don't want Tom to leave. I like him here. It all makes sense. We've grown so much closer since our trip to Paris. Even his dimples on the bedsheets beside me feel like they were meant to be.

I want this to last forever. The lukewarm mug of tea, the sound of a shower running, the messy bedroom, both too hot and too cold, the neighbour with his overloud leaf blower – this is life, right here, in all its annoying brilliance.

This is why I'm learning to live with all those nagging doubts: where does Tom disappear to? Why hasn't he introduced me to any of his friends or family? Why does he keep asking me about Ingrid Fox and Louis? Is his tidiness a way of masking some deep, internal pain which will come out if we get married?

I've stopped asking those questions. There are no good answers. I will just have to hope and trust and go from there.

As I sit in bed listening to the sound of the shower, my mobile rings and I see the Caller ID. It's Louis. I immediately wonder if something bad has happened to Gran.

'Hello?'

'Olivia, my dear,' he says. 'I don't want to disturb, but just wanted to let you know that I've told my lawyers to withdraw the case. The media will get hold of it, and you might get some calls and questions. I didn't want you to be caught by surprise.'

His voice sounds weary.

'That sounds like good news,' I say. 'In a way.'

Louis sighs. 'I've spent eight decades treating patients. I must have helped tens of thousands of people. I've heard patients talk to me about affairs, family break-ups, divorce, terrible childhoods, everything. And this is how it ends. A poor, tragic patient who sadly took her own life, and false accusations which will never now be disproved.'

There is something heartbreaking about hearing Louis like this. It's like seeing a parent getting old. This man saved my life as a teenager. He helped so many patients, including Holocaust survivors, carry on living when the future seemed impossible. It feels so unfair that he's had to deal with this. After a lifetime of heroism and good work, he ends up with the cloud of scandal hovering over him.

'Anyone who knows you doesn't believe the accusations,' I say. 'Ingrid Fox was a deeply troubled person. In the court of public opinion, your reputation has been cleared.'

'I remember you coming to my consulting room for the first time,' he says wistfully. 'You were like the daughter, or granddaughter, I never had. You've always been a great support to me, Olivia.'

'If I could be half the therapist you've been, then it will all have been worth it.'

'Don't be a stranger,' says Louis. 'Your grandmother is missing you. And say hello to the delightful TJ for me.'

The call ends and Tom emerges from the shower. I remember sitting at a café near Gran's flat smoking Gauloises when I was a teenager studying at the Sorbonne, and she said the key to life was being able to tell the good people apart from the bad people.

Tom smiles at me and leans down for a watery kiss, droplets from his hair brushing my nose. I think of Louis, and TJ, and how lucky I am to have all three of them.

But something is still nagging at me about Tom, no matter how much I try and silence this part of my brain. We are so intimate, so why does it feel like I don't really know anything about him? Why is he always so elusive, like sand escaping through my hands? And will our relationship survive once the mystery of it goes, or is that what we thrive on, our passion fuelled by the lack of boring, everyday reality?

I want to know more about Tom, but I'm also scared of what I might find out.

Who is he really?

75

OLIVIA

NOW

It's as we approach the Mémorial's main exit that Edward stops. There is a security monitor showing the street outside and Edward sees the figure on the screen before I do.

We're still in the reception area of the Mémorial de la Shoah. There is a large, older security guard slumped in his seat, slowly picking his way through a croissant and slurping an espresso. He is barely looking at the monitor. He is transfixed by the funny cat video playing on his phone. I recognise the video. The cat is called Maru and he is officially the 'most famous cat on the internet'. He is a Scottish Straight who lives in Japan and gets into all manner of adorable scrapes. I almost start watching it over his shoulder. TJ, needless to say, is obsessed.

'Liv . . .'

I look at Edward and see the concern in his eyes. I stop thinking of cute cat videos from Japan and get my head straight. This has been such an emotional evening. I check the time and see how late it is. Edward is still staring at the security monitor.

'What's wrong?' I say.

Edward turns to me. 'Do you remember a car following us on the route here?' he says. 'It was a blue saloon. It started tailing the taxi from the Palais Garnier. It stuck with us at every turn until we arrived here.'

'Paris is a big city, Ed,' I say. 'I'm sure it's just a coincidence.'

'Maybe. But I recognise something about that figure outside. I think he was the same person driving the blue saloon. And he matches the profile of the man who attacked me in the apartment when your grandmother was killed.'

'It's dark outside. You're getting paranoid. It could be anyone. We've just established that Gran wasn't Sophie Leclerc and, to be honest, I'm really done with this now. I need to get home and see my son. Let the police do their job, and let's bury Gran with the dignity she deserves, just like your dad said.'

I'm about to head outside into the final part of the Mémorial de la Shoah complex when Edward holds out a hand to stop me. I don't appreciate being manhandled. Yet I can see the fear in his eyes.

'Liv, trust me, just this once. I know I've seen this person before. Zoom in,' he tells the security guard. 'On that guy right there, go closer.'

'Ed, I told you—'

'I know you want to get home. I know seeing that death record was difficult. But you've got to see what I'm seeing. I swear that is the same man who attacked me in Montparnasse. He matches the description I gave to the police.'

I peer at the security monitor and see the man in question. He is standing opposite the Mémorial exit. He's dressed in civvies with a baseball cap pulled low and a pair of shades. He looks like just a tourist to me. He has earbuds in and could be anybody.

'You said yourself,' says Edward. 'If your grandmother wasn't Sophie Leclerc, then why did someone silence her? Why go to all the bother of killing an old woman?'

I look at Edward and see the same conviction in his eyes that I saw when Gran told me about her past as Sophie Leclerc. I don't want to believe him. I'm too stung from buying Gran's story. But, once again, those old bonds tug at me.

I had feelings for this man once, loved him even, if teenage dreaming can be called love. Whatever made him flee to New York all those years ago, he deserves my attention now. I might not trust him, but if he thinks he recognises the man then I should listen.

'What can we do?'

Edward thinks. 'I used to know some guys in the military, and he has the same posture and gait they teach at the parade ground. He could be ex-military. It could be nothing. But it could be something. I don't want to take that chance.' Edward takes out his phone.

'What are you doing?'

'I have an idea.' Before he dials, he turns to the security guard. 'Call the police and tell them an armed suspect is outside the Mémorial de la Shoah and poses a direct threat to life.'

He pauses, considering a last detail.

'Then do one more thing for me,' he says.

76

RENÉ

He is starting to lose hope. What is taking them so long? He is about to move back to the nearby street and monitor any other exits. He turns, ready to walk away.

Then, at last, the exit door for the Mémorial de la Shoah opens fully.

A figure emerges.

René wonders, for a moment, where the female target is.

He checks the key identifiers. The darkness doesn't help, but he can pick out the essentials like clothes, height, stride.

Except it is not the target, or even her male sidekick. Edward de Villefort is toned. This man is not. A gut hangs over regulation trousers. His is older and the walk is different. Yet his suit jacket is the same.

Something isn't right here. No, something is very wrong indeed.

It's the sort of sixth sense developed after enough ambush situations. If the enemy is good, then nothing gives them away. There is just silence and a sense of things being out of place, as if the world has lost focus. That is exactly how it is now.

Olivia Finn and Edward de Villefort should be leaving the building. Instead, there is this other guy.

Why?

René is about to retreat and regroup when, finally, the pieces fit together and he understands. The imposter stands there and gets out his phone. On closer inspection, the figure looks terrified. His hands are shaking as he holds his phone. Sweat is shiny on his forehead. He is trying too hard.

René replays the last ten seconds. The imposter was designed to get his attention. They need his attention because they don't want him to move out of his current position.

Which can only mean one thing.

The imposter is exactly that. A useless diversion, a well-placed distraction.

An anomaly placed here. But why?

Follow the logic. Find the answer.

Simple.

To stop him looking elsewhere.

René knows this. He's been in these situations before. He understands where the danger lies. Not from the two targets. Or not any longer. This is far, far worse than that.

The real enemy is right behind him.

Police.

A suspect outside the Holocaust Museum. Yes, he sees it now. An armed unit, shoot-to-kill. Maybe that's why they came here. It was a trap all along.

He turns to see if the snipers are crouched and hiding and waiting to take him out. They will be dressed in black with balaclavas over their faces, blending in with concrete and stonework until they disappear into the scenery.

Once upon a time, they were on the same side as him.

They will not shout a warning or treat him with the courtesy of a normal suspect. They will wait to see what he does and then send in uniformed officers to arrest him.

And that can never happen.

It is the one condition of the job he signed up to. Come back with your shield or on your shield. But never, ever be taken. Because prisoners end up talking. And the clients can't have that. The ones who are caught end up being killed by the ones who haven't yet been caught.

Either way, the client always wins.

René looks around him again.

He spots one sniper in position, then another cop getting a radio message and glancing in his direction. He knows that either the man or the woman must have called this in. The police will uncover his record. His real name. Everything he did before starting a new life under a new name in the Foreign Legion.

Muscle memory.

He takes a breath and says a final prayer. He should have walked away when he had the chance. René could have taken a different path. In that other life, he'd be decompressing after a hard day in front of the cameras, checking his socials, posting about his latest clothing range, a former special forces soldier who'd left the hard-knuckle work behind.

But he didn't, and he's here, and he has big men pointing big guns that will kill him in less than a second.

He reaches behind him to the back of his jeans for the Beretta.

Hands active, intent unknown, a fatal movement spotted by a shadow in the distance.

René knows what he's doing. He will die as he lived. That's

what he is good at. He wasn't much use at languages or algebra, but boy could he line up a target, calculate the variables and drop a hostile with the smoothest squeeze of a trigger you've ever seen. It was balletic, elegant, an art form all in itself.

He hums the chorus of 'Waterloo' to himself and smiles as he sings about not being able to escape even if he wanted to. Agnetha, Benny, Björn and Anni-Frid really knew what they were talking about. It's like they had mainlined his brain. The song allows him to focus. He can do this. Now will be no exception.

Four, three, two.

René turns and raises his weapon.

That's when the first shot is fired.

77

MYLES

When news reaches the headquarters of 'la Crim' about the incident at the Holocaust Memorial, Myles takes it all in. This is what frontline emergency work looks like – frantic, chaotic, and loud, a stampede of uniforms towards the cars outside.

'The call came through from Edward de Villefort,' says Vidal, grabbing his jacket. They have been listening to the audio recordings together and making notes. 'He claims the man who attacked him two days ago has followed him outside the Mémorial. Armed police are already deployed. They will shoot on sight if there is a danger to life.'

It's hard to remember much after that. One of the buttons on Myles's waistcoat flew off as he hurriedly put his jacket on and followed Vidal into a car and then sped through the streets of Paris with full blues and twos.

Midway through their journey, as they turned right, news came through that two shots had been fired and the suspect in question was neutralised.

Myles is always curious about those expressions. Neutralised suggests 'neutral', as if something exciting has become less exciting, which in some ways is true. But it is only neutralised for the people still living. The dead guy on the pavement doesn't feel very neutralised. In fact, he doesn't feel much at all.

By the time they arrive at Rue Geoffroy l'Asnier, the Mémorial de la Shoah is full of armed cops and police vehicles with their lights flashing. The crime scene is already cordoned off.

Myles sees Edward de Villefort and Olivia Finn standing by one of the police vehicles. There is another security guard who looks traumatised. He's holding a space blanket around his shoulders as he recovers. It's the first time Myles has seen Olivia in the flesh for a long time.

Captain Vidal shows his police ID and Myles follows him through the various cordons and barriers. Vidal goes over to the police vehicle and immediately takes over the scene. One flash of the 36 badge and all other police units back off.

'Any idea who the dead guy is?' asks Myles as they walk towards the body.

Vidal checks the time, wincing at how late it is. 'According to some of his tattoos, he's ex-Foreign Legion,' he says. 'They've fast-tracked his prints and got a match. We think his real name was René Visser. Recruits to the Legion usually take a false name to enlist, so he could be using a different last name now. He was on the run for a murder in Paris, before joining the Foreign Legion. My guess is he's now a gun for hire.'

Vidal nods to one of the forensics officers who covers the body. Vidal's phone buzzes. He reads another new message. 'Look, it's late and forensics will take over from here,' he says. 'If you're okay to wait, I won't be long.'

Myles nods, then Vidal hurries off to get briefed by the armed police team. Myles feels out of place. He always prefers figuring things out in his own office rather than grilling a suspect in person. He's like one of those method actors who only feels comfortable when pretending to be someone else. He's not much of a team player.

Myles is careful to stay on the sidelines and not draw attention to himself. He looks across and watches Olivia and Edward get into a police car. They will be driven back to the Lutetia hotel. Olivia has lost her grandmother and seen a man shot in front of her. Now her evening, or her early morning, is about to get even worse.

Myles waits by the car and prepares himself.

78

THE LUTETIA

1945

SOPHIE

'How did it happen?' asks Josephine.

Josephine has just returned to the room. Sophie is so tired she wants to sleep, but she knows the memories will keep her awake. So she sits on her bed and Josephine is opposite and they talk, just like they used to.

'Which bit exactly?' Sophie says.

'How you were taken.'

Sophie looks at Josephine and sees something different now. It's been that way ever since Josephine came back from her police interview. She is slowly morphing back into the Josephine that Sophie once knew from school.

Sophie can't talk about the camps, or not really, but she can talk about the night she and her father were arrested in Paris. Sophie sees it all now. There was no knock. That is what she remembers most. She hears the crash, the silence, then the chaos. The door left its hinges and the place burst with lights.

They went for her father first, then for her. She heard her father's voice shouting at them, trying to protect her.

There was a van parked outside the house. Sophie felt like an animal being dragged to the slaughterhouse. She glanced backwards. Her father was behind her with his hair messy from sleeping. Three men were dragging him away. She saw terror and sadness in his eyes. He looked embarrassed but, most of all, ashamed.

They were both bundled into the back of the van. The drive seemed to take forever. Eventually, they reached the entrance for the Drancy internment camp. She remembers that moment as if it is still happening now.

After that was the journey from Paris to Auschwitz. When they arrived, her father tried to touch her hand for a final time. She started calling out his name. But the decision had already been made. Her father was taken to the left. She was ordered to the right. There was no time for words but just a look. Then, almost as quickly, he was gone. Afterwards, she felt nothing any more.

Sophie finishes telling the story and then says, 'That was directly after speaking to you. I know you betrayed me and my father, Josephine. You are the only person it could have been. All I've never been able to understand is . . . why.'

Josephine pauses now. It's like her defences drop. She is working up to something, a major confession, and this, Sophie thinks, is when finally the truth will emerge. Josephine will confess what she did.

Josephine says, 'Sometimes we have no choice, Sophie. Sometimes bad things have to be done for the greater good.'

'What does that even mean?'

'Why do you think the Nazis were driven out of Paris? Why do you think the nightmare ended? Not because of the men who said nothing and now claim to have been heroes, but because of people like me who risked everything – their safety, their honour, their reputation, even their lives – to make terrible sacrifices to help their country win.'

'What are you talking about?'

Josephine dips her head. 'It's true that I had relationships with Nazi officers. It's true that I fraternised with the enemy. I cooed and flirted and went to bed with them. But not because I was some kind of whore. That was my cover, Sophie. I was working for the Resistance. My job was to target high-ranking Nazis and get them to tell me their secrets. The best way to do that was to make them vulnerable. So that's what I did. I couldn't tell you, or anyone else, or my cover would have been destroyed and I'd have been executed on the spot.'

Sophie doesn't know what to say. She tries to understand what Josephine is telling her. All along, she has been sure that Josephine was not just a traitor, but immoral too. She was a woman without a conscience. She slept with Nazis to save herself, and betrayed her best friend without a second thought. What if she has been wrong all this time? Then again, what if Josephine is still playing her? Can she trust anything this woman says?

'Even if that were true—'

'Which it is.'

'Why would you have to betray me?'

'The Nazis got paranoid that the Resistance was using women like me for honeytrap operations. They started following the women who slept with officers. I was followed, and the person following me saw our meeting together. I had to lie and tell them that I was meeting with you to get information on your whereabouts so you could be arrested and deported. If I didn't, then he would have known that I was working for the Resistance.'

'So you were happy to let me die so you could stay alive?'

'I justified it to myself by believing that my work was saving hundreds, even thousands, of people's lives. That the information I was gathering from the Nazi high command was helping save Paris and free France.'

'My father and I were just . . . what, then? Pawns in your moral crusade?'

Josephine is solemn, and quiet. 'There is no excuse for what I did that day, Sophie. There would also have been no excuse if I hadn't done it. That is the nature of war. People are forced to make impossible choices. They have to weigh up the cost of one life versus hundreds of lives.'

'If you were really in the Resistance, then why are you here?'

'Because I played the part of a Nazi whore so well that no one now believes me. The people in my unit in the Resistance were rounded up and shot just before the liberation. There is no one to vouch for what I was really doing. We operated in cells, only knowing the codename of our handlers, so we didn't know too much in case we were captured. I've been left to fend for myself, instead. Being here, and being given a clean slate, is my last hope. I can reinvent myself and start again.'

Sophie's anger builds now. She closes her eyes, and the memory of all the things she did comes back to her again. She remembers the smell of the commandant's study, the sight of his belt lying over the arm of the chair. She hears the prisoner in her hut begging for someone to help end her life.

'How do I know you're telling me the truth now?' asks Sophie.

'Because I have nothing left to lose,' says Josephine. 'I sacrificed myself for our country, and now the country has left me for dead. You are all I have left, Sophie. You were always so much better than me as a person. Forgive me, Sophie. That's all I want. Please . . . forgive me.'

Josephine looks as if she is debating whether to say the next bit.

'There's one other thing,' says Josephine. 'There's someone else you shouldn't trust.'

Then Josephine gives Sophie the name.

79

THE LUTETIA

1945

JOSEPHINE

She has said it. She has finally confessed and told Sophie the truth.

Josephine has spent so long bottling up her secrets that it feels like an immense relief to share something with another human being.

It is night again. They are both asleep, or pretending to be. Sophie has been quiet ever since Josephine told her the name, like she can't believe it, or simply won't.

Josephine drifts into unconsciousness. She is asleep, but the cries of the hotel keep her half-awake. She thinks about the police officer and the name she gave him. More and more, now, she wonders if that person is the real villain in all of this.

She tosses and turns and knows she is nearly free. She will lead a good life from now on and make up for all the bad things she has done. But she can only do that if she leaves this place alive.

It is later, much later, when she feels a presence nearby. Without asking, she knows it is Sophie. Perhaps she is finally ready to forgive Josephine. They were always having pillow fights when they were younger. Sophie was the strongest and usually won. Yes, maybe Sophie has forgiven her for everything and this is the first sign of a reunion.

Josephine's eyes are shut and she is still dreaming. Josephine almost wants Sophie to get into the bed with her, like they used to do, both of them sharing the other's warmth and protection.

Sophie, she calls out. Sophie. Fate has brought us back together here. We can be like sisters again. There is still hope for us, a future.

Sophie.

She feels the pressure getting tighter and tighter, like claws digging into her skin, and she tries to open her eyes now but she can't, or not easily; and, when she does, she can't see clearly at all.

She looks at the ceiling of the hotel room. It is ornate, almost regal, and such a contrast to the two of them, dirty and starved, reduced to this.

She should have been more careful, a kinder, better person. The terror of being abandoned made her into someone else, determined never to be hurt in the same way again. She is one of the eighty million killed by this war, a casualty who fell by the wayside, never got the recognition she deserved, shamed for a wrong she did to try and make a right.

Josephine looks straight into the eyes of her attacker and knows the mistake she made. The police officer must have been careless with his inquiries. But it is already too late. This is not a dream. She underestimated this person, thought she was the one in control, playing with another person's mind, when really it was the other way round.

She is being punished for the bad things she is meant to have done.

This figure is not trying to forgive her, but to kill her.

The shadow of death stalks this hotel.

Josephine will never leave alive.

DAY FOUR

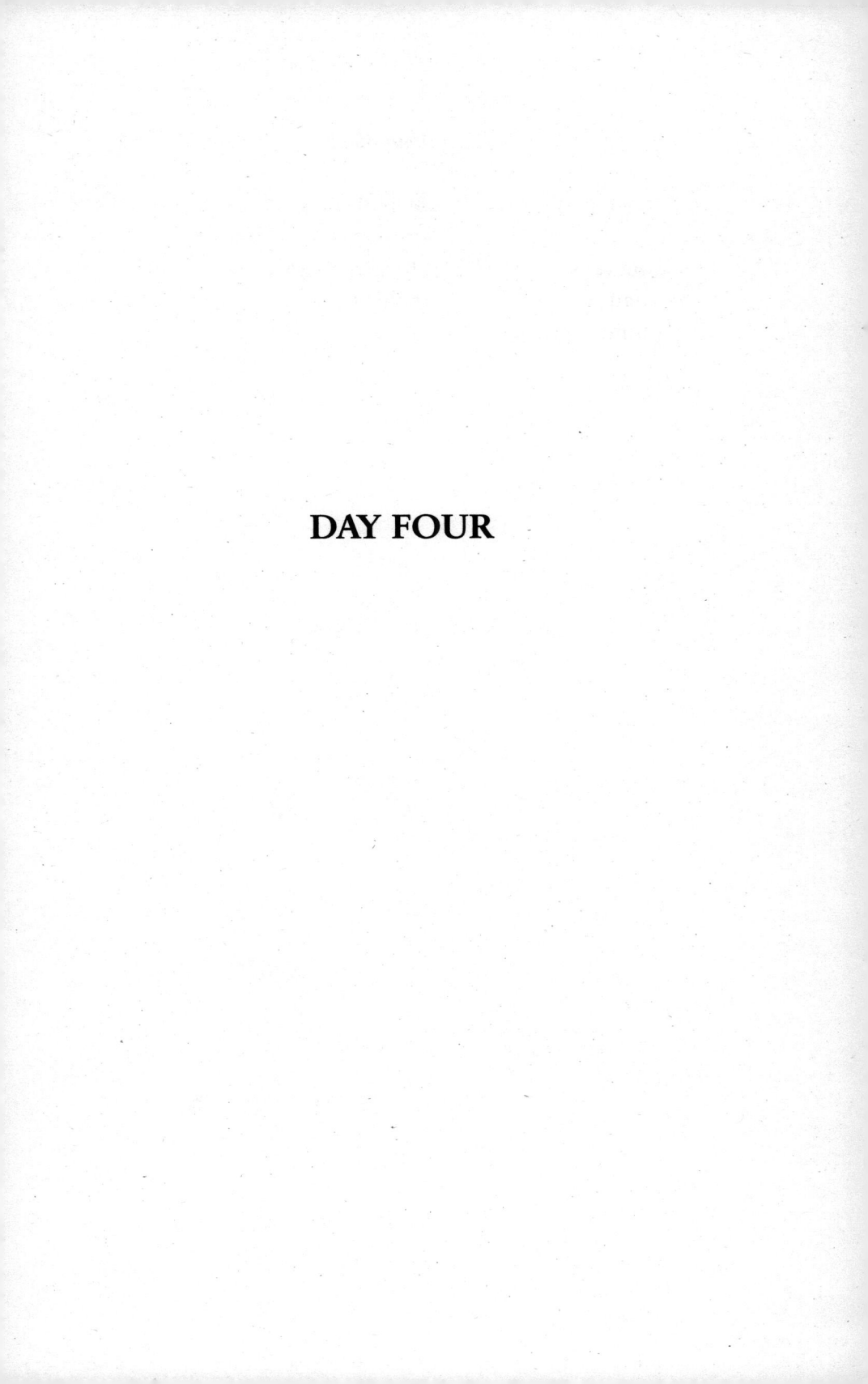

80

OLIVIA

NOW

As we go through the Lutetia's revolving wooden door and into the lobby, the events of the last hour go through my mind.

I can still hear Edward asking the security guard to make a call and the two of us going back inside the Mémorial de la Shoah and finding the alternative exit route with the help of the curator. We waited there until the armed police arrived and the security guard stepped out as a decoy and then the assailant himself was shot as he went for his weapon.

I've treated patients who've been through stuff like that. Once the shock wears off, the memories always come back to haunt them.

This memory won't be forgotten.

That man's death is now alongside Gran's and Mum's in my head. I'll try to forget it, but the memory will stick there. Death always does.

Given the time, the lobby of the Lutetia is empty. There is only the usual night manager behind reception and various cleaners. It reminds me of pitching up only a few days ago. So much has happened since then. Almost out of respect, Edward and I stand in front of the *Memory* painting. There are no tourists here elbowing us out of the way. It is just us and this painting, like a portal that allows us to travel back in time to the Lutetia as it used to be.

There is something about it that overwhelms me. I want to reach out and touch the painting to check that it's real.

I look at the figure of the young woman in the middle. I see the rest of Room 11 all around her. It all started with the painting, and now it ends here.

Who is the figure in the portrait?

What is the painting trying to tell me?

Is it Sophie or Josephine?

'You probably won't remember,' says Edward. 'But twenty years ago, just before I left for college, you came over to Dad's apartment in Quai Voltaire and we snuck off upstairs to talk about the meaning of life. I told you that I had feelings for you. Romantic feelings.'

I'm still reeling from everything that's just happened. It all feels like a blur. I've never seen someone get shot before, and I hope I never have to again. With Gran, then that man, I've witnessed enough dead bodies for a lifetime.

'Your exact words, if I remember, were that you loved me.'

Edward still looks at the portrait. 'And the next day, I was on a plane to New York and didn't come back to Paris for two decades. Not one of my classier moves. I've always wanted to say sorry for that. You must have thought I was a complete pig.'

'Which you were.'

'Which I was.'

'I heard the French authorities were about to arrest you for drug possession, and you fled Paris to avoid charges and let your dad sort it all out.'

Edward looks ashamed. 'The ultimate nepo baby. It's true. Dad heard that the police wanted to make an example of me. They'd arrested my dealer, and now they were targeting me and other rich kids like me, not just for possession but intent to supply. My dad helped me get on that plane to escape and start again.'

'So that's why you never said goodbye?'

'Yes. Back then, though, I really did have feelings for you. Everyone thought I was this ultimate party boy. Really, I was a mess inside. I was never good enough for Dad and everyone knew it. You, though, Liv, you were always so self-possessed, so sure of who you were. I envied that so much.'

I can hardly believe what I'm hearing. 'Wait a minute. You envied me?'

'Surely you knew that. It was obvious. I was this waster trying to escape life by getting high all the time. You were always level-headed. You weren't impressed by any of it. I always knew someone with your smarts wouldn't be interested in a party boy like me.'

I smile now. I've spent my entire adult life misremembering that night. It shaped my relationships, my self-recrimination, so many of the choices I made. 'Let's just say, that is not how I remember those years.'

'How do you remember them?'

'I was the shy English kid with braces and you were the Parisian love god who seemed to spend his entire school years dating supermodels. I didn't see through you at all. I wanted to be you. I couldn't have been more impressed if you'd single-handedly ended world hunger. Surely you saw that?'

'That's the funny thing about memories, I guess,' says Edward. 'The truth can be right in front of us, but we remember the emotion rather than the event itself.'

As Edward says that, I look back at the *Memory* portrait. I see the woman, the room, all the things I've looked at so many times before. Speak to me, Gran, tell me what I'm missing here. Who are you? What did you do all those years ago?

Behind me, I hear the tap of a cane on the floor of the hotel lobby and turn to see Louis walking up behind us. He is still dressed in his clothes from the opera. He looks at both of us with relief. At his age, it is an effort to walk like this, and I can see the strain on his face. What is he doing here?

'I've just heard about the Mémorial,' he says. 'Thank God you're both still alive. I came here from the opera house as soon as the news emerged. What happened?'

Edward tells him, and explains about the card in the Police Files.

Louis listens carefully. He looks burdened by the world. 'I'm sorry the Mémorial didn't prove helpful,' he says. 'But we must return to matters of the here and now. I'm afraid I have even worse news for you.'

He stops, gets his breath back, and then looks at me.

'The police are on their way.'

81

MYLES

Myles looks at the speedometer.

Vidal floors the pedal. The blues and twos are on but this hasn't yet been radioed in. Myles sits in the front passenger seat and closes his eyes. He's never been very good with speed, and Vidal isn't exactly smooth when it comes to corners. He can imagine this going horribly wrong and ending his life in an upturned Citroën with his face obliterated. He longs for his desk again in that airless office that smells permanently of chicken chow mein.

Of all those things, the missing button on his waistcoat is the thing that causes him most distress. Death is an inevitability. Untidiness is a choice. And Myles prides himself on making good life choices, even in death.

Myles checks his seatbelt and looks at the time. He wishes he'd never answered the call on his day off. Abandoning a schedule always leads to trouble. And now he's hurtling towards the Lutetia hotel having just seen the body of an ex-special forces sniper taken out by armed French police. They swerve another corner violently and Myles ends up hanging on for dear life.

Vidal skids right onto Rue de Sèvres. 'If the evidence in your recordings is verified,' he says, 'then it all depends on this source of yours.'

Myles kneads his temples. 'Yes,' he says.

'Presuming, of course, that there is a source and you didn't end up freelancing yourself and running a surveillance operation in a foreign territory.'

Vidal is smart. Myles knows he's been rumbled. Sharing the recordings with Vidal was a risk, but a necessary one.

'All good relationships have some secrets,' says Myles.

'That's what I was afraid of.'

Vidal doesn't slow down much as they turn left into Boulevard Raspail and then conducts the most perilous bit of all. He skids again through a full U-turn at Place Alphonse Deville before stopping with the Lutetia on their right.

'I need you to be sure, DI Forsyth. After this, you will return to Scotland Yard and leave this behind. I will be stuck here. If you're wrong, then I could lose everything.'

They get out of the car. Myles can see Ingrid's face again in the care home right before she left for her new foster family. And the tears when he met her so many years later and she told him what had happened. Lastly, he sees her body in the mortuary and her eyelids closed, and her foster family standing round her.

'Trust me,' he says. 'I've spent over a year on this investigation. I know who is behind all of this. If we don't move now, we'll lose them.'

82

OLIVIA

THEN

It is today that I come out with it.
I've been wondering how to say it ever since the morning when Tom stayed at mine. I spent most of last night in front of the bathroom mirror trying to find the right words. I know how rare it is to find someone you can imagine spending every day with. This is a secret I need to tell him.

Kyle, once upon a time, briefly made me feel like that. He was confident, funny, and he put on a good show before marriage made him lazy and revert to lowest common denominator Kyle; the towel-on-the-floor, leaving-the-toilet-seat-up Kyle; the person I had to ask for help with prams, car seats, nappy changes. He could have been different, but he didn't step up.

I blamed myself for not seeing that at the start. But I don't think he saw it either. You don't know what someone's made of until life demands it from them. Kyle was a great boyfriend, a youthful prodigy with immense talent who just didn't put in the shift to be a truly great long-term life partner, mainly because that's not what he wanted to be. He was happy being the prodigy, taking the easy wins, cruising through life.

Tom, though, could be different. I'm more sceptical now. I

don't believe in the fairy tale. But I also know I could go on a thousand dates with perfectly respectable men and not find that spark, the instinctive attraction, almost like meeting someone you've met before. I have to be emotionally honest with him though.

We're in a new coffee shop near home. It's called Espresso Yourself and Tom, sensing the nervous mood, breaks the tension by googling the worst pun names ever: Surelock Homes (a locksmith), The Lord of the Bins (waste clearance), Fiddler on the Tooth (a dentist) and, my personal favourite, Barber Streisand (a hairdresser). It's funny, and typical of him. He knows I'm nervous and knows how to calm things down.

He's also, typically, putting me to shame with his turmeric shot while I give in to an iced white chocolate mocha which is worth every sugar-laden sip. It's my own brand of Dutch courage. I wish we could just laugh over silly pun names and analyse drinks for their sugar content and enjoy this moment. But, as always, life has to get in the way.

If this relationship is going to last then I have to be honest with him. I want him to know the real me with all my flaws. Finally, I come out with it and say, 'Look, there's something I need to tell you.'

Tom smiles in that kind, gentle way of his. 'Early birthday present? Weekend trip to Paris? Hospitality tickets for the Chelsea game next week? All or none of the above?'

'It's about what happened to Mum all those years ago.'

He frowns now. 'Okaaaaay. How worried should I be?'

'I wanted to tell you. But I wasn't sure what we had here. Whether it was a short-term thing or something more. And, well, I've only told my therapist about this. So you're the second person on the planet to know. Not even Gran knows this. It's not something that will put me in prison, but it has shaped me more than I like to admit. To understand me as a person, I think you have to understand this.'

He looks concerned rather than suspicious now. He leans across and takes my hand tightly. 'Seriously, Liv, what's going on? You can tell me anything. You know that.'

I feel Tom's warm palm on mine, that sense of connection between us, and can't stand the idea of being on my own again.

I don't know if it's concern for me or concern for himself. But I trust Tom and I hope it's the first option. He's one of the good guys. Or I think he is. How do you know though? Is this when he shows his true colours? I will say these words and the texts will stop and the future plans will be cancelled.

I can't hold back the tears now. I don't notice them until my cheeks feel wet. I have cried alone so many times that it feels weird to be crying in front of someone else.

'Hey, hey, come on. Liv . . .'

This, finally, is what I hoped for. Tom wraps me in a big, powerful, desperate hug, like we're the only two people left on earth. I am about to tell him about something which has followed me for all of my adult life and hope that nothing bad will happen. I am opening myself up more than ever before.

He is stroking my hand again. He doesn't look emotional or panicky. I realise this is the flipside to the brainy part of him. He might not be great at showering me with compliments on the new book, but he's steady in a crisis. He will be methodical. He will show me love through acts of service.

I used to think I wanted the loud, showy, love-bombing type. That was Kyle all over. But, actually, I want someone who will cook me a meal, take out the bins, pay parking tickets, pick up TJ from school, wash the dishes.

That's what love means to me. I want someone who will still be here no matter what. I think Tom could be that guy.

It's time to be honest with him.

So I begin.

83

MYLES

NOW

Myles has heard a lot about the Hôtel Lutetia over the last few days. But this is the first time he's ever been inside the place. It's even bigger and more impressive than he imagined.

Myles never had all that growing up. His childhood was a bed and breakfast in the Lake District if he was lucky, with added chores and compulsory daily hikes. Sometimes he sounds like those *Monty Python* characters competing for the worst childhood story imaginable. But it's all true, even if he wishes it wasn't. The care home, the communal dorm room, the violence that always hung in the air. Fancy five-star hotels on the Left Bank in Paris just weren't part of his childhood.

The Lutetia, though, is something else. He's never seen a lobby and corridors so dazzling. It's like that Leonardo DiCaprio film *The Great Gatsby* where everyone's in a tuxedo with martinis in hand and taking bets on who's going to win the World Series. It's also the first time he's ever seen the *Memory* painting by Josephine Benoit in person. The portrait is the first thing any visitor sees after they emerge from the wooden revolving door. It is on the left-hand side, placed next to an odd metallic statue of Gustave Eiffel, who Myles presumes is the guy who designed the tower.

The portrait is above a bench and looks smaller than Myles imagined. It's got such a reputation that he always thought it would be some giant canvas. There is a plaque underneath it with the title, artist and date it was first shown. Getting a photo with the painting here is almost a rite-of-passage for tourists.

Myles takes in the portrait. He's seen a photo of it online, but nothing compares to the real thing. The young woman sits in Room 11 of the Lutetia hotel in her striped outfit from the concentration camps and the mess that the fleeing Nazi officers have left behind. There is the chaos of Paris outside and the total destruction of everything that she once knew. It is unbearably moving and sad but also hopeful. The mystery woman in the portrait is broken, but not defeated. There is a resilience in her eyes, a courage in the way she sits, a survivor of the worst that the world can possibly throw at her but still determined to rebuild her life and restore her old memories.

Myles sympathises with her. He endured a childhood in the care system, not a concentration camp. But there's a universal power to the painting. It speaks of suffering, trauma, the bad things that humans do to each other, but also the incredible goodness of the human spirit. It is a tribute to hope and redemption.

The spell is broken as he sees Edward de Villefort and Louis walking through the lobby and joining Vidal at the reception desk. Myles looks different now, but there's still a chance that Louis might recognise him. Myles has an instant dislike of Edward. He is arrogant, born with a silver spoon in his mouth, oozing privilege. Edward is the sort of person who will never know what it's like to spend hours ironing every crease and polishing shoes just to feel like they have enough armour to compete against people who grew up with all the advantages in the world.

Finally, he is close to the person behind all of this. The man who puts on a mask to the world while manipulating them.

Edward looks sullen and annoyed, while Louis nods politely, as ever. He doesn't seem to recognise Myles.

Myles feels a mix of relief and anger. 'Where is Dr Finn?' he asks.

84

OLIVIA

THEN

I'm glad I practised in front of the mirror. Without that, I'd be lost for words.

How do you say the thing that's been buried inside you for over twenty years?

'You asked before about why I've spent my life as a psychotherapist,' I say. 'What made me want to help other people deal with the trauma in their lives. And I've told you about Louis and Gran and moving to Paris after Mum died. That's the story I tell myself now, but it's not the whole story. It wasn't just that Mum died, it was also how she died. That was my trauma. That's what therapy helped me deal with.'

'Okay,' says Tom. 'Well, whatever it is, Liv, we'll get through it.'

I shake my head. 'I told you that I was the one who found Mum that day,' I say. 'I got home from school one day and she was there at the kitchen table with a bottle of sleeping pills next to her.'

'You did. And I can't even begin to imagine what that must have been like.'

'But there was something else as well. Mum was an addict. It didn't matter what it was, really, booze or prescriptions or smoking, she always took it to an extreme. I was her daughter, but sometimes I felt more like her carer, and all the pills and medicines were locked away each night to stop her overdosing.'

'That doesn't sound like much of a childhood.'

'It wasn't,' I say, blinking back more tears and forcing myself to go on. 'Only I had the key, and I would unlock the medicine cupboard and count out her nightly dose, then put everything back and lock the cupboard again. Religiously, I mean. I was just a teenager, but it was my responsibility. Her doctor warned me that if I didn't lock that cupboard then Mum, as an addict, would most likely overdose while I was out of the house. Sometimes it felt like her life was in my hands.'

'Liv . . .'

'Except the night before she died, we had a huge row. The biggest one ever. We were always fighting, but she was bitter and weak and lashed out to make herself feel better. I couldn't stand her criticising me when I was doing so much for her. I was sick of her, and that stupid house, and to be honest, in that moment, I wished she wasn't alive.'

Tom doesn't let go of me. But his eyes narrow. 'What happened?'

'That night, I was so angry. I counted out her dose but . . . I didn't lock the cabinet. The next morning, I had another chance to lock it, but I still didn't. I left the cabinet open, Tom. I stood in front of it and knew what would happen if I left Mum alone in the house that day, but I still didn't lock it. I left it open and then picked up my rucksack and went to school. Mum was still sleeping, as she always did. I shut the door and part of me hoped that I would never see her again. It was petty and stupid and adolescent, but it's a moment I've never been fully able to move on from.'

'It could have been an accident,' he says. 'You forgot to lock it, had your mind on other things, it doesn't mean it was deliberate.'

'No, Tom. I'm serious. I remember standing in front of the medicine cupboard with the key in my hand and deciding not to lock it. That memory is clear in my mind as if it was yesterday. Leaving it unlocked was a deliberate act. I did that twice. I couldn't take her shouting and swearing at me any more. I couldn't cope with her neediness, her blaming everyone else for her life choices, for making the whole world so miserable for me when it was her decision to bring me into this world. I was looking for a way out.'

'Seriously, Liv, you can't . . .'

'I killed her. All I had to do was lock that medicine cupboard so she couldn't reach the pills and she would probably still be alive today. But I didn't. I wanted her out of my life. I left the cupboard unlocked knowing full well she would try and open it and, once she did, she would grab all the pills she could and overdose. I even remember locking it before the police arrived to try and cover my tracks. I might have been a kid, but I knew exactly what I was doing. It was intentional.'

'And you were how old when this happened?'

'Seventeen.'

'I see.'

He picks up my right hand now and holds it. He looks at me in that gentle way I first fell in love with. I'm pushing him away, I know I am, because part of me can't bear to be this vulnerable, this trusting in another human being. I realise that a teenager can't be held morally responsible for not locking a cupboard. But the letter of the law doesn't matter to me as much as the emotional weight it carries. Mum's death changed my life.

There is a before and after. No matter how much I try and forgive myself, nothing works. I keep returning to the memory.

I have a terrible sinking feeling in my stomach. This is it. I have gone too far. Louis understands, but he's the only one. Tom will carry on seeing me, but there will be some small part of him that withdraws from me, even if it isn't a conscious decision.

'If this was your way of trying to break up with me, Dr Finn, then it backfired spectacularly,' he says.

I laugh. I can't help it. I don't understand. The memory of standing in front of that medicine cupboard has haunted me for the last two decades. In my darkest moments, I've called myself a murderer, a killer, someone who let her own mother die rather than helping her.

That single act of teenage selfishness has defined my own image of myself. Louis is the only person who I ever talked to about it. That is why we have such a deep bond. He is the one person on earth who knows why I'm my own worst enemy.

'How can you love me after knowing that?'

'You were an angry teenager forced to care for your mum when it should have been the other way round,' he says. 'Only one person caused that overdose, and it wasn't you, Liv. If anything, you were the one who needed someone to care for them. You were only a child, for God's sake.'

He kisses me then, a proper teary, meaningful, life-affirming kiss, until when I open my eyes and see him again I realise that I had no choice but to open up like this, to risk everything and see if this was real. That is what love means. It involves total emotional transparency. There can't be barriers or walls. And, now, I am certain about this, or as sure as I'll ever be. He's seen me as I am and is still committed.

Normal life barges in again. It's almost four and he has another meeting. I have to pick up TJ. We agree to meet again tomorrow and talk through it all. We kiss goodbye, hug tightly again, resolve to make plans for our future.

I send him a text that night. For the first time ever, I say I love him. He says he loves me too. This day has gone better than I ever thought it could.

That night I go to bed happy.

It's the last time I ever see him.

85

OLIVIA

NOW

I reach the ballroom and am nearly at the private exit, hoping to get out of this hotel before the cops find me, when the lights flick on suddenly. I want a moment to myself. I can't deal with the police again, not right now. I need to collect my thoughts.

The lights are blinding, at first, and it takes a while to get used to them. I hear the sound of the ballroom doors closing and being locked shut. There is a man standing in the doorway of the grand ballroom.

He is tall, with a brush of sandy hair, but in a smart suit now with tortoiseshell glasses and a waistcoat and neatly trimmed beard.

I know him, but I don't know him.

This is the man I once thought wouldn't even own a suit. The military muscle has gone and he looks larger, like an athlete in the off-season, and wears shined shoes and dresses with a care that didn't seem possible.

But he has the eyes of the person who brought me tea in a novelty mug with 'World's Okayest Husband' on the side, who told me his problems at the Memory Unit, and who brutally ghosted me after I told him the truth about my past.

He moves slowly towards me. I still think of him as Tom. But that was clearly a fake name. This is the same man who planted the bugs in Louis's phones at Quai Voltaire. He pretended to be a patient to get close to me before the trial. He almost certainly wasn't working in an official police capacity. He was freelancing. That means his motive was personal and must have been connected with Ingrid Fox.

Suddenly everything I said to this man takes on a different meaning.

'I promise you I can explain,' he says, and I realise that his voice, like his eyes, is the only thing that hasn't changed, the bit of him that was real. 'But we don't have much time.'

'Who are you?'

He takes out a warrant card from his jacket pocket and holds it up. 'Detective Inspector Myles Forsyth.'

'Do your bosses know about what you did? I'm guessing Mr Tom Lomas wasn't an official cover identity?'

'No,' says Myles. 'It wasn't.'

'You were the one who planted the bug in the consulting room at Quai Voltaire. You posed as a patient at the Memory Unit. You were trying to gather dirt before the defamation trial to help Ingrid Fox win.'

'Yes.'

He looks so different now. It's amazing what a sharper haircut, a proper suit, even more facial hair can do. He's like a completely different person. But those eyes are the ones I fell in love with. I let him deceive me for all those months. Did I want to be deceived? As a therapist, I've seen that happen with patients. They know where danger lies, but they still run towards it.

'Why?'

'Ingrid was my sister,' he says, at last. 'Or that's what I always called her. We grew up in the care system together. I saw what happened to her. I saw what that man did to her, the things he made her believe. That trial was the one chance to get justice. Without you, who knows, my sister might still be alive today.'

I'm taken aback. I don't understand. 'Her accusations were false. She was unstable.'

'No,' he says. 'Ingrid wasn't the one with false memories. You are.'

'What are you talking about?'

'Olivia, your entire life has been based on false memories. You've believed what he's told you. That's how he's got away with it for this long. You were in therapy with him just like she was. Don't you see . . . he's the one behind it all.'

I'm about to reply when there's a sound outside the ballroom doors.

86

MYLES

Myles is still reeling. It's impossible to take in. More memories come back. He remembers all those times in the care home with Ingrid and the games of rock paper scissors they used to play. He remembers the shame of not being able to protect her and how he felt when her body was found. He failed her before the trial, and he failed her afterwards. This, now, is his way of trying to make it right.

'DI Forsyth!' yells Captain Vidal outside. 'Let me in. I'm ordering you, on behalf of the DNPJ, open this door!'

Myles knows they don't have much time. Vidal could order back-up at any moment. The entire hotel will be surrounded with uniformed officers. Myles has no jurisdiction here, and Olivia is a witness in a murder case. He tries to get his head straight and figure out what to do.

'What are you talking about?' says Olivia.

'You're the memory expert,' says Myles. 'You think you're immune from false memories. You sit there in your ivory tower and diagnose everyone else's problems. But, really, you suffer from them more than anyone, Liv. That's what I found out. That's how he manipulates his patients and gets a hold over them.'

'You're not making sense.'

Myles takes his phone out and holds it up. 'On this phone are audio recordings from the bugs I planted inside Louis de Villefort's phones. They capture the phone conversations between Louis and your grandmother. He keeps mentioning a secret buried deep in her past that only he knows. That she murdered someone during the war in Room 11 of this hotel. That she killed the real Josephine Benoit, and Louis is the only one who knows what a terrible person she is and what she is capable of. It's what we now call coercive control.'

There is more banging on the locked doors of the ballroom. Captain Vidal and Louis will get the night manager from reception to unlock the doors. They have seconds left before those doors fling open. Both Myles and Olivia will be apprehended. All this will be over.

'What are you talking about?'

'He lies, Liv. He lies about everything. He probably even lied about being in the Resistance. He coercively controlled your grandmother for eighty years. But he couldn't control the effects of her dementia. When she went public, and she was clearly beyond his control, it was easier to have her silenced. The same was true of Ingrid. What better way to frame your accuser as delusional and neurotic than for her to take her own life before the end of the trial? Why else do you think someone as senior as Captain Vidal attended the scene here in this hotel? Louis treated him years ago, just like he treated so many other powerful figures. Once he had control of their minds, he had control of them too. He made them all believe they'd done something terrible in their past and that only he could help them. He lied to get power over people.'

There is more banging on the door. It is Edward this time.

'Liv, for fuck's sake, open the bloody door!'

Vidal's voice joins him again now, as does a third voice, that of the night manager. There's the sound of keys being tried for the ballroom doors. They will be through here at any moment. Vidal is also on his radio co-ordinating back-up. Officers from the DNPJ could surround the hotel at any moment. There will be armed police too. Both of them could end up like that Foreign Legion soldier.

'I still don't understand,' says Olivia. 'Why would Louis do any of it?'

'For the same reason that bad men do bad things,' says Myles. 'Gaslighting, coercive control, call it any name you like. It gave him power. Nothing is more powerful than the therapist and the patient in the consulting room. Ever since he started treating people as a medical student in this hotel, Louis de Villefort has revelled in the psychological power of his position. Like all narcissists, Louis needs to be the centre of attention. In his consulting room, with him as the therapist and the patient vulnerable, he was god.'

Just at that moment, the key to the ballroom doors turns in the lock.

Olivia looks at Myles and both of them make a decision.

87

THE LUTETIA

1945

SOPHIE

'Sophie . . . SOPHIE!'

She is being shaken awake. She isn't sure if she is asleep or not, but she looks up and sees Louis standing over her. How has he got in here? Then she remembers that the medical staff have keys in case they need to subdue a patient suffering from flashbacks. Is that what's happened here? Louis looks worried, scared even. It is light outside but the curtains are still closed.

'What is it?' she says. 'What's happened?'

Louis withdraws and puts his hands through his hair. He looks anxious. But not for himself. For her. This is her last day in the Lutetia. She will undergo her police interview today and walk out of that door as a free woman. Surely, he should be celebrating?

'You really don't remember?'

She is still foggy, and it takes her a moment to adjust to where she is. She looks around Room 11. She is still in the hotel. There is the bed to her left.

That's when she sees it.

Josephine is lying on the bed next to her. But she isn't moving. There is a pillow beside her head. Josephine's eyes are staring up at the ceiling and the rest of her body is rigid.

It is just like Sophie's memory from the hut.

Her greatest fear has become real.

She can see the other prisoner begging Sophie to help her and the way the prisoner's body looked once it was done. Sophie begins to feel a horrible sense of dread go through her, as if the past has been repeated.

She usually checked that Josephine was breathing. But she didn't last night. What happened?

'I don't understand,' she says, looking at Louis. 'I don't—'

Louis comes over to her again and crouches by the bed. He has tears in his eyes. He holds her hand tightly, as if scared he might never see her again.

'This is my fault, Sophie, I should have got you treatment sooner. I thought if you could just hold on until today then we could get you out of here and I could look after you myself. But that was naïve. I feared this might happen and I didn't do enough to stop it. I'm sorry, Sophie, I'm so, so sorry.'

Sophie can't bear to look at Josephine on the bed again. She can feel her body trembling now as she takes it all in. She remembers wanting to do it, and those memories of the hut when she did do it, and in between there is a gap around what really happened last night.

'Did I—?'

Louis looks sadder than he has ever looked before. 'Yes, Sophie,' he says. 'You must have done. This morning, I was waiting for you in the lobby downstairs. When you didn't turn up, I came to the room. That's when I found her.'

'She's definitely dead?'

Louis nods. 'I checked her pulse. She's been gone a while. You must have done it during the night sometime.'

'But I don't remember—'

She stops before completing the sentence. The gap in her mind is filling up now. She remembers what she did at the camp, then what she thought about doing here, and now the rest of it comes back to her.

'She was telling me something last night. She said she was in the Resistance, and that you were lying, and that you are the one I should be wary of. She said she'd told a police officer and that you'd be investigated and arrested.'

'Of course she said that,' says Louis. 'She would do anything to put the blame on others. Perhaps that's why you killed her. Deep down, you were just trying to defend me. You stood by the bed, you took the pillow, you pressed down. You didn't mean to hurt her, but . . .'

Yes, Sophie feels the memory forming in her mind. She thinks about standing by Josephine's bed, taking the spare pillow from her own bed, and then pressing down with all her might while Josephine wriggled and kicked, until finally the kicking stopped. Maybe that's how her subconscious worked. She was outraged by Josephine's accusation against Louis. She was defending Louis in a way she had never managed to defend her own father.

'I killed her,' she says, at last, staring at the body. 'I killed her. I did it.'

'Yes,' says Louis, wiping away a tear. 'I'm afraid, Sophie, that's the only possible explanation.'

88

THE LUTETIA

1945

SOPHIE

Louis sighs and then, seeing her distress, he reaches for her and holds her tightly.

'We have to think quickly here, Sophie,' he says. 'It won't be long before the police in the hotel discover the body. They will want to question you. Your police interview is scheduled for today. If they find out you killed someone, they will never let you leave the Lutetia. They will do what they always do to women who they class as unwell and put you away in an asylum somewhere. You know what those places are like. I can't let that happen. I *won't*.'

She feels sick. She spent so long wanting to be free from the camps that the idea of an asylum seems even worse than death. She can't go to a place like that. She can't.

'But what about the things Josephine said? She told me you lied about being in the Resistance. She—'

'Sophie, listen to me. Josephine was an ill woman. She was never in the camps. She betrayed you. If you don't listen to me, I can't save you.'

'What do I do?' she says, as Louis relaxes his grip on her and stands up again. He is pacing, thinking, still running his palms through his hair. 'I can't go to an asylum, Louis, I just—'

She breaks down. It's like a selection from the camps again. Those deemed fit enough for society are sent to the right, those deemed too frail are sent to the left. She survived all those selections, by whatever means necessary, only to end up on the wrong side of the final selection back here in Paris. Her body isn't injured this time but her mind is. Those bad memories have made her do such a terrible thing. In the middle of the night, she has enacted her worst thoughts and killed the woman who was once her best friend.

'Please, you have to help me. I won't be taken. I just won't.'

Louis stops pacing. He takes a deep breath.

'Perhaps there is one way,' he says, looking at Josephine's body and then back at Sophie. 'I mean . . . it could just work. It's something we used to do in the Resistance.' He pauses, thinking some more. 'Josephine passed her police interview yesterday, yes? She has stayed on to get her official papers before she is allowed to leave?'

'Yes.'

'You still haven't been interviewed yet?'

'No.'

'Okay, we'll have to move fast. The minute the police find the body, then we lose control of the situation.'

'Anything,' she says. 'Anything other than being taken to one of those places. Help me, Louis, please.'

Louis sits beside her on the bed now. Outside she can hear the sound of other guests and one of the Red Cross officials. Louis puts his arm around her and lowers his voice.

'Follow everything I tell you,' he says. 'If I get caught helping you, then I could be implicated too, and then there's nothing I can do.'

'I'm sorry, Louis. I'm sorry for putting you in this situation. And . . . for doubting you.'

'Never mind that now. Josephine was always persuasive. She was an actress, after all.'

'You really would do this for me?'

'In sickness and in health, for richer, for poorer . . . it's what true love means.'

Sophie has seen hell, and could be back there again, but she has a partner by her side now and that is the hope she clings on to. She lost her father in the camps, but she won't lose Louis. Together, they will survive somehow.

'Now listen carefully,' he says. 'This is what we're going to do.'

89

THE LUTETIA

1945

SOPHIE

Sophie Leclerc is dead. Long live Josephine Benoit.
If anything, it is almost a relief to leave Sophie behind, psychologically at least. The real Sophie Leclerc died the moment her father was separated into a different line at Auschwitz. There was no Sophie after that. She is the woman from the camps who made the terrible decisions needed to survive – cooking for the commandant and his family, watching that belt draped over the chair in his study, helping a fellow prisoner in her hut die by smothering her, slowly losing any traces of her own humanity.

The Sophie who loved life, walked in the moonlight, skipped to school and had joy in her heart died a long time ago.

She gets ready to leave the Lutetia now. Their identities have been swapped. Sophie Leclerc is now the body upstairs waiting to be found. Josephine Benoit has been cleared for release and can walk away a free woman. Her three days of captivity here are over. She has a final lunch in the magnificent ballroom then gets ready to leave.

As she stands in the lobby, about to depart, a French police officer standing by the front desk mutters goodbye to his colleague by the desk and approaches her. He is polishing his glasses with a handkerchief.

'You're leaving?' he says.

She freezes now. Has someone already discovered the body in Room 11? Will they question why Sophie has Josephine's papers letting her leave this place?

'I have my papers,' she says. 'Today is my last day here.'

'What will you do now?' he says.

She is confused until she realises that the French police officer must think she is Josephine and that he and Josephine must have met at the hotel yesterday. Sophie and Josephine were always identical, but with the shaved head and rags it is even more difficult to tell them apart, especially for someone with glasses and poor eyesight. The body in the room has been left with the official papers belonging to Sophie. That's how they will identify the body.

'I've always wanted to try painting. And you?'

'I wanted to talk to you about our conversation yesterday.'

She tries to stay calm. She is just inches from the doorway and freedom. She thinks about Louis and the asylum and knows these next few seconds could decide everything.

'I see.'

'It's about that name you told me,' he says. 'Louis de Villefort. You said that he was a collaborator who is now falsely claiming to have worked for the Resistance. We've been compiling a list of known Resistance fighters, and we can't find his name among them. Of course, it's impossible to be sure given how fragmented the Resistance was and is. They have no proper structure or documentation. He is a medical student, and is treating patients here, so it'll be tough to get my superiors to go for it unless you have some concrete evidence about his work as a collaborator. But I must warn you to be careful, mademoiselle. It's possible he has friends in high places and if word gets back to him that he is suspected of collaborating and lying about being in the Resistance then he could come after you and try and silence you.'

She wants to get away from here as fast as possible. Josephine must have been spreading more lies. Yes, Josephine was the collaborator and Louis was in the Resistance. That is what Louis has told her, and that's what must be true.

'I was mistaken,' she says. 'I got the name wrong. I'm sorry, but, yes . . . it was a mistake.'

The police officer looks confused and is about to speak when he is called away by a colleague on the reception desk. She continues through the lobby towards the entrance and watches more new arrivals queuing on Boulevard Raspail. She hurries through the revolving door and out onto the Left Bank. She tries to comprehend what he just said.

It is a clear sunny day and, for once, there is the faintest sense of hope in the air. The only possessions she has are Red Cross coupons to buy new clothes and official papers to begin again. The burden of being Sophie Leclerc – camp survivor and orphan – is gone, like shedding an old skin. Instead, she is now officially Josephine Benoit, cleared by the police, ready to melt into the heat of Paris and start her life again.

She turns and takes one last look at the Lutetia. She wonders how long it will take before the body is discovered and questions asked. According to Louis, the police here are quietly told to record any deaths in the Lutetia as having occurred in transit, to avoid tarnishing the hotel's reputation. The body will be named as Sophie and the death recorded as happening on the journey from Auschwitz to Paris. Only she and Louis will ever truly know what went on in Room 11 at the Lutetia hotel. Hers is just one of hundreds, even thousands, of stories in this place, the lives permanently changed by the chaos of war.

She wonders again about the police officer's comments. Did Josephine say Louis might be lying about being in the Resistance? Is it a coincidence that Josephine died so soon after she made the accusation? The police officer thought she was Josephine and warned her about the dangers Louis posed and what he might do if someone suspected him of collaborating and exposed his lies.

But, no, she can't think like that. Josephine was the traitor. Her claims to have been working for the Resistance were false. Everyone knows she was a Nazi whore. They saw her entering all the grand hotels on the arm of an officer. Sophie isn't sure what Louis actually did in the Resistance, but it was probably something very secret and underground.

Louis is her saviour. He is the true Resistance hero. He is the one she must believe. He has said that she must get well first before they resume their relationship. He will be her therapist and treat her. Once he's finished his medical training, he is planning to set up a new consulting room above his apartment in Quai Voltaire. She will be one of his very first patients.

Louis, her darling Louis, won't let her be taken off to an asylum. He will always protect her. She has been through so much trauma. It will take a long time to heal, if she ever does.

It is mid-morning and the next bus pulls up outside the Lutetia and the crowd of relatives gather round. They all peer in through the bus windows, straining to see the faces of relatives, hoping that today they will be reunited with their loved ones.

Louis has found her a small apartment in Montparnasse where she can stay while she recovers. He said it's best to lie low for a while. She asked for some painting materials to pass the time. She will stay inside, nurse her wounds, and paint. She will visit him for therapy sessions and get used to her new life as Josephine rather than Sophie.

'You can enter now! One at a time! No pushing!' shouts the Red Cross worker.

The queue slowly begins to form. The survivors look hollowed out. There will be more screams tonight, lots more pacing. Each of these people have a tragic story to tell. There will already be rumours about which among them is a collaborator. Scores will be settled, and more bodies found.

Sophie continues walking along the Left Bank and towards the rest of her life.

Behind her, at the Hôtel Lutetia, another day begins.

90

OLIVIA

NOW

I barely have time to understand what's happened. Suddenly so much of my life shifts just slightly and makes sense in a new way.

I see myself as a teenager walking up the steps to the consulting room at Quai Voltaire still shocked and traumatised by Mum's death and the way Louis promised to help me understand my trauma. And how he analysed my memories of what I did just before Mum died, and focused on the medication and the pill bottle. He went over and over that single memory, taking an angry teenage thought and turning it into an iron-cast truth.

And now he is standing there. The doors are open and Louis is beside Captain Vidal and Edward. Louis, the wise old man who I looked up to more than anyone, is stooped with his cane and that magnificent sweep of snowy hair.

I imagine him in his sessions with Gran and the lies he made her believe, and how my entire career has been moulded by this one figure. The best way to hide your own crimes is to accuse other people, deflecting attention, the ultimate double-bluff. I think of all the memories he claimed to have recovered in therapy, and the people he accused, and the destruction of families and parents. And I am not sure what to believe any more.

'Olivia, my dear, step away from that man,' says Louis, waving his cane in the air. 'He's the one I warned you about. Do not trust him. Olivia, listen to me, do not believe a word he says.'

But, already, I am backing away and moving towards the man I still think of as Tom, yet who I now know is DI Myles Forsyth.

'Is it true?' I say. 'Are you the one who ordered Gran's death? Did you make her believe she was a murderer, just like you made me believe I was responsible for Mum's suicide? Was Ingrid Fox telling the truth? Did I defend you, when all this time you were just using me?'

Louis shakes his head, but he no longer looks like the gentle old man. There is a fierceness in his eyes. 'I don't know what lies this man has been telling you, my dear, but you're not in a good state. I'm not surprised, at least not clinically speaking. The shooting at the Mémorial earlier has stopped you thinking clearly. Five minutes in my old consulting room, and I could help you.'

So many other thoughts go through my mind. Did Louis take advantage of me when I was a vulnerable teenager? Did he take advantage of Gran when she was a traumatised survivor of the concentration camps?

I look at Captain Vidal now and remember what I was told about his role in a police shooting. I imagine Louis making him go over and over and over it until, deep down, he came to remember it differently. What if the consulting room at Quai Voltaire isn't a place of healing, as I've always believed, but the engine room for decades of gaslighting and coercive control? If you control a patient's memories, then you control the patient too. You can manipulate their past, and therefore their future.

The final part of Louis's mask drops now. He looks angry, savage almost, not used to being openly challenged like this. 'I'm a healer,' he says. 'Ever since my work after the war in this hotel, all I've tried to do is help people.'

I see Captain Vidal is more cautious now, reflecting on his own relationship with Louis and then looking at DI Forsyth.

Louis turns to Vidal. 'You're not buying any of this nonsense, are you? They're playing you, just like they did during the trial. I'm the scapegoat here. None of this is true. Lies, a goddamn pack of lies.'

It's then, standing in this grand ballroom, that the past seems to come alive again. I see Gran as she was then with her shaved head and her striped rags. She is eating her portion of bread, drinking water, and opposite her is Louis, the medical student posing as her saviour, making her dependent on him, using her to feed his monstrous ego.

Out of nowhere, Gran's voice suddenly fills the room.

91

OLIVIA

The voice is coming from Myles's phone. This, I realise, must be one of the audio recordings from the phone conversations Louis had with Gran. I can hear Gran's frail, shaky voice and the unexpectedness of it pierces my heart with more pain and emotion than I've ever felt before.

The memory keeps coming back to me, says Gran's voice, with its ghostly aura. *I can't remember where my keys are, or what my name is, but this memory keeps springing up. I'm in Room 11 at the Lutetia and I'm waking up on my final day of captivity in 1945. You're standing over me. I look across and see Josephine's body on the bed beside me. You tell me that I acted out during the night. But, the thing is, I don't remember it. I remember going to sleep and I remember being woken up. I remember being told about what I did, but not actually doing it. I realise the distinction now. My dementia means I can't remember the present, but other memories from the past are coming back to me.*

Then there is Louis's voice on the recording. He tells Gran that she is mistaken. That her dementia is confusing her. They have been through this, he says wearily, so many times before.

Her mind is losing its capacity to remember anything, and now she is blanking out bits of old memories to protect herself.

But she knows what she did that day. Who else could have done it? She went to sleep with dangerous thoughts about harming Josephine and acted on those thoughts during the night. Josephine was the person who denounced Gran to the Nazis. She was responsible for the death of Gran's father. Gran killed Josephine out of revenge and then took her identity and her papers in order to escape the hotel and avoid being sent to an asylum. Louis was the one who helped her remember. That's why she's been so reclusive all this time. Gran murdered someone and Louis has been protecting her.

'Stop!' says Louis, now, nodding at Myles to pause the audio recording.

There is silence in the ballroom. The wind clatters through the open casement window, almost like a reckoning. I feel the last of my doubts falling away. The truth hits me all at once. I look at Louis, the man I have always trusted more than anyone, and see a stranger staring back at me.

'It might be impossible to prove. But my guess is that the real Josephine did work for the Resistance,' I say now. 'She knew you were a liar and a fraud. She was trying to expose you as a collaborator who lied about being in the Resistance and you couldn't let her do that. She also told Gran about her suspicions. So you devised a clever plan. You killed Josephine in Room 11 of this hotel and then persuaded Gran that she did it, killing two birds with one stone, and convinced Gran to cover up her crime by stealing Josephine's identity and making it look like the dead woman was Sophie Leclerc.'

Louis is silent. 'You always were so naïve, dearest Olivia,' he says, 'just like your grandmother. Deep down, you wanted to believe the best of other people. You didn't see the world like I did, like all of us did during the war. I did what I had to do to protect myself.'

'No, you abused patients. You gaslit them into thinking you were the one indispensable part of their lives. You did it to Gran, and you did it to me. You did it because you enjoyed the power. You fed off it.'

I continue staring into Louis's eyes as Captain Vidal makes the arrest. I watch as Edward stands there a broken man watching his father being taken away.

I feel Myles beside me as this vast ballroom stretches out around us and, for a brief moment, the ballroom once more seems to be filled with those survivors from eighty years ago in their striped clothing with their quiet, tragic dignity. Then, just like that, they slowly disappear, until the room is just as it is, refurbished and modern and ready to make new memories again.

The past can't hurt me any longer now.

It's finally over.

SIX MONTHS LATER

92

OLIVIA

NORFOLK

TJ's hand is hot in my own. We are walking down the gravel lane towards the cottage. The Norfolk coast stretches out in the distance. We are the only two people in the world here. There has been so much tragedy, but we are here to reclaim things, to make it good and happy again. I am back where this all started at Fisherman's Cottage.

TJ is excited and talkative today. 'Would you rather . . .'

I smile and wait for the question. The sea breeze is refreshing. It is cold, damp and wonderful.

'. . . have snow for Christmas or presents?'

I pretend to think. 'That's a good one. I know what your answer will be.'

'What?'

'Snow.'

'Nooooo!'

'Really? Does that mean you want . . . *presents* for Christmas?'

TJ smiles goofily. 'I want the new England shirt with TJ 10 on the back.'

'I thought you wanted the PSG one to embrace your quarter Frenchness.'

'That was ages ago. I want the England one. Not the old kit but the new one. The one they're using for the World Cup.'

'I know that too.'

TJ nods. He likes to be clear on such important matters. 'Good. You promise you won't forget?'

'I promise.'

''Cause no one wears the old kit any more, Mum. I have to have the new one.'

It's Mum now, never Muuuuuuum or Mummy, and I'm slowly getting used to it. He is seven and, as he often reminds me, not a little kid any more. I've turned from being doorkeeper, driver and disciplinarian into camp counsellor mode, respecting his space, knocking before I enter his bedroom, consulting him about plans rather than just scooping him up and leaving the questions for later.

It's all new and very disconcerting and it seems completely wrong that in another seven years he'll be fourteen and will no longer want to know me. I spent so long wishing for the end of the nappy-changing days that I didn't bank on the rest of it speeding up so fast. Now I'm trying to slow things down again.

'I've told Santa in no uncertain terms that anything other than the brand-new England top is unacceptable,' I say.

But TJ is no longer listening. He's already distracted by the sight of the waves and the sea stretching out in front of us.

We reach the cottage. There is a small path from the cottage down towards the shingly beach and then the sea. TJ looks at it in awe. He starts tugging my hand. He doesn't even have to say anything. I can see the question in his eyes.

'Fine. On two conditions—'

TJ nods, though I can tell he's still not listening.

'Don't go into the water. And make sure I can see you from the cottage at all times. No running off. Be. Careful.'

'Yes, yes, yes, yes.'

'TJ, are you—'

But it's too late. He runs off down the path towards the beach and the sea. We recently watched the *Free Willy* films on Amazon Prime and he's been obsessed with whales, the water and the sea ever since.

I keep him in my eyeline until he reaches the beach and starts trying to build a sandcastle. It is very warm for the time of year and TJ has never cared much about the cold. I open the front door of the cottage. Fisherman's Cottage only has two small bedrooms upstairs and a tiny kitchen and sitting area downstairs. The window looks directly out onto the beach so I can see TJ.

I never want this moment to end.

I take the little jar of ashes from the kitchen counter and then make my way outside again and realise that it is finally time.

I watch TJ running down the beach, his blond hair ruffled by the wind, his shoes caked with sand, and a look of pure, innocent joy all over him. I hold the urn with Gran's ashes, as if it's part of her, and know that it's up to us now.

Me and TJ, the next link in the chain.

We will have our brief time and then it will be TJ's children and their children and on and on it goes. That is how memory works, after all. I have my great-grandfather's eyes, the nose of a distant uncle, the funny big toe from Gran's side. I am made up of the memories of the people who came before me.

I am their legacy.

I look at the urn and I see Gran – Sophie, now, who became Josephine – standing next to me. She is no longer dressed in the camp uniform with her head shaved, but smiling at me with long brown hair and her own clothes. She watched over me at the Lutetia and is here to say goodbye.

I think of all the hours I spent undergoing therapy in that room at Quai Voltaire and the way Louis made me feel guilty for Mum's death. Did I deliberately leave the medicine cabinet unlocked? I'm not so sure now. I've been over that memory so many times that it has changed out of all recognition. Those sessions were meant to help me; they ended up harming me even more.

I wait until the wind calms down and then step forward and unbottle the urn. I gently scatter her ashes along the seafront so that she is always here with me and TJ. When I finally dare to look back, I see that the figure has gone now, her errand completed. She has helped me solve the mystery of who she was, in life and death, and who I am too.

She taught me how to live and now I must pass it on. That, in the end, is the most important thing she gave me. Money and status and power – none of those things survive us. They are not the things that memories are made of and never will be.

At the end of the day, what survives is love.

IT'S THE CRIME OF THE CENTURY...

Don't miss the hit international bestseller from Matthew Blake

SUNDAY TIMES THRILLER OF THE MONTH

ANNA O

Innocent sleep walker...

Or a sleeping killer?

'Irresistible'
LEE CHILD

'Stunning'
DAVID BALDACCI

'Ingenious'
THE TIMES

MATTHEW BLAKE

Also available to buy now